State of Innocence

Inspired by True Events

S.K Mason
Debra Scacciaferro

ISBN: 978-1-953735-87-4

Melange Books, LLC
White Bear Lake, MN 55110
www.melange-books.com

Published in the United States of America.

Cover Design by Caroline Andrus

To my grandmother, Claudiane. I wish this book had made it out on time for you to see my first fiction in print. I know you'll enjoy it from where you're resting now. All my love
xoxo
SK Mason

———

For my husband Jim DeFelice, whose love, faith and humor have sustained me through the crazy ups and downs of our shared writing life.

Thanks also to my long-time writing buddies S.K. Mason, Lorraine Ash, Karen Phelps, Judy Reene Singer, Maria Gil, Laura Liller and Linda Gould, for all your encouragement, feedback, wisdom, advice, and laughter.

Xoxo, Debra Scacciaferro

PART I

DEATH OF INNOCENTS

"We do what we can do, and we leave the rest to the angels and the gods."

— LORRAINE ASH (LIFE TOUCHES LIFE)

CHAPTER ONE

Alexia Rodriguez-Mackenzie had never been to a funeral before, so the five-year-old didn't realize that her baby brother was dead. All she knew was that Lando had gone to visit Jesus in Heaven, and for some reason, Daddy blamed it on her.

She stood in the snowy cemetery, her hand clutching her grandmother's gloved one, while Father Estanzia droned on and on and on.

"This precious baby, Orlando Rodriguez Mackenzie, not even a year old, now dwells in the house of the Lord. Commend his spirit to you, Oh Lord, on this day, the Twenty-Third of March, in this year of the Lord 2010."

"*Abuelita?*" Alexia whispered, her teeth chattering. "How much longer?"

"Almost over." Her grandmother gave her hand a quick, reassuring squeeze.

Alexia nodded and shivered again. Even with her warmest black tights under her dress, her legs were numb. The sky was winter gray, heavy with clouds. Her mama sat in a metal folding chair, crying, her nose red, her pretty brown eyes smudged with tears. Daddy stood next to her, holding Jayleen, who buried her face in his shoulder.

It wasn't fair. "Abuelita, how come Jayleen gets to sit with Mama and Daddy, and not me?"

"Jayleen's little," said her grandmother. "You're a big girl."

Alexia sighed.

"We pray to the Blessed Mary and the Holy Father," the priest continued. "Please comfort him as his own mother and father here on earth did."

Mama cried louder.

"And we pray to the angels in Heaven to love him as his sisters here on earth did," the priest continued.

Alexia didn't like that. Would the angels be Lando's new sisters? It wasn't fair.

"*Abuelita?*" Alexia whispered again, her teeth chattering. "How much longer?"

"Almost over." Her grandmother gave her hand a quick, reassuring squeeze.

"The Shepherd of lost little lambs has taken Orlando home with him to live in Heaven. Though he was with us for only a short time, Lando will be missed and remembered forever."

And with that, Father Estanzia made the sign of the cross over the white box with the silver cross painted on it.

Daddy said Lando was sleeping in that white box. But how could he be, when Abuelita said he was in Heaven visiting the Blessed Virgin and Jesus? If she and Jayleen were very good girls, Abuelita said, God would make a miracle happen and they would get to see Lando again.

"*Abuelita?*" She squeezed her grandmother's hand, wanting to ask her about the miracle.

"Sshhh!" Her grandmother raised a gloved finger to her lips, then pointed to the white box being lowered into the grave.

Alexia turned to look back at Mama. A tall man dressed in a black suit was holding white flowers. He had a round face, with a sad smile. He laid one flower in Mama's lap. He held one out to Daddy. Daddy wore black jeans and a tie and a borrowed black jacket from Mama's cousin, Carlos. Alexia had never seen Daddy dressed this way. She and Jayleen wore their Christmas dresses. Daddy put Jayleen on Mama's lap, then took the flower and walked over to the big hole where the box was.

Alexia didn't want to look at the box. Her tummy felt funny, like she might throw up. She started to shake all over. "*Abuelita!*" She tugged on her grandmother's hand. "*Abuelita!*"

"Sshhh, *miha!*"

The man stepped over to them now, holding out a flower. *Abuelita* took one, but Alexia put her free hand behind her back. She wouldn't touch the flower.

"*Miha!*" her grandmother scolded gently. "What's the matter? You have to put a flower on the grave for your brother."

"No!" Alexia's heart was pounding so hard, it scared her. Wrenching out of her grandmother's grasp, she broke free, running as fast as she could.

She ran out of the cemetery toward the big brick church. When she got to the steps by the front door, the Monsignor stepped in front of her, knelt down, and caught her by the shoulders.

"Where are you running to, my child?" He smiled down at her.

Alexia stared up at him. She was breathing hard, each gasp of cold air making her chest ache. Her voice wouldn't work right. The buzzing in her ear drowned out everything else. She began to shake all over.

"My poor child, what's wrong? Have you lost your parents?" The priest glanced up, looking toward the parking lot. "Maybe this is your Daddy?"

She turned to look. A man with a bushy gray beard in a long black coat, his hands deep in his pockets, stared at them, grinning as if he knew her. Oh, but she knew him. She'd seen him before. The night all the bad stuff happened.

"No," Alexia said, shaking her head. "No, no, no!" Alexia tried to run back the way she had come, but the priest held her hand, preventing her from breaking free, trying to question her further.

"Alex!" Daddy's voice was sharp as he ran toward her. "Alexia!"

"Is that your father?" the priest asked.

"Daddy!" Alexia cried.

Monsignor let her go, and she rushed toward her father.

Daddy grabbed her by the arms. His face was angry. "What the hell's wrong with you? Runnin' off like that! You upset your mother. You can't just run anywhere you want."

"Sorry, sorry!" Knowing there was no way she could explain, Alexia hung her head in shame. But at least she felt safe. She glanced back, where the strange man was now talking to the Monsignor.

"Daddy. The bad man is back."

Daddy looked over, too. His hand shook. "Goddammit!" He tightened his grip on Alexia's hand. "Come on. Funeral's over. We're going home."

———

Much later that night, after all the sad relatives who had crowded into their tiny house left; after Abuelita tucked Jayleen and Alexia into their bunk beds; and after the light finally went off in Mommy's and Daddy's bedroom Alexia crept down from her bunk. Trying not to make a sound, she tiptoed over to Lando's empty crib.

When the floor creaked, she stopped, heart pounding, listening for the squeak of Daddy's bed, expecting any moment to hear Daddy's feet hit the floor.

But the house stayed quiet. Carefully, she stepped up onto the bottom rail of the crib bars, hoisted herself up, swung her leg over, and fell over the side onto the sagging mattress. She folded her hands together, her eyes fixed on the framed Sacred Heart of Jesus picture on the wall, faintly lit by the night light.

"Jesus? Can you hear me? God bless Mama and Daddy and Abuelita and Jayleen and Lando and Floppy Dog. And can you please send Lando home when you're done playing with him?"

She listened for a moment, wondering if she should say something else.

"I'll be a really good girl," she added.

She listened again, staring hard at the picture. She didn't know what else to say that would convince Jesus.

"Doesn't he want to ever come home?" Her chin quivered. "Doesn't he want me for a sister anymore?"

Alexia's eyes stung with tears. Her throat swelled up with sadness.

"Please, please, please!" she whispered fiercely, squeezing her hands in prayer so tightly that they shook. "If you send him back, I promise I'll watch over him forever, and hide him in the closet if that Bad Man comes back here again."

CHAPTER TWO

It was only human to stuff shame or tragedy way down into the darkest recesses of our psyche, where we could pretend it couldn't affect us anymore. Where we could lie to ourselves that it never happened.

But Kimberley Mason kept the remnants of her personal tragedy close at hand, in a pale lavender box in the top cubby of her bedroom closet, to remind herself that life is more fragile than we can imagine. It was the first thing she glanced at every morning and the last thing she bid a silent goodnight to, reaching on tip-toe to stroke it with her finger.

On special days like this morning, when her daughter Gabrielle should have been two-and-a-half years old, Kimberley carefully pulled down the box, set it on her bureau, and folded back the lid with trembling hands.

She could hear the steady spray of the water from her husband Ammon's shower. The children were still asleep. Kimberley had just enough time to enact her monthly ritual honoring her daughter's brief, innocent life, marking the passing of time as close as she could to her other's children's milestones.

Kimberley smoothed the white baby blanket her mother had sewn and embroidered with lilacs. Lifted the white silk cap worn at her infant's hospital baptism. Stroked the tiny satin shoes that matched the nightgown they had buried her in. She fingered the pile of condolence cards, wrapped with a pastel silk ribbon. She gazed at the four birth photos. There were one each of tiny Gabrielle held in the arms of Kimberley and Ammon; by her two older siblings; by Grandma and Grandad; by Aunt Charlotte.

They had all known that the genetic defect would take her within days, if not hours. Yet, even with time to prepare, the moment of Gabrielle's last breath had shocked Kimberley, provoking an unexpected anger at a God that could let such a thing happen. She had since made her peace with God, or at least she liked to think so. Removing the round, white, orchid-scented candle, which her sister Charlotte had hand-scripted with the words "Beloved Child," she set it on her bureau. Lighting it, Kimberley closed her eyes and prayed to her child in heaven. She even prayed to God.

Temper my grief so that it helps me to help others in pain, Lord. Make me an instrument of your peace. Help me use this loss as a way to help other families and especially to help all the innocent children who come for help.

Blowing the candle out, her gaze following the thin plumes of smoke lingering in the air. "Love you, Gabrielle," she whispered. "Watch over us all, today. Especially your baby brother Jack. I'm starting my new clinic job today and he's starting day care. Have fun with the angels."

Before Ammon emerged from the bathroom, the memory box was safely in its cubby, and Kimberley on her way to rouse her sleepy-headed children for school and start breakfast.

———

Downstairs, Kimberley tucked six-month-old baby Jack in one arm, then grabbed a carton of orange juice out of the refrigerator.

"Morning Kim," Ammon said, planting a kiss on her cheek. "I'll take Jack," he added, lifting the baby out of her arms.

Jack worked his jaw, letting go with an ear-splitting wail.

"Mommy! Mommy!" cried Paige, galloping into the room, closely followed by younger brother Tony. "Can you make blueberry pancakes?"

Ammon swooped Jack through the air, making airplane noises to calm him.

"Look, Daddy, look!" Tony lifted his arms, zipping around the kitchen table. "I'm an airplane, too!"

Jack bawled louder.

"There's too much noise in this house!" Paige complained, covering her ears.

Ammon plunked the howling infant into his highchair and buckled him in. "Must be hungry." The microwave timer buzzed loudly. "Can you get his cereal?"

Kimberley didn't answer. She had gone into one of her fugue states, staring out the bay window at the brightening sky. She noticed her own reflection for a moment. Her fine, sandy brown hair was getting too long. The flowered pattern on her new blouse struck her as too busy for her thin frame and medium height.

"Kim?" Ammon gave her a sharp look, disturbed to see his wife transfixed and oblivious to the uproar of the kitchen. "You all right?"

"Oh!" Startled, Kimberley whirled around. "What?"

"Timer went off. His grub is cooked." He scooped up Tony as the four-year-old zoomed past on a third lap around the table, guiding him gently into a chair. "Enough, mate. Time to settle down and eat."

"Timer. Yes." Kimberley snapped back into the present in fully engaged Mommy mode. Pulling on an apron to protect her blouse, she retrieved the warm cereal and set it down in front of her husband.

Ammon caught her by the wrist. "Thanks, Kimmy." His dark brown eyes penetrated hers with an unspoken question.

"Everything's fine," Kimberley reassured him, flashing a quick smile. "Still need my father to pick up the kids today?"

"Yeah. Got that science club meeting after school, today. Biosphere project." Ammon gently wrestled the baby spoon from Jack's chubby fist. "Here now. Let go, Jackie. Good boy." He looked up at Kimberley. "I should be back around four-thirty, thereabouts."

"Why aren't *you* picking us up today, Mommy?" Paige asked.

"Today's Mum's day for working late at the clinic," Ammon answered. "So, let's hear a big cheer for Granddad!"

They obliged him. But even the sweet scene couldn't erase the one ache beneath the surface of Kimberly's composure. *Gabrielle.* She closed her eyes briefly, overcome by the overwhelming ache of loss.

She opened her eyes to find Ammon staring at her with an expression of concern. "Something wrong?" he murmured again. His hand smoothed back a stray wisp of hair from her cheek.

"I was thinking about a new case I start today." The words came out calmly, although she hadn't intended to mention it. Setting down her mug, she folded her arms around Ammon's waist, burying her face against his shoulder.

"What case?"

"Well, it's a SIDs case. I was going to mention it last night, but I forgot." She glanced up, feeling Ammon go rigid.

He was giving her that look; the guarded one that tells her he is bracing for disaster. The look that always spurred her to downplay the worst.

"It's nothing," she said softly. "It's a family grief situation. You know I can't say too much about it, but it may, possibly, you know, bring up some old feelings. And I figured you should know. That's all."

Ammon stiffened. "Do you have to take it?"

"I want to take it." Kimberley pulled back to look up at him. "Jon thought of me first. He said I'd be able to offer these young parents wisdom and guidance out of my, I mean, out of *our* own experience. He really thinks it's a good opportunity for—"

"Well, I don't," Ammon protested quietly. "Look how upset it's making you."

"It's not making me upset. Honest. It's just that I was thinking of how to help them, and one thing led to another, and I was remembering Gabrielle and..." Kimberley's voice trailed off. "She would have been two-and-a half today."

Ammon's eyes widened for a moment, as if he were calculating the date. "Right, right. I know," he murmured, drawing his wife closer, holding her for a long moment. But when they parted, he shook his head ever-so slightly, with an exasperated sigh. "I know being a therapist is important to you. But I don't pretend to understand why you need to keep opening up old wounds." Sighing again, he leaned in to kiss her forehead lightly. "As long as it doesn't affect you or the kids."

"Time for school!" Ammon called. "Everybody got their lunches? Backpacks? Jackets? Tony, stop mucking about with that syrup jar. Let's go! Let's go!" He scooted the children toward the front door. "The Mason family bus is leaving on time!"

Paige and Tony grabbed their belongings, then rushed to Kimberley for a quick kiss on their way out the door. Ammon collected his keys and briefcase while Kimberley brought Jack and his diaper bag to the car. She buckled him safely inside, then helped Paige and Tony into their car seats. Finally, she kissed Jack's cheek, wiping a thread of drool from his mouth.

"I love you," she cooed, tucking his light blanket around him. "Mommy loves you."

"Love me, too, Mama?" cried Tony, always hungry for her attention.

"Of course, Sweetie." She threw him a kiss, then one to her daughter. "You too, Paige! I love you all!"

"What about me?" Ammon asked.

"Love you the most," Kimberley said.

Firmly, she closed the door.

"Have a good day!" she called, stepping away as the car backed out of the driveway and headed down the winding road of their subdivision. She continued waving, leaning against the door frame, until the car disappeared from view. Only then did she finally allow the tears she'd been holding back all morning to flow, mourning her own child as she prepared to help another family mourn theirs.

CHAPTER THREE

"Connor?" Isabella Rodriguez called from the top of the stairs.

There was no answer, just the drone of the television. She started down, pausing when the living room came into view. There was Connor, sprawled on the couch, still watching Court TV and texting on his cell phone, his red hair mussed as if he'd been massaging his scalp again. A burning cigarette smoldered in the metal ashtray. She sighed as she reached the landing.

"Connor Mackenzie!"

"What's up?" He didn't look at her, intently scrolling through his messages. The one from charter boat owner Jeff Elken interested him.

> BOAT REPAIRS FOR U TOMORROW.
> CAN U GET HERE BY 6 AM?

About time, Connor thought, texting back to say he would be there.

"You all right?" Isabella moved closer, trying to get a look at his screen. "Who you texting?"

Connor ignored her, shifting away from her gaze to bring up a text sent by his cousin Gil.

No word yet

Connor frowned, tapping in a reply.

KEEP ME POSTED

"Who you texting?" Isabella demanded again.

"Jeff." The lie slipped out easily. Conner looked up at her and smiled. "He needs me on the boat tomorrow."

"Oh, that's good." Relieved, Isabella went over and kissed him on the cheek. "Alexia and Jayleen are ready to go. What about you?"

"What about me?" Reaching up, he pulled Isabella down next to him.

She ran her hand lightly against his chin, feeling the prickly two-day old stubble. "Scratchy-face," she teased gently. "You gonna shower and shave before we leave, right?"

He caught her hand and nuzzled her warm palm. Then he pulled her close to kiss her mouth.

Isabella giggled softly to indulge him. "*Te amo*," she murmured. Then she pleaded. "Come on. We have to be there in an hour."

He kissed her again, slowly, savoring the softness of her lips, lightly scented with apricot-flavored gloss. "You taste nice," he murmured, running his hand along her silky hair. "Do we have to go?"

Isabella pulled away, frowning. "Yes, Coriño. You know we do." She searched his blue eyes, but he only shrugged and sank back against the couch.

"I've been thinking." Connor reached for his cigarette, which was almost burned to the filter. "I don't know. It's just…" He shrugged and inhaled. "What's the point?" Stabbing out the cigarette, he slumped back and stared up at the ceiling. "Going to some therapist…that's not gonna change anything."

Isabella considered her next words carefully, using her most soothing tone of voice. "The whole family has to go. That's what the school psychologist said. Otherwise, it's not going to help Alexia."

"I've heard that shit before." His voice was steel. His eyes were blue ice, avoiding her gaze.

"This is different." Repressed anger flooded her stomach with acid. Still, Isabella managed to keep her voice soft, soothing. "I know you don't like to talk about...but..." She bit her lower lip. "But we have to all of us go."

"Why can't you just take the girls? You don't need me." His eyes strayed to the television screen.

Angrily, Isabella grabbed the remote and switched off the TV.

"Hey!" A flash of annoyance flickered over Connor's face. "Come on. I did that support group thing you wanted. Asshole. He had no right to say what he said about me. Prick!"

"This is different." She reached over and took his hand, tracing the prominent blue veins along his arm. "This therapist, Mrs. Mason, she's gonna help Alexia. She's gonna help us get past this."

"I'm past it." Connor pulled away, annoyed that Bella was pushing the issue. "I just don't want to keep talkin' about that night. Okay? Is that too much to fuckin' ask?"

Isabella froze. She had the distinct sensation of being underwater, submerged beneath the surface of their lives, with a gulf widening between her and Connor. The loneliness of it left her unable to express what she really felt. She was tired of his evasions, of his broken promises, of his selfishness. So she simply let his question hang in the air until he couldn't stand the silence between them.

For Connor, seeing Isabella, his beautiful, brown-eyed girl, withdraw like that triggered memories of his own emotionally unavailable mother. He knew what was at stake here. Knew it in his bones. If Alexia didn't snap out of this, didn't stop sleeping in that damned crib, didn't stop freaking out at school, that damned social worker would make trouble. She could say he was an 'unfit parent.' Could even call in Child Protection. God, he hated them all! All the f—ing busy bodies. Of course his daughter was sad, he fumed silently. Who wouldn't be sad when their baby brother died? She just needed time.

"Why can't everybody just leave us the hell alone!" He thumped the cushion in frustration. He raked his fingers through his hair, his scalp tingling. Shaking out a cigarette, he fumbled with the lighter. His hands trembled. He was pissed, both at Bella and himself. He hated feeling trapped and he hated feeling weak. He took a long drag off the cigarette and held it in. He wished it were marijuana.

"You *said* you'd *come*." The uncharacteristic accusation, sharp and pointed, was out of Isabella's mouth before she could stop it.

Connor exhaled slowly, making the smoke trail out of his nostrils. He reached for her hand, but Isabella drew it behind her. "Come on," he wheedled. "Don't be like that."

"You promised!" Isabella held her breath, fingering the silver locket that held a photo of Lando inside, a rare present from Connor. He'd given it to her just yesterday, totally out of the blue. "You promised me, Connor. You promised to step it up. Make a commitment to your daughters after everything that's happened. You gotta be stepping it up, or that social worker's gonna take our kids away from us." She shook her finger at him. "You said it yourself! And I'm not about to let that happen, at least without a fight!"

Connor stared at his nails, which were bitten down to the quick. He began to pick at a cuticle.

"Is that what you want?" she accused him, her accent growing stronger with her despair. "Ay *Dios Mio*! We just lost our son. You wanna lose the girls, too?"

Her words penetrated his torpor. *She might be right. Going to this stupid therapist might just get the social worker off their backs.*

"Okay." He took a deep breath, then grudgingly nodded. "I'll go and shave. And then, maybe, if I feel like it, maybe I'll go with you."

"Come on now." Isabella tugged at him. "I got your clothes laid out on the bed. And there's a fresh towel and razor in the bathroom."

Connor rose unsteadily, leaning against her for a moment.

"Connor?" Isabella glanced anxiously into his eyes, relieved to see his pupils were normal. "You all right?"

"I'm good." He straightened, kissing the tip of her nose. "You're the only one," he murmured, cupping his hand against her cheek, rubbing her skin with his thumb. "The only one I'd do this for. You know that, right? I'm doing it for you."

"I know." Forcing a smile, she pushed him toward the stairs. "You got twenty minutes. We don't want to be late."

Connor nodded and slowly started up the stairs. His legs felt heavy, like an old man's.

Isabella watched him anxiously, until he reached the top and disappeared from view, silently praying that she could get him to the clinic before he changed his mind and screwed everything up again.

CHAPTER FOUR

"Good morning, Mrs. Mason!" Receptionist Emma Wu flashed a quick smile at Kimberley as she entered the reception area. "Your first appointment has already checked in."

Kimberley found her pile of blue folders on the end of the worn oak reception desk. A neatly typed list of appointments showed a full schedule. Along with tonight's support groups, it would keep her going steady until nine in the evening.

Flipping open the first folder, she read the name. Mackenzie. Inside were two documents. A school psychologist report on Alexia Rodriguez-Mackenzie that said the child showed signs of depression, severe withdrawal, and meltdowns over the recent sudden death of her sibling. A Medicaid letter authorized up to ten sessions for family grief therapy, and ten for the child's individual therapy sessions.

The SIDs case.

She asked Emma to point out the Mackenzies.

"Let's see." Emma scanned the room. "That couple by the magazine rack? See them? Filling out forms?"

The couple looked very young and sweet, their heads bent over the clipboard. A red-headed child stood next to the father, pulling at his sleeve.

"Up, up, upsi-daisy!" she cried.

The father looked up, then gently shook his head.

Kimberley smiled at the sweet exchange. But her full attention focused on the dark-haired child snuggled against her mother's side, sucking her thumb with a vacant, forlorn expression. Her mother absently stroked her hair.

That must be Alexia. Poor baby. We have some hard work to do here.

———

"Here we are!" Kimberley led her new clients upstairs. Swinging open the door to her office, she moved quickly through the small, dim room, switching on table lamps and the floor lamp behind her desk. "Welcome, everyone! Please make yourselves at home."

The Mackenzies hung back. The youngest stepped across the threshold, tentatively scanning the room. Catching Kimberley's eye, she shyly wiggled her fingers in greeting.

"Come on in," Kimberley said. "Sit anywhere you like." Busying herself at her desk, she gave her new clients time to carve out their own space in their own way, which always gave her a strong first impression of the family dynamics.

The youngest, Jayleen, tugged on her father's hand. "Daddy, can I sit in the rocking chair?"

"Sure," Connor said, smiling as he followed Jayleen inside to lift her onto the cushioned seat. He rummaged in his pockets, retrieving miniature cars, a red fire truck and a blue van. The child eagerly opened her hands to receive them, then settled down to roll them along the arm of the rocker. Connor nodded with an expression of quiet pleasure.

He dotes on her. Kimberley mentally filed that observation away.

"Nice set up," Connor remarked, settling his tall body onto the couch. "Plenty of room for all of us." He patted the cushion, inviting Isabella to join him. With the eldest daughter still clinging to her leg, Isabella lurched over to the couch, finally nestling next to him. Alexia settled at their feet. Isabella reached in her diaper bag and fished out a coloring book and crayons.

"Color in your book, Alex," her father said.

A bit sharp with her, Kimberly mentally noted. *And she doesn't respond. Listless.*

Kimberley was now fully engaged, mentally primed to soak up everything about the family. She thought of the therapy process as similar to doing a jigsaw puzzle, where all the bits of information were scattered. It was her job to coax them out, sort through, and piece them together until they reveal the whole picture of family or personal dynamics.

Her first impression was of a family smothered in a heavy blanket of grief. Her heart instinctively went out to them, as she discussed how the sessions would work.

"You're younger than we figured." Connor's eyes met Kimberley's gaze for a mere second before flickering off again.

"Did you expect someone older?"

Connor shrugged. "Not really." His eyes roamed the room.

"I see you went to three group sessions for grief counseling after your son died." Kimberley consulted her notes. "How did that go?"

There was a long pause. Isabella murmured that it didn't seem to help Alexia.

"I'll say!" Connor snorted. "That old guy that ran the support group? He didn't like us much." His eyes darted to Isabella. "Weren't his type."

"I don't think he disliked us, Connor," Isabella demurred.

Connor dismissed her comment with a wave of his hand.

"Did talking to other parents going through the same thing help you, Isabella?" Kimberley persisted.

"They weren't the same as us," Connor said flatly. "They were talking about suicides, kids dying in a car accident, cancer. It was f-ing depressing, if you wanna know the truth."

Isabella glanced at Connor and shrugged. Her eyes had that

absent look that Kimberley recognized from the bereavement classes she and Ammon had attended.

She's thinking about her baby, the way she keeps touching her locket. Using it as a soother.

Kimberley plunged on with some questions intended merely as an ice breaker to put the family at ease. But Connor hurried the process along with brief, almost curt answers. The girls were five and three; parents in their early twenties; they had met at high school at the Newburgh Free Academy; Connor was three years ahead of Isabella. No, they weren't married. They'd moved in together just before Alexia was born. Connor worked part time doing boat maintenance and crewing on charter boats in the Newburgh marina. He said it with pride. Isabella was taking one night-class a semester. She wanted to become a nutritionist.

Throughout the process, Connor seemed to vacillate between defensive and boastful to silent and wary as a hunter. His eyes constantly scanned the room. Isabella reminded the therapist of a dancer: languid and yielding, yet poised for some sudden, dramatic move.

As a couple, they were physically striking. Slim and petite, Isabella had a smooth cafe-au-lait complexion, full lips, dark eyes, and glossy black hair. Connor was lanky, with a long body, hawkish features, pale complexion, blue eyes, and red hair. Although clean shaven, he seemed an indifferent dresser in a faded gray thermal pullover, worn jeans with fraying hems, and brown hiking boots scuffed beyond repair. In contrast, Isabella was all understated elegance on a limited budget, dressed in a turquoise sweater over jeans embroidered with a sprinkling of white flowers. Kimberley wondered if she embroidered them herself.

The little ones were also a study in contrasts. Alexia favored her mother, while Jayleen had her father's blue eyes and red hair, as well as her mother's coffee complexion. Both girls were dressed in bright, coordinated sweater tops and leggings. They appeared healthy and well-taken care of.

"Well, what would you like the focus of today's session to be?" Kimberley asked.

The couple exchanged glances.

"It's Alexia. She's been very sad since, well, her brother…" Isabella's voice trailed off.

"We're concerned about her," Connor cut in sharply. "Very concerned. Yeah. It's why we came."

"Would you like to talk about your son?" Kimberley said.

Connor visibly stiffened. No one said a word. Isabella touched her locket. Alexia sucked her thumb harder. Jayleen bent her head lower and rolled her cars back and forth across her lap.

"Lando died in the night," Isabella finally said, sniffing loudly. "Last month. He was only…" She took in a sharp breath, as if choking back tears. "Only eight months old."

"I'm so sorry," Kimberley murmured. "I know it's a very traumatic time. That's what I'm here to help you with."

Connor put his arm around Isabella, drawing her closer so that she could rest her head against his shoulder. He lowered his chin against her hair with a sigh. They clasped hands, entwining their fingers together, presenting a bittersweet study in deep grief.

"I was having this dream." Isabella's voice sounded as if it were coming from faraway. "I woke up, and I thought of the baby, because he hadn't cried for his feeding, you know? He usually slept in our bed."

"And would have been, but your mother was the one said he needed to be in a crib," Connor said.

"Umm-hmm." Isabella nodded. "So we started letting him sleep in the crib. Like, the day or two before?"

"Yeah. Two days before," Connor agreed.

"Right." Isabella fingered her locket. "And so when I woke up that night, I was wondering where the baby was, and Connor wasn't there either."

As Isabella rambled on, Kimberley sensed that the bereft mother was circling around the subject, approaching it sideways. *Still too raw to address directly.*

"He had a cold," Isabella continued. "The baby, he was fussy all day, you know. Sneezing and all stuffed up. I hated to leave for my class. I just…I just felt so bad for him." She stopped suddenly, looking over at the therapist. "Do you have children?"

"Four." Kimberley nodded. "About the same ages as yours."

"Then you know."

"I do know." Kimberley has a sudden impulse to mention Gabrielle. *Don't make this about your grief.* "I do understand."

Somehow that seemed to reassure the bereaved mother. The words tumbled out. Isabella had opened the door to the children's room and smelled something bad. She had thought at first one of the girls must have been sick.

"I mean, it wasn't a baby smell, you know?" Isabella's voice cracked. "There was, there was vomit. It was, was all over Lando's sheet."

Vomit? When Kimberley had researched SIDS, the diagnosis was considered to be just the opposite: a case of a death with no obvious symptoms. *Wouldn't vomit indicate some other cause?* She made a small note on the pad on her lap.

Isabella coughed, then retched, struggling to clear her throat. Rummaging frantically through the diaper bag, she pulled out a juice box, hands shaking as she struggled to peel the plastic wrap off the miniature straw.

Connor grabbed it, biting off the wrap, and spit it out. Poking the straw into the box, he offered Isabella a sip.

Kimberley studied the girls. Kneeling on the rocking chair now, Jayleen rolled her cars along the rim of the chair's back. Alexia was still crossed legged on the floor, her head bent over her open book, impassively coloring Disney princesses.

"He was cold," Isabella finally said, describing the moment she found her son. "When I turned him over and saw his face, I knew he was dead. I really don't remember anything else."

Kimberley shuddered involuntarily. There was absolutely no response from the girls. *Are they even listening? Or just numbing out with coloring and cars?*

Her attention returned to Isabella, who was crying now, roughly brushing away her tears with the back of her hand. The gesture roused Connor, who reached for a box of tissues from the side table. As Isabella dabbed at her eyes, Connor stroked her hair.

"I heard her screaming." Connor's voice was monotone, disconnected from any emotion. "It was so loud, I'm thinking somebody must've broke in, you know. Attacking her or some-thin' bad." His eyes seemed to be focused on some invisible point in space and time, even as he continued to stroke Isabella's hair. "When I got there, she was holding the baby, screaming her head off. Then she just…I don't know…just folded up. Just fell down. You know?" He looked over at Kimberley and for the first time, settled his gaze on hers. "I caught her before she hit the floor. Then I laid her down. We called nine-one-one. Started doing CPR on my son. I did all that."

"That was good, Connor." Kimberley returned the young man's gaze with an encouraging nod. "And how soon did they respond?"

"Couldn't tell you." Connor's shoulders twitched. "I was still doing CPR when they pulled up. I uh, I told Alex, run down and let 'em in."

Kimberley's hand rose to her mouth involuntarily, but she stifled a gasp. *That poor child let paramedics into her house? She watched her mother faint? They heard their mother scream?*

Connor's eyes narrowed, as if he sensed disapproval. "How was I gonna go?" he said, his voice hoarse with frustration. "Had my hands full. I was the one trying to save him."

"It's okay," Kimberley said, almost by way of an apology for her reaction. "It's… It's… I can only imagine what you were going through."

"Yeah, I don't think so. You know what? The EMTs, they didn't do a thing for him. I'm thinking of suing." Connor thrust out his jaw and studied Kimberley for a moment. "Yeah, 'cause they just came and took over. But not even a minute goes by and they stop. Said my son was gone. I was pissed. They shoulda' kept trying. But no! They called it. They wrapped him up, took him away. And that was it." He leaned in suddenly toward Kimberley, his tone dropping into a whisper. "That was the last time we saw my son."

Kimberley couldn't fathom why no effort had been made by the emergency technicians to help the family through the ritual goodbyes and symbolic 'handing over' of the deceased. It was certainly the norm in stillbirths. *Why would a SIDS death be any different?*

But these were not the questions to ask the Mackenzies right now. Instead, she offered her condolences on losing their sweet baby.

"Thank you," Isabella whispered, stroking her locket once more.

"What a pretty locket."

"Connor got it for me." Isabella smiled.

"Is there a photo inside?"

"Two." Isabella nodded. "Lando and my Dad. We named the baby for my Dad. He died when I was little." She looked up at Kimberley. "And now both of them are—" She moaned, reaching for her bag with a shaky hand. "Somewhere in here there's a photo of Lando. "She rummaged around for a moment. "Here it is. His christening picture."

She handed it to Connor, who stood up and laid it carefully on the therapist's desk.

"Give her this one." Isabella passed on another photo. "It's one we took before...before, well, you know."

Kimberley studied the photos. "He's a beautiful baby."

"Yeah, yeah," Isabella agreed. "He's all Connor, even down to the Mackenzie red hair."

Connor squirmed. Isabella brushed his reddening cheek with the tips of her fingers. "You loved having a boy, after all us girls."

Connor gave a tight smile and nodded, shifting uncomfortably.

Animated by her happy memories, Isabella gushed out a string of anecdotes. Lando had been so smart. Connor had brought home a different toy car for him every day. He and the girls would lay all the toy cars out in front of the baby to see which he would choose.

"It was always the red fire engine," Isabella said proudly. "The one Jayleen's playing with. That was his favorite. Whenever a fire engine came down the block, he'd get excited. He'd say 'fa-fa.' He was trying to say fire engine. So smart! I told you right? My father was a fireman."

The children looked up, the first time they betrayed that they were listening to the conversation.

Kimberley decided it was time to talk directly to the girls. "What other games did you like to play with your brother?"

The question was met with a long silence.

"Peek-a-boo," Alexia finally said, her soft, hesitant voice a shade above a whisper. "He liked playing peek-a-boo with me. Through the crib bars."

"I've played that with my babies." Smiling and nodding to show encouragement, Kimberley had the urge to gather this sweet, vulnerable child into her arms. "It's so much fun, isn't it?" A ghost of a smile flitted across Alexia's lips, as she nodded solemnly.

Pleased at the small breakthrough, Kimberley glanced at the clock, then guided the session to its close.

"Thank you so much, Isabella and Connor, for sharing these beautiful pictures," she said, handing them back to Isabella. "I think you've made a good first step toward being able to heal the grief. And I'm sure, as we go through the process, you'll be able to talk about it more easily each time we meet."

"Talk about it more!" Connor exploded, sitting upright as if ready to bolt. "What makes you think we want to go over and over what happened that night? We're only here because of Alex!"

He stared at Kimberley, openly hostile, as if daring her to

judge him. As if he was trying to provoke her. "Does that make me some kind of bad person? Huh? That I don't want to keep dredging up that rotten night?"

"No, no," Kimberley reassured him. "It's a natural reaction. I do understand that the process of therapy can be very uncomfortable for some people."

"Uncomfortable? How about stupid?" He leaned forward to confront Kimberley, as Isabella shrank back into an embarrassed retreat. "Talking can't ever bring Lando back!"

Kimberley knew she had to reach deep into her own hard-won experience to find a way to help this angry young father.

"Sometimes, stuffing the pain deep inside only makes you feel more alone. More upset. The more alone you feel, the harder it is to deal with the pain." Kimberley was no longer speaking as a therapist, but from her own hard-won experience. "Grief starts to smother your emotions. It makes you feel helpless. Scared. Although it seems counterintuitive, Connor, talking about the pain is often the only way to release a lot of those bottled-up bad feelings. And that will help make the pain go away eventually."

She could see Connor wasn't buying it.

But Isabella wore a hopeful expression. "Do you think maybe, that's what Alexia needs to do?"

"Yes." Kimberley nodded, glancing over at Alexia, then Jayleen. "Yes I do. And that's something I can help her with. Something we can all help her with. Talking about the happy times spent with Lando can go a long way toward helping Alexia and Jayleen replace the bad memories with the good ones. You saw just now how it worked."

She forced herself to look at Connor with compassion. His head was tilted back, his expression sullen.

"It might help you, too, Connor," she suggested gently.

Connor sat up. With an air of cool appraisal, his eyes raked over her, up and down, in a way that chilled Kimberley and made her feel totally exposed. And when he finally spoke again, his voice dripped with sarcasm. "Well, Miss Kimberley, we'll just have to see how good a therapist you are, then."

Kimberley felt as if he had flung down some kind of challenge that she couldn't afford to lose.

CHAPTER FIVE

It was nearly ten when Kimberley pulled into the driveway that night. The light in the kitchen was still on. She could see Ammon through the dining room window, piles of paper stacked around him, his head bent over the one he was marking.

Exhausted from the long day, she hauled her briefcase and a bag of groceries from the back seat. The night sky was clear and cold enough that her breath formed a thin trail of condensation. She looked up, taking a moment to admire the star-flecked sky and seek out the Big Dipper, the first constellation her father had taught his daughters to find. Ever since she was tall enough to peer through the lens of his telescope, he had shown them the wonders of the heavens, naming the stars and planets, pointing out the rings of Jupiter, the moons of Saturn, and the quicksilver threads of meteor showers as they burned through the void. They had even seen comets, gaseous and haloed, hanging in space, as breathtaking as if they were the Star of Bethlehem.

As a child, Kimberley had imagined that when she put her eye to the scope, she was peering into God's brain, with the stars as the manifestations of his love. After Gabrielle had died, friends had registered a star in her name. Ever since then, Kimberley thought of the stars in a more bittersweet way, as millions of heavenly souls, winking down on their loved ones. Sometimes the thought was comforting.

Tonight, it was not.

———

"Kimmy?" Ammon called softly, as he heard his wife come in through the garage door at the back of the kitchen. "Need a hand with the bags?"

"No. I didn't get much. Just stopped off for milk, a loaf of bread, and Paige's favorite cereal." She kept her voice low, so as not to wake the children. Quickly, she put away the groceries. Walking into the dining room, she moved up behind her husband, kissing the back of his neck. In this moment, she was so grateful for her life with him. Grateful for everything they shared.

"Nice," Ammon murmured, as she hugged him. "How'd it go?"

"Pretty well," she said, noncommittally, slipping into the chair next to him. "Big pile you got there, Professor Mason." It was her teasing name for him.

"Unit test," he explained with a sigh. "I'll be at it another hour, I guess." Yawning, he stretched his arms over his head. "So what about the SIDS case?" His expression was calm, but his eyes searched her face.

Be careful what you say, Kimberley thought.

"It's pretty straight forward, I think, for the parents. But their daughter is going to need a lot of attention. Oh, if you saw her face, Ammon! She was the saddest little thing."

Ammon's eyes widened in alarm.

"But I'm sure I can help her," Kimberley quickly reassured him. "I feel as if I made a connection with her today."

Ammon remained silent, gazing at her for a last moment before returning to grading papers.

Unwilling to give up his attention so soon, Kimberley changed the subject. "How did Grandpa do with the kids, today?"

"Happy Days, apparently. Kicking Tony's Nerf ball 'round the rug when I came home." He chuckled, turning to face her with an indulgent smile. "He used the laundry baskets for goals. Clever. Wish I'd thought of that."

She laughed. "I hope the laundry wasn't in them!"

"No worries. Your father was grand enough to wash up two loads," Ammon said. He turned back to his papers, his pen methodically going down the line of answers. "Good bloke, really, he is. We're lucky to have him around, eh?"

"Yes." *Daddy's always there when you need him,* she thought. "Wish I could have seen them." She yawned, rising. "I think I'll go up to check on the children. Then I'll read in bed. Do you mind?"

Ammon looked up. "Nah." He smiled. "As long as you're okay."

"I'm fine," she said, kissing his forehead. "You worry too much."

"I know," he said, making a face at her. "It's my job."

Placing her shoes on the mat by the staircase, Kimberley padded lightly upstairs. Gently, she tiptoed into Paige's room and kissed her daughter's forehead. Paige was perfectly composed, even in sleep. She lay in the exact center of the bed, the covers pulled precisely to her chin, a placid smile on her face.

"Sweet dreams, my sweetie pie," Kimberley whispered before closing the door.

In Tony's room, Kimberley stepped gingerly. Sure enough, her foot came in contact with a rubber ball, which veered away into a dark corner. Her next step was squarely on a stuffed animal. Picking it up, she saw it was Eeyore, the depressed donkey from the Winnie the Pooh collection. She laid it on the top of his dresser, next to Tigger.

"There you go, old friend."

In the soft glow of the night light, she could see that Tony was out of his covers, as usual. He had turned nearly sideways across the narrow bed, one leg thrown up against the wall, the other splayed out, his arm flung over his head. His breaths came in short puffs, as if he were fighting dragons or running a train in his dreams.

Gently, she rearranged him properly, settling his head on the pillow and tucking the blanket around him. She knew he wouldn't stay that way. Even as she kissed the top of his head, he began to squirm in his sleep, and one arm shot out from under the covers.

Such a little monkey, you are, in perpetual motion.

The ritual 'last check' on her slumbering children usually filled Kimberley with a sense of peace. But tonight, as she reached the baby's nursery, she froze. Her chest constricted. Isabella's words invaded her mind.

He was cold.

I saw his face and I knew he was dead.

Kimberley shivered. She tried to banish the words and the disturbing images they conjured, but they played in an endless loop. She knew she was being irrational, projecting the anguish of her clients onto her own life. Still, she couldn't stop her heart from racing as she pushed the door open and hurried to the crib.

The blood rushed to her head. Her ears filled with fluid, distorting the sound of her breathing. She stood over Jack's crib in dread.

This is silly. Relax.

Gripping the railing, she strained to hear if Jack was still breathing. She started to reach for him. Her hand trembled. She was afraid to touch him for fear that Isabella's words, *he was cold,* would be true.

Forcing herself to bend lower over the crib, she caught the clean scent of baby powder and Johnson's shampoo. She brushed the tip of her finger against his silken cheek. It was warm. She moved her hand near his mouth and stood there for a long time, waiting for her irrational terror to dissolve under the steady rhythm of Jack's hushed breaths.

CHAPTER SIX

"This place is busy today!" Isabella held open the door of *Casa Rosita* for her mother and the girls. The restaurant was the most cheerful on Broadway, with pink chairs and yellow tables set against aqua walls. Everything was festooned with garlands of silver mylar. Noisy groups of diners packed the place. The delicious aroma of Mexican food piqued Isabella's appetite.

"I hope we don't have to wait too long for a table," Beatriz Rodriguez complained. "I only have an hour between shifts."

"*Abuelita*, will they run out of quesadillas?" Jayleen asked anxiously, tugging on her grandmother's hand.

"Never, *Pequeña*. Rosita would never run out." Beatriz shifted from foot to foot. "Ooh, my feet are killing me." She waved at one of the busboys cleaning off tables. "Can we sit there, Miguel?" she called out. He nodded and Beatriz nudged the girls forward to claim the table even before it was cleared.

After settling in, they ordered lunch without bothering with a menu: quesadillas with chorizo and cheese for the girls, chicken enchilada suizas for the women.

"Iced tea for my daughter," Beatriz said. "Chocolate milk for my granddaughters. Coffee for me. Nice and strong. I just finished my shift at St. Luke's, and I have a second shift tonight."

Isabella cringed at her mother's complaints. In her head, she heard Connor's familiar condemnation.

Your mother tells everybody her business.

But the waitress only clucked her tongue in sympathy. "*Es una lástima!* Such a shame. You need all the caffeine you can get."

"You know it," Beatriz agreed.

The two women chuckled in commiseration.

Isabella felt ashamed. In her mind, she argued with Connor in her mother's favor. *Why shouldn't she talk about her work?* Especially here, where Rosita and her crew were almost like family. Mom and Rosita had been school friends, two eight-year-old Mexican girls newly arrived and totally bewildered by American culture.

"Ah!" Beatriz sighed, fastidiously smoothing her pink floral smock over her pale green scrubs, the uniform for the preemie ward. "Now, I wonder what is in my bag, today?"

The girls sat up in anticipation, Jayleen wriggling in her seat. Beatriz made a show of rummaging through her canvas tote. Slowly, she pulled out a half-finished sweater in rose-colored yarn that she was knitting for Alexia.

The girls oohed and aahhed. Beatriz held it against Alexia to check the fit. She allowed the girls to stroke the fabric and voice their approval before folding it back into the tote.

"That's all!" she teased. The girls knew better, holding their breaths for the anticipated treat. They were rewarded with a pack of crayons, a mini book of stencils, and two small pads.

"To share," Beatriz instructed, gazing at the girls with quiet pride.

"What do you say?" Isabella prompted.

"Thank you, *Abuelita!*" the girls chimed in, pouncing on the art supplies.

"That was a really nice treat, Mama," Isabella added. "You shouldn't spoil them."

"Just a few things from the dollar store." Beatriz shrugged as if it meant nothing, but Isabella could see she was pleased at the girl's reactions.

"How did things go with the therapist yesterday?" Beatriz added, switching to Spanish.

It was another habit that always annoyed Connor. He often complained that her mother was deliberately excluding him which, Isabella had to admit, was true.

"Fine," she answered in Spanish. "She's really nice."

"But is she good?" her mother emphasized.

"I think so." Isabella shrugged. "I mean, Connor and the girls seemed to like her."

"As if that's anything to go by," Beatriz answered dismissively.

Isabella bit back a retort. Actually, she wanted to say, Connor knew a lot about therapists and social workers: from his own family's experience, they were useless at best, troublemakers at worst.

"More importantly," her mother continued. "What's the course of treatment she's going to take with Alexia?"

Isabella shifted uncomfortably. "I don't know yet. It was only the first session." Seeing her mother's look of disapproval, she quickly added, "She's going to work with Alexia on Tuesdays after school. So, probably then she'll have a plan."

"And how many sessions did Medicaid allow?"

"Ten for the family. Same for Alexia," Isabella conceded, feeling as if she were being cross-examined.

"*Only* ten?"

"Well, they might extend it for Alexia, depending on how it goes."

The waitress brought their meals. Isabella was grateful for the interruption. She busied herself cutting Jayleen's quesadilla.

"Oh, by the way, I found this book at the library for you." Beatriz reached into her tote bag, then slid a large book over to her and tapped a finger on the title. Isabella stared at the book. *Psychological Assessments of Childhood Trauma*. It sounded way above her head and too depressing to even think about.

"Thank you, Mama." Isabella sighed. She groped for the right words. She knew her mother was only trying to help, but sometimes she pushed too damned hard. "I know you mean well."

"I only thought this would help you understand whatever the therapist says," Beatriz said defensively. Her posture was ramrod straight. Her head held high with wounded dignity. "Information is important. To get around in this world—"

"I know." Isabella finished her mother's well-worn aphorism: "You have to know how things work."

"Yes, *Querida*." Beatriz gave her daughter a stern look. "You really do."

———

Someone bumped hard into the back of Isabella's chair as she was just starting to enjoy her meal.

"Ty! Apologize to the lady, right this minute!" commanded a slim black woman, struggling to maneuver a stroller and two young boys past Isabella's table. Turning around, she did a double take. "Ohmigod, it's you! Isabella!"

"Danielle!" Isabella recognized her effusive classmate from last semester. She stood up and the two hugged.

"Where you been, girl?" Danielle said. "I hardly see you anymore. You taking another nutrition class or what?"

Isabella shook her head. "Comp 101 this time."

Danielle snorted and waved her hand. "I already did that one. These your kids?"

Before Isabella could answer, Danielle turned back to her own boys. "Sit down, Ty. Right there. And you, Jay-Jay. Sit down with your brother now. Take off your jackets." She turned back to Isabella. "Boys! They never listen to a word I say. They're too wired. Girls are better. Look how nice your girls are behavin'. Sometimes I tell you, I'd trade in my boys for girls any day."

The words stung Isabella. She touched her locket. She'd give anything to hold Lando one more time.

Danielle unhooked the infant car seat and set it on the table. "This one's an angel," she cooed, removing the baby's pink hat and jacket.

Isabella stared at the baby, which triggered a whirl of emotions, from jealousy at seeing someone with a newborn to stunned disbelief. Danielle hadn't looked pregnant back in December.

"When did you have her?" Isabella managed to ask.

Hearing the strained tone of her mother's voice, Alexia quietly put down her fork to watch the two women.

"She's my sister's!" Danielle laughed. "Her name is Neisha." She fussed over the infant. "She's the prettiest little thing."

Isabella froze. "Congratulations," she managed to say before lapsing into silence.

Alexia crept to her mother's side. Wrapping her arms around Isabella's waist, she pressed her cheek against her mothers.

"God, it's nice to hold a baby again," Danielle babbled on as she lifted the infant to show her off. "They're great when they're small enough to stay put. Right, you sweet baby girl?"

Isabella opened her mouth, but no sound came out. She felt faint. The babble of voices, the light, even the delicious aromas faded away. Only the pressure of Alexia's embrace kept her from descending into the state she called 'the pit'.

"You just had a baby, right? A boy, wasn't it?" Danielle glanced around the table, as if looking for the missing child.

Isabella wanted to die. She couldn't reply. She couldn't move.

Alexia tightened her grip, as if determined to keep her mother in the present.

Beatriz coughed politely to get the woman's attention.

"Danielle, is it? Hello, I'm Isabella's mother. I guess you didn't know, but…" Her voice was low and soothing, as if she were giving bad news to a patient. "We lost Orlando. He passed away last month."

Danielle looked stricken. "Oh." She glanced at Isabella, then back at Beatriz. "Wow. Sorry. That's just... Girl, I'm so sorry," she ended lamely.

For a moment, no one spoke.

"Hey, Mama! Can we order?" asked one of the boys, as a waitress arrived at Danielle's table.

Danielle nodded. "Go ahead." She turned back to Isabella. "I, uh, I gotta get the boys some food now. We should talk, okay? I mean, if you need to talk, you know? I'm around."

She gave an awkward half smile, then sat down at her own table with her back to Isabella.

———

Beatriz watched in amazement as her granddaughter took charge.

Alexia led Isabella back to her seat, urging her to sit, even placing the fork back in her mother's hand. She'd never seen Alexia and Isabella act this way, as if suddenly their positions were reversed.

It wasn't natural, she thought. It wasn't healthy.

"Mama, please eat something," Alexia urged.

For Isabella, the world seemed to recede. Even Alexia's voice was faint. She knew she was descending into the familiar funk of depression but was helpless to stop it. She took tiny bites of the enchilada. It was wasted on her now. She might as well be eating cardboard. The iced tea tasted bitter.

She reached out and stole a sip of Alexia's chocolate milk. Even its sweetness was muted.

"Are you all right?" Beatriz gently laid a hand on Isabella's wrist.

Her daughter nodded. Beatriz saw that her eyes were unfocused. She seemed a million miles away.

Alexia slipped over to her grandmother's side, her face grave. "Mama wants to leave, *Abuelita*," she whispered into Beatriz' ear. "We should go home soon."

Beatriz stared at Alexia for a moment, stunned at her grand-daughter's maturity. The scene she had just witnessed was disturbing. Isabella was more depressed than she had realized. Still, she was immensely proud of Alexia.

"Si, *Pequeña*. Finish your lunch. I'll ask for the bill."

———

After returning home from the restaurant, Isabella had fallen asleep on the couch. At three o'clock, she finally roused herself, throwing on a jacket to bring in the last of the laundry from outside. Ten garments hung from a line strung between the cherry tree and the weathered boat shed Connor's great-granddad had built.

Jayleen was riding her rusted red tricycle in circles around the battered plastic playhouse that Connor had rescued from cleanup day last October. She had worn the grass into a dirt path.

"Where's your sister, Jayleen?"

The child shrugged without a pause in her endless circuit.

Isabella just sighed.

With the laundry basket tucked under her arm, Isabella trudged up the staircase. Her thoughts strayed to dinner, mentally sorting through her staples: canned broth, black beans, and a box of Jiffy Corn Muffin mix.

She pushed open the door to the children's room. The crib's railing had been lowered. Alexia was curled up inside, sucking her thumb. Lando's favorite stuffed animal, 'Floppy Dog,' was tucked under her arm.

"*Miha*," Isabella crooned, setting down her basket. "What are you doing here? Huh? You should be playing in the backyard with your sister."

Alexia didn't answer. Her brown eyes were pools of sadness, her cheeks stained with faint tracks of salty tears. Isabella knelt by the crib, poking her fingers through to touch her daughter's hand.

"Oh, Sweetie," Isabella murmured, stroking her daughter's hair. "I know. I know just how you feel. You're missing Lando just like I am, aren't you?"

Solemnly, the child nodded.

Isabella sat back on her heels and gazed at her daughter. Even at this age, Alexia was beautiful. She was Isabella all over, didn't everyone say that? Jayleen was Daddy's girl with his blue eyes and reddish-brown hair, but Alexia was Mama's girl.

"You're my best friend, you know that?"

Alexia nodded again, her body relaxing slowly under her mother's soothing touch.

"Daddy and *Abuelita*, they mean well, but they don't suffer like we do. They don't understand how deeply we feel things, do they?"

Alexia raised her arms. Isabella stood up and lifted her out of the crib.

"Oh dear," Isabella groaned. "You're getting too big for me. You're growing up so fast." With Alexia's legs wrapped around her waist, Isabella carried her daughter over to the bed, sank down and began to rock her gently, crooning a lullaby. Alexia snuggled closer, burying her head against the hollow of her mother's neck. They stayed like that, rocking back and forth, until they heard the kitchen door slam, and the sound of Connor's voice.

"Hey, Bella? Where are you?" Connor sounded excited. "I got something to tell you!"

"Up here," Isabella called.

Alexia flew from her mother's arms and scrambled back over the rail into Lando's crib.

"Daddy doesn't like you being in the crib. If he sees you, you'll be in trouble," Isabella scolded.

Connor's heavy footsteps could be heard coming up the stairs.

Alexia burrowed deeper under the baby blankets.

Isabella flew to open the door, hoping to head him off, but Connor had already reached the landing.

"Guess what?" Connor's blue eyes sparkled. He winked at her, grinning. "I got a job at the docks, full-time, now through the whole summer!"

"That's great!" Isabella threw her arms around him, trying to angle herself out into the hallway to prevent him from seeing Alexia. "Doing what?"

"Same stuff as usual. But I'll be crewing steady. Jeff Elkin's brother-in-law is in the hospital with cancer. I'm going to fill in for him." He lifted Isabella and spun her around in the hallway. "He wants me to start next week, getting the Dutchman II ready for some eagle watching cruise he wants to do next month."

"That's great news, Connor!" Isabella hugged him tightly, lifting her face to him, praying that Alexia had climbed out of the crib by now.

Connor kissed her over and over, spinning her twice more. "Things are finally going my way for a change," he crowed. "I think we got a pretty good shot at getting in on some of that river-front money, you know?"

"Your grandpa would be so proud of you, Connor!" Isabella felt relieved, especially now that Connor was standing with his back to the girl's room.

"Yeah, wish the old guy was here to see it. It's going to be good. He's paying me ten bucks an hour! That's enough to put some more into Grandpa's old boat. Boy, I'd like to see her cruise the Hudson again one day."

"Ten? Oh my God, Connor!"

"Yup!" He grinned, stepping back from her to give a little victory shuffle. "Wanna know the best part?"

She nodded, giddy with so much good news.

"It's all under the table. So no taxes."

And no unemployment, either. Isabella's heart sank, although she kept her smile frozen in place. She didn't dare voice an objection; not when he was in such a good mood.

"Where are the kids? I want to tell them the good news."

"Oh, they're around, uh, somewhere."

Connor's expression changed to suspicion. He turned around and stalked into the room.

Isabella hurried after him, pulling on his arm.

Connor shook her off, planting his hands on the crib's railing, planting his feet as if balancing himself against rough seas ahead.

"Didn't Daddy tell you to stay out of the crib, Alex?"

Alexia didn't move. She sucked her thumb harder as if bracing for the worst.

"Connor, please?" Isabella pleaded.

"This nonsense has got to stop, Bella! I'm doing my part. I'm working full time. But I come home, and you're depressed. She's in the damned crib, defying me. Nobody's watching Jayleen."

"I'm sorry," Isabella whispered. "I'm sorry."

"It's no good, this way," Connor insisted. "I told you, we gotta take down the crib. Pack his clothes away in the attic. The toy dog. His cars. All of it."

Alexia hugged Floppy Dog tighter at his words.

"I don't want to forget my baby!" Isabella cried.

"That's why I gave you the locket," Connor said. "Why isn't that enough? Why do we have to have his stuff in our face all day, every damn day? It's too hard!"

When Isabella didn't answer, Connor turned back to Alexia. "Give me the dog, Alex. I don't want you girls playing with his toys anymore!"

"No!" Alexia cried, clinging tighter to the stuffed animal.

Furious, Connor leaned in and wrenched Floppy Dog out of her arms, stalked over to the closet and flung it on the top shelf.

Alexia howled with rage when he slammed the door shut.

"This shit stops right now!" Connor cheeks flushed with anger, his eyes narrowing. "If you won't keep her out of the crib, Bella, I will."

He lunged after Alexia.

She screamed, rolling deeper into the blankets.

He grabbed hold of the fabric, dragging her toward him.

Isabella screwed up her eyes, hating what she knew was about to happen.

Alexia clutched at the bars and howled in protest. She tried to kick, but her legs were tangled. She bucked and writhed instead.

"Goddammit Alex!" Connor was breathing hard. "Let go!"

"No! Noooo!" The child held on tighter, jerking her body repeatedly.

"Connor! Please, she's not ready," pleaded Isabella, raising both hands against her throbbing temples. "She's not ready."

Connor ignored her, struggling to get a better grip on the agitated child, who began shouting out, "No! No! No!" like a yapping dog.

"Let go!" he commanded.

"Connor!" Isabella felt paralyzed, not daring to interfere, but desperate to stop the noise. The houses were so close together, she was sure that the old lady next door would hear. "They'll call protective services. Please, this is not the way to—"

"Stay out of this, Isabella!"

He yanked hard.

Alexia screamed as her fingers were ripped from the bars. Her body flailed wildly as Connor struggled to hold on to her.

Isabella covered her mouth, biting her fist to keep herself from screaming. The pressure in her temples increased, signaling the onset of a migraine. An aura of rainbow colors pulsed around the fringes of her vision.

Connor lifted his daughter out of the crib and flung her onto her bed. With a tremendous yelp, Alexia hit the mattress, then bucked violently. Her head cracked against the wall.

For a long moment, no one moved. No one spoke. No one cried out.

Alexia's eyes opened wide, then she slowly sat up.

"She's fine," Connor said. "Aren't you, Alex?"

"No she's not. Are you Alexia?"

Alexia looked down at her feet and sucked her thumb harder, retreating further into herself.

CHAPTER SEVEN

Alexia had not spoken for days, when Mama told her it was time for another session with Miss Kimberley. She had dragged her feet on the walk over, so that Mama scolded her twice for scuffing her shoes.

She dragged her feet going up the staircase to Miss Kimberley's office. But to her surprise, Miss Kimberley opened a different door.

Inside was the prettiest room Alexia had ever seen.

"Wow! This is some beautiful room, hey girls?" Mama smiled at Alexia. "What'cha think?"

Alexia sucked her thumb and hung back by the closed door, watching as Mama and Jayleen checked out the room.

"This is our children's therapy room," Miss Kimberley said. "I hope you like it. The whole staff and lots of volunteers helped decorate it. In fact, you are the first one of my clients that I am bringing in here!"

She smiled at Alexia, as if expecting her to smile back.

Grownups always did that. I'm not smiling back.

Alexia did like the red and blue walls. She liked the yellow border that ran around the middle of the walls. She liked the big bookcase filled with toys, puppets, games, and books.

Mama pointed out a cat-shaped clock, with a long tail that moved back and forth. Alexia looked away.

"Did you see the dinosaur mirror?" Miss Kimberley walked over to its place on the wall.

"Me, me!" Jayleen shouted, and ran over to it. She stuck out her tongue and licked it.

"Jayleen! Stop that," Mama said. But she laughed, so Alexia knew she wasn't angry.

The room reminded Alexia of her classroom a little. Miss Kimberley seemed nicer than her teacher, but she still didn't want to be here.

Jayleen ran to the table in the center of the room. "Mama look! Somebody drew a lion on this chair!" She ran around to the next chair. She gasped. "Hey! There's a cat on this one! And Mama! See? That one's got a horsey!"

"They're stencils," Mama said. "I never thought of doing stencils on the furniture."

"Why doesn't everyone choose a chair?" said Miss Kimberley. "What chair do you want, Jayleen?"

"Could I have the lion?" Jayleen popped into the seat and leaned over the table to trace the outline of a stenciled figure. "Mama! Look! The table gots a lion on it, too!"

"Wow!" said Mama. "I think I'll take this one, with the little white lamb." She eased herself into the small chair.

"Which chair would you like, Alexia?" Miss Kimberley asked.

Alexia shrugged. Daddy had warned her not to say anything that would get her in trouble.

You gotta watch yourself.

Say the wrong thing, they can take you away.

Give you to some foster family that don't care nothing about ya.

Saying nothing, Alexia thought, was safer.

But Mama and Jayleen were telling her to pick a horse chair or the butterfly chair.

Alexia ignored them, walking slowly around the table. She sucked her thumb harder, wishing she could go home. What if she picked the wrong chair? One had a dog painted on it. She decided to sit in that one. It reminded her of Floppy Dog, but the ears were all wrong and it was black, not brown. She missed Floppy Dog. Daddy took him away and hid him high in the hall closet, where she couldn't reach, not even with the stepstool.

Miss Kimberley sat down across from Alexia and smiled. "Okay. How would you like to play a game?"

"Me! Me!" Jayleen cried, jumping up and waving her hand. "I want to play."

Mama laughed. That reassured Alexia a little. Mama hadn't laughed in a while, so she must like the therapy lady.

"This is a matching game," Miss Kimberley picked up a box from the table. It held two decks of cards. She put them into two stacks. She fanned out one stack, which had pretty pictures on them. Then, she turned over the first card in the big deck and laid it face up.

"These are the frame cards, which have words printed around the border. This one says 'funny,' see?" Miss Kimberley explained, pointing to the letters. "Now, I'm going to ask you, Jayleen, to choose one of the picture cards that you think matches the word 'funny'."

Jayleen wriggled closer, getting up on her knees to get a good look at the cards. She pointed to a sweet-faced, smiling clown in a sunny yellow suit with red buttons and a green bow tie. "Mama, don't it look like the helpful clown in The Little Engine book?"

Mama nodded. "You're right, *miha*!"

Alexia held her breath, wondering what would happen if Jayleen had made the wrong match. Would Miss Kimberley take her away, like Daddy said?

But Miss Kimberley praised Jayleen. "Very good job," she said. "Why did you pick him?"

"He gots a yellow flower in his hat!" Jayleen giggled. "And he gots red hair, just like me and Daddy!"

"Excellent!" Miss Kimberley said. "You are very good at noticing details." She laid the clown card on top of the larger one, so that it formed a frame around the picture. "And that's how you make a match."

"Oh, isn't that clever," said Mama. "Your turn, Alexia."

Alexia pulled her arms behind her back. What if she couldn't make a good match? What if she made the wrong match and Miss Kimberly gave her away to a foster family?

She watched Miss Kimberley choose another big card, laying it face up on the table.

"Do you know what that word is, Alexia?"

Alexia shook her head.

"Can you spell the letters?"

Alexia's hands trembled. "L?" she whispered, glancing quickly at Mama, who nodded. "Umm, O?" she whispered a little louder.

Alexia's brow furrowed in deep concentration at the third letter. It was a hard one. "Umm, U?"

Mama frowned and shook her head. Alexia held her breath, now trembling so hard, her teeth shook. The therapy lady would yell at her. Take her away from Mama.

But Miss Kimberley was still smiling.

"V," prompted Mama.

"V," echoed Alexia. She looked down again, staring hard at the card. She knew the last letter. "E!" she blurted out.

"Good job!" Miss Kimberley said. "Do you know what that spells?"

Alexia bit her bottom lip, trying to stop herself from crying. She didn't know the answer. She hung her head in shame. She wanted to run from the room. She wanted to go home.

Mama leaned over and whispered in her ear. "It spells love."

Alexia sniffled. "Love?" she whispered uncertainly, still not daring to look at the therapy lady.

"Very good," Miss Kimberley said. "So now, out of the

pictures that you see here, can you find one that would make a good match? Like Jayleen did?"

Alexia looked doubtful. She was almost paralyzed with fear.

"Go ahead," Mama urged.

"You can use my clown," Jayleen offered.

Alexia reached out with a trembling hand to spread the cards further apart. She studied each card intently. The tick of the clock sounded awfully loud. Her finger lingered on a picture of two dancing figures, but she passed on until she came to one of two girls in pretty dresses, their arms around each other, heads touching.

"That one," she said shyly. Then she froze, hanging her head, in case she had done the wrong thing.

"What a lovely match!" Miss Kimberley put the cards together. "What makes you choose that card, Alexia?"

For a long moment Alexia didn't answer, wondering what would be the right thing to say. She glanced at Mama, who blew her a kiss.

"Tell the lady, *miha*. It's all right."

Alexia gazed up at Miss Kimberley. She looked deep into the lady's eyes and realized they were as kind as Mama's and Abuelita's.

"I picked it," she said. "Because it's like Mama and me."

Kimberley had decided that she would use the remaining time in the session to work one-on-one with Alexia. The child had seemed to respond a little.

When Isabella and Jayleen left, Kimberley was dismayed, but not surprised to see Alexia immediately revert to her guarded demeanor. She literally shrank down into the chair, her dark brown eyes fixed on the table in front of her. Her head sank into her hunched shoulders, as if she were trying to hide. Her hands rested listlessly in her lap.

"Do you play games at home?" Kimberley asked gently, putting the cards back in the pack.

"Sometimes." Alexia's voice was barely above a whisper.

"What kind of games do you like best?"

Alexia was silent.

"My family likes to play word games. Like, if I say yellow, you might say banana, because bananas are yellow. Or maybe you'd say the word sun, because the sun is yellow."

Alexia didn't comment.

She looks like a frightened rabbit, frozen in place to pretend it didn't exist.

Kimberley tried another approach. "Well, we played my game. Now, you get to choose a game from the ones on the shelf."

Alexia kept her eyes down. She shrugged.

"Well, come on over here and let's see what games we have." Kimberley rose, keeping her voice casual, absolutely non-threatening. She held out her hand. "Come on. Let's see what's here."

Alexia rose from her chair, shuffling slowly around the table. Avoiding Kimberley's outstretched hand, she approached the bookcase, stopping about a foot away, keeping her eyes angled to the floor, her hands clasped behind her back.

"We have lots of different games," Kimberley said, pointing out a few of the cooperative learning games. Mermaid Island had a beach theme. Count Your Chickens was a farm game. Neither one elicited a flicker of interest from Alexia. She pulled the Feed the Woozle game down to show Alexia, but the novelty of popping silly snacks into the mouth of the orange Muppet-like creature aroused no enthusiasm.

"How about this one?" she asked. "Lost Puppies."

Alexia's head came up.

"Do you like puppies?" Kimberley hoped she had finally found a connection. "Well of course you do. You chose the puppy chair, didn't you?"

She began to lay out the game pieces, pleased at the minor progress they were making.

"See, the board is the neighborhood," Kimberley explained. "These are the streets where the puppies got lost, and these are the houses they live in. And these are the cards we use to find them. Do you have a dog at home, Alexia?"

Alexia shook her head, taking a step toward the table.

"A toy dog?" Kimberley asked.

Alexia hesitated, then slipped into the chair. She nodded.

"You do have a toy dog?"

Alexia nodded again, this time more confidently.

"That's great. We have those at my house, too," Kimberley said. "Now, we're set. Would you like to turn over the first card?"

Alexia studied the board in silence. Sensing her fragile emotional state, Kimberley resisted speaking too soon, pushing too hard. The only sound was the rhythmic tick-tock of the cat clock's pendulum tail. Just when Kimberley figured the game was a bust, Alexia reached out and turned over a card, giving a little gasp at the image of a long-eared brown puppy with a white patch over one eye.

"Floppy Dog!" Alexia cried. Her mouth dropped open in amazement, then spread into a delighted grin. Snatching up the playing piece, she clutched it to her heart. "Floppy Dog," she crooned.

Little by little, Kimberley coaxed Alexia to talk about the dog.

"Daddy put Floppy Dog in the closet," Alexia burst out angrily. "I can't reach him."

"Why did he do that?"

"He said it was no good."

"What's wrong with Floppy Dog? Is he broken?"

"No." Alexia laid the card on the table, stroking it with one finger. Tears welled up in her eyes. "'Cause he makes us feel bad."

"He makes you feel bad?" Kimberley echoed the child's words, using a technique called reflecting. Sometimes it helped the client hear what they were saying and reevaluate it.

"He makes Daddy feel bad," the child corrected, inserting her thumb in her mouth.

"Floppy Dog is a toy," Kimberley reiterated. "And it makes Daddy feel bad."

The child nodded sullenly. She took her thumb from her mouth. "The crib is bad, too."

Kimberley suddenly understood. "Oh, was Floppy Dog Lando's toy?"

Alexia nodded.

"And it makes Daddy sad to see Lando's things in the house?"

Alexia's tears spilled over, dripping down her cheek.

"Does Floppy Dog make you feel bad?"

"No!" Alexia whispered in a hoarse voice, choking on her tears.

"You love Floppy Dog?"

"Yes." The word came out in a low moan. She gazed up at Kimberley with a haunted expression, before breaking down completely.

Every maternal instinct in Kimberley took over, washing away the rules about avoiding physical contact with young patients. She crouched next to Alexia, hugging her shoulders, comforting her as she sobbed uncontrollably.

"There, there, Sweetie," she murmured, feeling as if she were rocking her own daughter Paige. "There, there, honey. It's okay to let out the sadness. You are safe here. It's safe."

Alexia cried in great moans and racking sobs. She went limp, arms dangling at her sides, as she let out the anguish she had been guarding so stoically for so many weeks.

When she had exhausted her emotions, Alexia sniffed loudly. Kimberley handed her a tissue and helped her blow her nose. "I'm just going to the sink over there for a washcloth," Kimberley said quietly, pointing to the back of the room. She stood up. To her amazement, Alexia took Kimberley's hand and slid off her chair.

The child trusts me!

Kimberley cooled the child's forehead and washed her tear-stained face. They returned to the table with seventeen minutes remaining in the session.

"Would you like to draw a picture of Floppy Dog to show me what he looks like?" Kimberley asked. "I have some paper and crayons."

"Yes, please." Alexia threw her entire body into the project, swaying in the chair, even climbing up on it to get a better angle.

"So this is Floppy Dog," Kimberley enthused. "Oooh, I like how you drew him. You're really a good artist, Alexia."

With a shy smile, the girl pushed the picture over to Kimberley. "You keep him."

"Why thank you!" Kimberley said, touched by the gesture. "But, wouldn't you like to take this home with you?"

A shadow crossed Alexia's solemn face. She shook her head. "Daddy will only put it in the closet."

CHAPTER EIGHT

The following week, Connor and Isabella arrived alone for their next session, looking relaxed and cheerful. Connor, once again, choose the couch. Isabella snuggled next to him, kicking off her shoes, and tucking her legs up under her. Connor put his arm around her shoulders.

It was sweet, Kimberley thought, how they gazed into each other's eyes, nodding as if in answer to unspoken questions, as attuned to each other as any long-married couple, despite their youth.

Perhaps today's a good day to bring up the subject of Floppy Dog and the crib. Getting Connor to understand his daughter's needs would mean real progress.

"Welcome," Kimberley began. "Last week you shared the reasons you were seeking counseling. What I have found with other clients is that the first session is often emotionally draining, and people sometimes leave my office in a daze." With a wry smile, she added. "Or even with a big headache."

Her little joke elicited a gruff chuckle from Connor, and a blush of embarrassment from Isabella.

"I'd be curious to know how you felt when you left here last week."

The couple exchanged a glance. Isabella tucked her hand under Connor's thigh.

"Pretty good," Isabella said. "Like, somebody was finally listening to us. It didn't feel like you were judging us for being too young, or for what happened." She turned her head to look up at Connor. "I felt..." She hesitated. "Well, hopeful. Like, things could get better, if we stuck together."

The last phrase bothered Kimberley. "What about you, Connor?"

"Sure, okay, uhm." He spoke casually, but his glance at Kimberley was guarded. "So, I was glad Bella felt good about it. And you seemed like you care. So it's good."

"That's great." Kimberley smiled encouragingly. "You know, sometimes after a session, emotions come bubbling through to the surface. I wondered if you wanted to talk about any emotions you've dealt with since the last time we met. Connor, what about you?"

"Sure. Okay, so... I don't, you know, feel that much different since Lando died. But sometimes, I see somebody with a baby, you know, 'specially a boy, and it's like, how come my kid's not here? They got theirs, I don't got mine. Not fair."

Kimberley kept her expression neutral as she gently reflected on his response. "Yes, life can certainly seem unfair. And I'm hearing that it brings up feelings of frustration to see other people with their babies. Is that right?"

"Yeah," Connor agreed.

"Does it ever make you feel sad, Connor?"

"Sad?" He looked startled, as if no one had ever asked him that question. His eyes darted to the therapist, then away to some mid-point between them. "I guess. It makes me sad when Bella— when she's sad." He turned to her. "You know what I mean," he told her pointedly. "Seeing you and the girls all sad when I get home, it's like...why did I bother to come home?"

His words seemed to shatter Isabella's composure. Her chin

quivered. She looked away, tears welling up in her eyes, clutching her locket.

"*Mio Dios*, I know," Isabella moaned. "Connor says I'm too sad. I know. I guess I shouldn't keep thinking about Lando over and over. I should be stepping' it up, gettin' myself back together." She looked up at him, her voice pleading. "I keep blaming myself that he died."

"Why do you feel it was your fault?" Kimberley asked.

"It wasn't," Connor interrupted. "It wasn't nobody's fault. It just happened." Connor drew Isabella closer in a protective way. Reaching for a tissue, he wiped away a tear from her cheek.

"Are you familiar with the stages of grief?" Kimberley asked them.

They stared at her blankly.

"With every loss, we go through grief," Kimberley said quietly, thinking of the day she'd held her own dying daughter in her arms.

"*We?*" Connor's voice held a tinge of sarcasm.

Kimberley regarded him for a moment, weighing whether to mention Gabrielle. Deciding it was more important to stay detached, professional, she launched into a brief explanation of the stages of grief: shock and denial, anger, bargaining, depression, and acceptance.

"We don't always go through the stages in order," she added. "And we may go through a phase more than once. Children especially can get stuck in a phase, and that's where therapy can be helpful."

Connor's eyes flickered briefly in her direction.

"To give you an example," Kimberley continued. "Shock would be when you found the baby died. You might not have processed what was happening. Your body and mind may have shut down."

"Yes!" Isabella sat bolt upright, nodding emphatically, as if she had just had an epiphany. "Lifting him up, I could feel he wasn't... Oh my God, my head went all crazy. I couldn't think..."

She shivered, clutching Connor's hand. "I felt, like, paralyzed or something." She pressed his hand to her heart, as if to stifle the onslaught of emotions. "That was shock," she murmured, as if understanding it for the first time. "I was in shock."

"What about you, Connor?" Kimberley said. "Have you experienced that stage of shock or denial?"

"Yeah, okay, so…" He shrugged again. "When we, uh, got home from the hospital, I went into the kids' room and expected him to still be in his crib. It didn't seem real. Felt like, uh, I was in a movie or something. I mean the girls were in their beds, but he wasn't."

"Yes, exactly," Kimberley explained. "Your heart and head tells you, no, it can't be really happening. You can't hear what other people are saying. So maybe you just shut down. Stop listening. Stop processing. That can turn into denial."

"That's how I felt when the EMTs said Lando was dead," Connor added. "I thought they should have just butted out if they didn't want to try harder to fix him. I mean, I could have started his heart again. I've seen it done on TV a thousand times."

The room was quiet for a moment, each parent, including Kimberley, lost in their separate memories of grief. She remembered her own moments of shock hearing her baby had a fatal genetic flaw; of Ammon's uncharacteristic denial of the test reports as they searched for information on a cure; and their anger at realizing there was none.

"Denial puts a lot of strange thoughts in our head," Kimberley finally said. "And denial sometimes leads to the bargaining stage." She was speaking from her own experience now, as their loss merged with her loss. "Praying to God, begging him not to take our baby away. Promising to be better parents. Asking him to take me, instead of—" She stopped herself from saying Gabrielle's name. This wasn't about her grief, but the Mackenzie family's grief. "Something like that," she ended lamely.

Connor snorted. "Waste of time bargaining with *God*." He practically spat out the name.

"Sometimes it's not God," Kimberley countered gently. "It's the EMTs, or the doctor."

"No," Connor objected, shaking his head. "'It is what it is.' That's what Gramps always said. You just accept it and move on." he emphasized, looking directly at Kimberley. "Which is what we're *not* doing here."

His accusation stung. Kimberley had an impulse to scold him. *You're not the only one who's lost a child!* But she kept her composure, realizing it as part of the anger stage. "Moving on doesn't happen overnight, Connor, especially after something as traumatic as losing a baby. It takes time in order to process it all, so you *can* accept it and move on. That's what we *are* trying to do here."

Connor snorted again.

"We're trying to recognize where in the process we are, and how differently everyone handles these stages." She forced herself to smile at this man whose defensiveness was only aggravating the situation. "For instance, sadness and anger, sometimes one partner's anger can provoke sadness, and the other partner's sadness can provoke anger."

Connor's jaw began to work, clenching and unclenching.

"Yeah, yeah, exactly!" He leaped up from the couch, his blue eyes blazing, as Isabella stared at him. "Everybody pisses me off with all their *good* intentions. They all got this *sad* face, this *sad* voice. It's phony. At least to me it is."

He stepped toward Kimberley, smacking both hands flat on her desk.

"Sometimes it makes me so mad, all I want to do is kick my truck, or throw the goddamn basketball at the shed until I can't feel anything anymore! When I see somebody with a baby, I want to take it away, and say, see how it feels!"

"I see how upset this makes you," Kimberley said gently. She was intimidated by Connor's tall frame leaning over her desk. "Do you think you can sit back down?"

He looked at her, startled. "Oh, yeah. Sure." With an embarrassed smirk, he sat at the farthest end of the couch away from Isabella, looking as if he would jump up again at the slightest provocation.

Kimberley switched the focus off him, asking Isabella for her perspective.

"It's mostly a feeling of sadness." Isabella folded her arms in front of her, as if to hold herself together. "It seems to swallow me up. It's like when people are trying to get me to stop thinking about my baby, I go into, sort of, well . . ." She hesitated, searching for the right word, gripping her arms tighter. "It's like a trance. I feel like I'm falling back into the dark hole, and all I want to do is just have someone hold me and listen to me talk about Lando."

"And does anyone do that for you?" Kimberley asked gently. "Hold you and listen to you?"

"Oh, well, sure. I mean, Connor holds me. He listens sometimes." Isabella's hesitancy belied her words. Then she smiled. "And Alexia. I'm really grateful that my daughter's always there for me." She laughed lightly. "She's like my best friend."

Kimberley sighed. It was going to be a delicate task to wean Isabella off her unhealthy dependence on her daughter, especially if Connor didn't offer Isabella a proper outlet for her grief.

———

Kimberley explained how comforting people can speed the process of getting through these emotional stages of grief, something she thought Connor would appreciate. Especially children, she emphasized, who may not understand the concept of death or the normal stages of grief.

"So they may act out in many ways that seem wrong or inappropriate to their parents," she continued. "Refusing to go to school, for instance. Alexia might worry that she'll come home, and Mommy and Daddy and Jayleen will have disappeared."

"Did she say that?" Connor demanded.

"No," Kimberley corrected herself. "It was just a 'for instance.' But one thing she did say was that a toy that comforted her has disappeared. Floppy Dog. Is that the right name?"

Connor frowned, but Isabella nodded.

"She may be clinging to the toy, or as you mentioned last time, to Lando's crib because she can't handle the fact that he isn't coming back. Death is a hard concept for children. Maybe it calms her to have something of his to cuddle with. She can fantasize that he's still here with her when she's sleeping in the crib. Or that she can talk to him through Floppy Dog."

As Connor's frown deepened into a scowl, she quickly added, "That's not a bad thing."

"You're weirding me out!" he insisted. "Talking to the dead?"

"Yes, for you," Kimberley agreed. "But for a child used to fantasies and storybooks, anything that helps her to cope with the loss and work through those stages of grief is crucial to help her 'accept and move on,' as your grandfather put it."

Connor didn't reply, but his shoulders and jaw visibly relaxed.

"But if the crib and the toy, or any coping strategy for that matter, is labeled wrong or unacceptable, Alexia may never get through the stages-of-grief process." Kimberley looked from one to the other. "Do you understand?"

Connor shifted uneasily. Isabella leaned over and laid her hand on his arm.

"I mean, the teacher has already labeled Alexia's withdrawal as bad," Kimberley emphasized. "But your acceptance and support can overcome that and is far more crucial to her getting better."

Isabella looked hopefully at Connor.

"Yeah, yeah. Okay. I get it," he finally gave in. "I'll give her back Floppy Dog. But that crib's gotta go back in the attic." He glanced from Isabella to Kimberley. "Next week, the latest."

"I think that's a good compromise, Connor," Kimberley reassured him. "What do you think, Isabella?"

The mother hesitated, her facial muscles betraying conflicting emotions. Still, she ended up agreeing that it might work.

"I see that you and Connor have different ways of dealing with emotion," Kimberley continued, bringing the conversation back to the couple's problems.

Through skillful questions, she learned that Isabella's family thought it was wrong and scary to show anger, while Connor grew up in a house where anger was a weapon used to control and gain dominance. A trait that Connor insisted he had never used toward Isabella or the girls. She learned that Isabella's family handled sadness by working hard to take their mind off it. But she, as the youngest, had been indulged when her father died.

"Did your mother comfort you?"

"Sometimes," Isabella said softly, hugging herself, rubbing her arms. "Sometimes at night, after her shift, she'd sit up in bed with me. Stroke my hair. Hum a lullaby. She'd fall asleep with me. I felt safe then. It was, you know, not so lonely for us."

"You're the youngest child?"

"My older sister's in California," Isabella explained. "She left when I was fourteen."

"I see. And Connor, what about your family? What was encouraged, emotionally?"

"Encouraged?" Connor drew in a long breath, still staring at the ceiling. "Nobody encouraged any of us to do nothing. I tell you one thing, though. No crying. That was a rule. Not even when the bastard whipped us with his belt or threw us across the room. Not one whimper, or he'd give you something to really cry about."

The words came out defiantly.

He glared at Kimberley, his eyes cold, his pupils narrowed.

She flinched. *This man doesn't know how to grieve. More likely, he's scared to grieve.* "And sadness?" she asked him.

He barked out a harsh laugh. "Mom was the Queen of Sad. Shit, she went around with her f-ing sad face on all day. Like that helped anything. Half the time, she was, like, not even there."

"And so sadness, for you, is a useless emotion," Kimberley said.

"You got that right." Connor fell back against the couch, his jaw clenching and unclenching. "You're either doin' something or you ain't."

"Have you felt any sadness yet for Lando?"

"Whaddaya think? I'm f-ing human!" He leaned forward, fixing her with an angry stare. "I felt sad. Yeah, sad when there's something real to feel sad about. At the funeral. I felt it right here," he smacked his heart with his knuckles. "I just don't wallow in it, the way…" His head swiveled toward Isabella.

"The way I do?" Isabella said, fear contorting her features.

"The way my mother did, every useless day of her life. Okay?" He stared accusingly at Isabella. "Don't be like her."

"Okay," Isabella whispered, shrinking back into the couch.

"Okay," he agreed sharply. "Cause the last thing I need is *you* turning into *her*."

CHAPTER NINE

"Happy Birthday to you! Happy Birthday, dear Charlotte…"

Crowded in with family and friends around her parents' dining room table, Kimberley held Jack higher to see the blaze of candles that covered the entire surface of the homemade cake. Hard to believe her sister, Charlotte Wynworth, had hit the "Big Three-O." Kimberley would be there herself in three years.

Kimberly's dad, Ian Wynworth, started the traditional birthday countdown.

"Are you one? Are you two? Are you three…?"

The guests picked up the chant, with Ammon's strong baritone booming in Kimberley's ears. His arms were snug around her waist, his body pressed warm against her back.

"Are you ten, are you eleven?" Kimberley joined in, bouncing Jack up and down in time to the count.

When they reached thirty, Charlotte made a face and held up her hands for quiet. "Here goes." She made a show of inhaling.

"Can she do it?" Ian called out. Everyone laughed right on cue as Charlotte blew with all her might. And right on cue, again, their father leaned over to help blow out the last few candles.

"Still counts!" Ian announced, to the exclamations of protests and the children's giggles and groans.

Then it was Lee Wynworth's turn to hand her eldest daughter the silver cake knife. "First cut is for good luck."

Charlotte carefully sliced down through the layers of cake and cream.

"Don't want to drop cake on your lovely silk dress, now," said Lee, holding a flowered dessert plate close to the cake.

"Where's your apron, Missy?" Ian joked.

Charlotte laughed, transferring the slice neatly onto the plate. Lee passed her a fork. There was a slight hush as she took the first bite, holding them in suspense for a moment longer.

"Uhm!" she finally pronounced, swooning a bit for effect. "The best cake yet, Mum! Scrumptious!"

"Chocolate ganache, just as you asked for," Lee said as she took over the slicing chores. "Who's having cake?"

"Aunty Char! Aunty Char!" Tony cried, wedging his way through the crowd, waving a scrap of paper at her. "I made you a card all by myself. See! I signed my whole name! Right there!"

"Wow! You did!" Charlotte bent down to give Tony a kiss. "Great job, Tony Bony!"

Holding Jack on her lap, Kimberley enjoyed watching the rest of the birthday rituals play out. Presents were opened and held up for admiration, with hugs and thanks warmly bestowed to everyone down to the smallest child. She was proud of Paige, who had not only helped her grandmother set the table earlier but had taken it on herself to line up Charlotte's cards in a display along the buffet table. Watching Ammon deep in conversation with her father, she was glad they got along so well.

"You're a lucky boy, Jack," she murmured, feeding him a bit of cake. "You've got a wonderful family to grow up in."

She wondered what lessons the Mackenzie children absorbed from their parents and relatives? How much could she really learn about her clients by seeing them in a neutral office setting? Wasn't she missing vital information by not being able to observe their family rituals? Maybe she should talk to her boss about the possibility of home visits.

"Kimberley?" Ammon's voice broke into her thoughts. When she looked up at him, he gave her a quizzical smile. "You're a million miles away," he said. "Jack's gotten into the icing."

"Oh, my gosh!" Looking down, she was surprised to see Jack's face and hands smeared with chocolate.

"Here, I'll take him." Ammon lifted the baby from her arms. Kimberley's mother bustled over with a wet dishcloth to clean up Jack.

"Thanks, Lee," he told her.

"My pleasure. There's my little man, all clean now," Lee cooed to the baby, pinching his chubby cheek. "Such a little imp you are, my Jackie. Grammy loves you, darlin'." After a quick kiss, she disappeared toward the kitchen.

"Time for a game of soccer, my boy," Ammon said, swinging Jack up into the air, just missing the chandelier.

"Ammon!" Kimberley cried out.

"What?" Ammon turned, snuggling the baby gently into the crook of his arm.

"He almost hit his head!" she accused, reaching out for her baby.

"No he didn't. He's fine." Ammon gave her a funny look. "What's the matter with you?" When she didn't answer, he turned his back on her. "Grandad's waiting on us, Jack. Let's go kick the ball around some, eh?"

———

Kimberley was trembling, her cheeks burning with adrenaline and embarrassment. What was wrong with her? She was snapping at Ammon more and more these days. But he could have hurt Jack.

"A cup of vanilla tea?" Lee Wynworth stood in the doorway, gazing quietly at her daughter. "I was just going to put on the kettle. Or would you prefer cocoa?"

"Tea sounds good." Kimberley jumped up. "I'll help."

"Relax," her mother urged. "Just sit."

But Kimberley was too agitated to stay still. She began to clear plates. Everyone had gone to the backyard, except for Mrs. Linden, a longtime neighbor. The three women busied themselves stacking dishes in the dishwasher, washing, and drying the more delicate china serving pieces. Kitchen conversation turned to light chatter: new books, news of old neighbors, gardening plans.

Kimberley only half listened, watching through the kitchen window as Tony played soccer with the grownups. In his zeal to keep up with the bigger players, Tony darted underfoot, got knocked to the ground more than once, and caught in a tangle of kicking legs.

She opened the window. "Ammon, are you sure Tony should play?"

"No worries, Darlin'," he reassured her. "We won't bounce him off our heads."

"It's not tackle football!" her dad echoed.

When Tony slid into the rose bush after the ball, Kimberley ran to the back door. "He's going to get hurt, Ammon!"

"He's fine, Kimberley," Ammon once again reassured her, as Tony scrambled off with the ball.

The third time, when Tony crashed into his grandfather, she ran to the back door.

"Ammon! Make him stop!"

Ammon glared at her, stone faced. "He. Is. Fine."

"All good here!" Ian chimed in, lifting Tony into the air and spinning him around. "He's built like a little bulldozer, Kim."

"I'm sure Tony's fine," Kimberley's mother said, patting her daughter's shoulder. "Ammon's so good with the children."

"Easy for you to say, Mum," Kimberley snapped. "You never had boys."

As soon as she said it, she regretted it. Her mother, who looked as if she had been slapped in the face, turned and walked away.

"Mum, I'm, I'm sorry," Kimberley called after her.

What was wrong with her?

———

Kimberley returned to the kitchen sink to finish washing the last of the china. She paused only once to gasp when she saw Ammon lift Jack onto his shoulders and dribble the ball to the makeshift goal. Turning away from the window, she caught her mother and Mrs. Linden sharing concerned glances.

When the clean-up was done, their neighbor excused herself to see the game. Kimberley got out two mugs and spoons.

Her mother brought the old, flowered teapot to the table. "I'm afraid there's a crack in the lid," she said. "It was Aunt Catherine's, you know. I miss her so."

They poured the tea and measured out sugar and milk. The tinkling of the good silver spoons masked the awkward silence between them.

"You don't seem yourself," Lee finally murmured, studying her spoon. "What's wrong?"

"I'm sorry I snapped at you, Mum. I'm just tired." Kimberley reached for one of her mother's ginger tea biscuits. "I didn't think two days a week at the clinic would be so exhausting."

"Your Dad said you're there till all hours."

Kimberley nodded. "Nine-thirty to nine-thirty. It's a full load."

"Fair dinkum!" Lee's eyebrows lifted as she uttered her favorite Australian phrase. "Overlong days. Are you sure that's all that's bothering you?" her mother persisted. "You seem...well, rather curt with Ammon today."

"No, it's fine. I just..." Kimberley hesitated, wondering whether she should mention the SIDs case, then deciding against it. "I'm just not getting enough sleep, that's all." She noted her mother's doubtful expression. "So, what about your garden? What are you going to plant this spring?"

"I'll show you." Rising, Lee went to her kitchen bookshelf, returning with several gardening catalogs. Opening one, she flipped through, found the right page, and slid it over to Kimberley.

"There," she pointed to a selection of lilacs.

"Don't you have lilacs in the front?"

"Yes, but I was thinking of planting these by the back fence for the grandchildren. Where we took out the old cherry tree?" Lee looked down at the page. "So many new varieties. I thought I'd choose a different one for each grandchild."

"They're all so pretty," Kimberley agreed.

Lee pointed to one. "Little Boy Blue Syringa. I think that one for Jack."

Kimberley chuckled at the name. "Perfect."

"And this one, Old Glory, big purple sprays, for our Tony," Lee went on. She turned the page. "And here. Sweetheart Syringa, Classic Double Pink. That one's for Paige, don't you think?"

"Where's mine and Charlotte's?" Kimberley teased.

"I only have room for four." Lee tapped another photo. "I thought this one. The white one? With just a hint of blush around the edges? It's called Fiala Remembrance. It blooms late in the season." She hesitated a moment. "I thought that one would be for Gabrielle."

Kimberley's throat tightened at the name of her dead daughter. Hand to her heart, she struggled to breathe. Then she began to cry.

"Oh, Fair Dinkum! I shouldn't have brought it up. Oh Kimberley!" Her mom reached for her daughter's hand.

"It's fine!" Kimberley said. "Really, fine!" She raised her head and squeezed her mother's hand. "It will be just beautiful."

"Are you sure?" Lee studied her daughter's tear-streaked face. "I won't do it." Lee's voice cracked with emotion. "Not if it's too much for you."

Kimberley squeezed her mother's hand again, gazing into her kind hazel eyes. "Oh Mum! Why is it so hard to move on?"

———

Ammon sipped a Guinness stout, as he relaxed on his in-laws' stone patio. He was sweating from the friendly game and ran his fingers through his tousled hair. The men had been teasing each other about their soccer abilities. Little Tony had draped himself across Ammon's knee, hanging on every word.

After the game everyone went inside for snacks except for Ammon and Ian.

"Something wrong with our Kimberley?" his father-in-law asked casually. "Seems a bit out of sorts."

"You noticed, eh?" Ammon gulped down the last of his drink.

"Another one?" Ian asked, reaching for the cooler.

Ammon hesitated. Usually, he limited himself to one. "What the hell."

Ian popped the top off the bottle before handing it to Ammon. "So what's going on? Is she, well, you know?" He was alluding to the unspoken word 'depressed'.

Ammon sipped the foamy beer, wondering how much to say. "Sort of."

"I don't mean to pry, you know that, mate." Ian pursed his lips, looking at a squirrel chattering above his head on a maple branch.

Ammon nodded. He took a bigger swig. The heady brew felt good going down the back of his throat. "She's got this case at the clinic. Couple with a…with a dead baby."

Ian's eyes widened.

"I tried to talk her out of taking it on, but . . ." Ammon took a smaller gulp. "Seems to be bringing up all the old feelings again. I catch her standing over Jack's crib at night, like she's afraid it will happen to him."

Ian's frown deepened. He too, took a long swig. "Bloody hell." His body seemed to sag, the beer bottle dangling from his fingertips.

They both lapsed into silence.

Then Ian roused himself with a long breath. "She probably just looks at it as a challenge. A way to prove she can cope now." He started to laugh gently. "One thing I know about our Kimberley, she doesn't back down. She's a fighter, she is, especially in helping others. Like her Mum, she is."

Ammon wasn't laughing. "I don't like it."

"I know what you mean." Ian looked at his son-in-law seriously. "Things happen...tragedies and the like. I've seen my share. And, well, you shouldn't blame yourself. There's nothing you can do, mate, aside from just keeping your head. But we're here for you, Ammon. You, and Kimberley, and the grandkids, whatever happens. You know that."

"I do." Ammon smiled at his father-in-law. "And I'm grateful, Ian. You've been grand, and I'd be a bloody whinge not to thank you and Lee for all you do for us. But..." He took a deep breath, blurting out his worst fear. "God, Ian, we were just getting things back to normal after losing Gabrielle. I just don't want this to push Kim back over the edge. Not to mention, I worry about her safety in Newburgh. There was a shooting on Broadway a few weeks ago."

He drained the last of his beer, tipping it until the final drop dissolved on his tongue.

"Bloody hell," Ian murmured sympathetically.

"Yes, bloody hell," Ammon agreed.

CHAPTER TEN

Connor felt good to be back working for his old boss, overhauling the Dutchman II for a new season. He was completely in his element, focused on his task, breathing in the promise of spring in the unseasonably warm temperatures. A soft breeze whispered off the Hudson River.

Jeff Elkin's twenty-eight meter long, thirty-passenger boat had been lifted by crane out of the water onto a bare, cracked cement lot near the huge green warehouse dock. It sat on a framework of metal bracing, which allowed access to the bottom of the hull.

Connor was checking each metal fixture to see what was corroded.

"Gonna need a new one of these," he called out to Jeff, holding up a piece of rusty metal. "She's finally corroded right through." He jabbed his screwdriver deep into its center to make the point.

Jeff looked up from where he was filling a gouge in the hull, using a fiberglass gel. "When Mikey gets back, *if* he ever gets back, he can pick up a new one," he groused. "Damn kid's been gone three hours. What the hell is he doing?"

Connor nodded. Grabbing the clipboard, he looked over the maintenance list, marking checks next to transducers, pitot tubes, and the exterior surfaces of the thru-hull fittings. By the entry for the strainer, he wrote: "Replace."

"So, you think you'll get enough people to make this eagle watching thing pay off?" Connor asked.

Jeff's expression brightened. "Already got eighteen reservations. Paid in full!"

Connor laughed. "That many people want to pay to look for eagles?"

"Amazing, huh?" Jeff said. "I heard back from four different bird groups so far. They're all interested. It's worth getting the boat ready so early, if we can get two or three trips booked out of this. Extends the season, you know?"

Anything that brought in more work sounded good to Connor. Before Alexia was born, Connor had crewed regularly for Jeff and his brother-in-law and business partner Omar Beckner. He'd always enjoyed being around both men, who had known his Gramps. While seasonal, it was the closest to a regular job he'd ever had. Elkin had always run a small operation: a few rental motorboats in addition to the Dutchman II. Business ebbed and flowed like the tides. When it ebbed, Connor had been reduced to a couple of weeks last April to ready the boats for the fishing season, with a bit of crewing on the odd weekend. It had been a blow, and not just financially. He felt better on the water. Less angry, more at peace with things. This year, things were looking up.

"How's Omar doing?" Connor asked.

"Not so good. Chemo's bad stuff." Jeff grunted, working more gel on a metal trowel to get it to the right consistency. "He keeps saying he'll be back in time for the bird trip."

"Will he?" Connor was startled. *Would that mean he'd be cut from the crew?*

Jeff puffed out a mournful breath. "Nobody's got the heart to say he won't."

"Oh. Too bad." Not knowing what else to say, Connor

grabbed a rag and a can of lubricant to start on the propeller and shaft.

———

The two men worked in an easy silence, intent on their work until they heard a crunch of wheels on gravel. Mikey Beckner drove up in a blue Chevy Silverado pickup truck.

"Hey, Uncle Jeff! I'm back!"

"What took you so long? Stop at the bar again, Screw-up?" Jeff said, throwing down his rag in disgust.

"Nah!" Mikey grinned. "The place was busy."

"Get that stuff unloaded." Jeff wasn't smiling back. "Connor, give him a hand."

"Aye, aye, Captain!" Mikey tossed off a mock salute.

Jeff's scowl deepened as he resumed filling in gouges. "Good thing your father ain't here," he muttered.

The two young men hauled out buckets of paint and boxes of supplies, stacking it all near the boat.

"Hey," Mikey said suddenly, as he reached into the truck for another box. "Friend of mine said some old guy's been asking around about you."

Connor froze. "Who?"

"Dunno." Mikey shrugged. He hoisted the box to his shoulder and turned.

"What'd he look like?" Connor demanded, the bile rising in his throat.

"Dunno. Wasn't there." He started to walk away. "He just said—"

Connor grabbed the kid's arm, stopping him. "How old?"

"Yo, back off!" Mikey said. "Make me drop this?"

Connor released his grip.

"Whas up with you, bro?" Mikey groused, shifting the box on his shoulder. "Somebody after you?"

"Nobody." Connor shrugged. He looked away. "Just don't like surprises."

"How 'bout good surprises?" Mikey said, as he headed off.

Connor didn't answer.

"Ran into your cousin Gil."

Connor stared at the acne-scarred, skinny seventeen-year-old. "How do you know Gil?"

"Brother, I know everybody." Mikey set down his box, throwing a quick glance in Jeff's direction. "Ran into him just now down Rudy's Place," he whispered. "Stopped there for a quick beer, but don't tell my uncle," he added conspiratorially. "Said to tell you he'd be there tonight. Come by."

Connor grunted, lifting a heavy box of washing solution onto his shoulder. He didn't really trust Mikey. He was a smart ass and a big mouth, who wore his pants too low, and his baseball hat turned backwards. He knew Jeff only gave him odd jobs because he was family.

"Actually," Mikey said. "He said to tell you to stop at Rosie's for a taco and a few beers after you get done today. His treat."

Connor shook his head. "Promised Bella I'd be home for dinner." But even as he said the words, he felt resentful. He imagined how nice it would be to have dinner with just Gil.

His good mood soured. He knew what Bella would say: Let Gil come over to the house instead. But that wasn't his cousin's style.

Maybe he could see Gil after dinner. *Forget that, too. She's got her damned class tonight!* He'd be stuck home with the kids. But as he thought about it more, he figured maybe he'd slip out after she got home. She'd be pissed, though, if he came home drunk or high.

Shit! Got that appointment with therapy woman in the morning.

Connor's resentment grew the more he turned it all over in his mind. He wanted to see Gil in the worst way; go out and get happy. But everybody would be mad at him: Bella, the therapist, and his boss; probably even Mikey'd be there to snitch on him.

Seagulls screamed overhead. Connor grudgingly hefted the last box onto his shoulder. He looked up, watching the birds dive and swoop around the dock, looking for food. He envied them, just lazing on the wind, scavenging for their supper, then soaring out along the steel blue water. Amazing creatures, birds; no one and nothing to tie them down.

He dumped the box next to the others, then grabbed a rag to wipe his hands. He had worked hard today. He'd go home for dinner, like he promised. But he *sure was* entitled to meet Gil for a quick drink tonight. Just one beer. Two, maybe. After the kids were in bed. That was all. No harm could come from that. He'd sneak out the backyard, climb the boat and jump over the fence, out of sight of that nosey old bitch across the street.

If he played it right, Bella wouldn't even have to know.

———

"Damn you, Connor Mackenzie!"

Home from her night class, Isabella stared at the kitchen table in disgust. A swarm of ants crawled over two plates streaked with cherry pie filling and crumbs. More had drowned in the milk pooled at the bottom of two plastic cups. She choked back a gag reflex.

It wasn't like Connor to just leave dirty dishes out. He hated ants. Even if he didn't always wash and dry them, he'd always soak the plates in the dishpan. Resentfully, she grabbed a paper towel and began squashing the ants. Retching, she scraped the mess into the garbage, and then washed everything in hot, soapy water. It was only as she was drying up, that it occurred to her that the house was unusually quiet for ten o'clock.

Where was he?

Of course, the last two nights Connor had fallen asleep in the middle of a TV show; unusual, since he'd always been a night owl. Her mood softened as she got out the broom to sweep the floor. He had worked long hours all week on the boat. She'd walked down to the warehouse the other day, after taking the girls to daycare, to watch him painting the hull. Seeing Connor at work always turned her on, watching his muscles ripple in his tee shirt as he stretched, putting his entire body into the rhythmic motion. She was gratified, too, when his boss told her he was glad to have Connor back on the team. That had meant a lot to her. She wavered now in her earlier, harsher judgment. Maybe Connor had been so tired tonight, he'd just gone to bed after tucking the girls in.

Turning out the lights, she took off her shoes and tiptoed up the stairs, recalling how sweet Connor had been at dinner earlier, how attentive to the girls, and how deeply he had kissed her when she left for class.

She pictured herself sliding under the covers, waking him with soft kisses, massaging his shoulders, moving down his body, arousing both of them into passionate, hungry lovemaking. By the time she reached the top of the stairs, every inch of her body was raw with need and anticipated pleasure.

The bedroom door was open, but the darkness was complete. She crept inside, aching for that first exquisite touch of her lover's skin.

"Connor?" she whispered.

There was no sound.

She strained to hear him breathing; strained to make out the shadow of his form, feeling her way with hands outstretched so as not to bump into anything.

"*Te adoro,*" she murmured, kneeling on the bed. Leaning over, she felt for him and had a shock of sudden, cold clarity: Connor was not in bed.

She sat up, pissed. That's why the house was so quiet. He wasn't even home.

"God damn you!" she cursed softly, feeling as if someone had stabbed her in the gut. It all made sense now: he'd been sweet just to throw her off guard. He must have slipped out of the house as soon as she left, leaving the girls alone to have their pie and milk and get themselves to bed. That's why the ants were in the kitchen and the plates still on the table. She'd been a fool to believe he would stay home as he'd promised; a fool to believe him when he said he'd see Gil some other time.

She slammed her fist into his pillow. But her next thought made her freeze: *Ohmigod! The girls!*

She flew to her daughters' bedroom, fueled by an unbearable sense of déjà vu. From the glow of the streetlamp outside the window, she saw instantly that both girls were safe in their beds. But were they all right? The reassuring sound of their breathing brought tears to her eyes.

She made the outward sign of the cross, fingertips to forehead, heart, left shoulder, right shoulder, then palms together, whispering her thanks to Jesus. Inwardly, she still raged at Connor's betrayal. She knelt by each bed to caress her daughters' hair and rearrange their covers, stifling an urge to wake them just to hear their sweet voices.

"My angel," she whispered to each, touching her lips to their forehead. "*Te adora, miha!*"

Closing their door, Isabella returned to her bedroom. She switched on the bedside lamp, and stared at her bed, the covers smooth and untouched. She gulped down angry waves of emotion.

How could she ever trust him again?

After what happened with Lando, she'd actually believed Connor would take his responsibilities seriously again. With the new job, she'd actually convinced herself that he was back on the right path.

Estúpido! Idiot! You dope! You dummy!

She sank back on her heels, clamping one hand over her mouth as if to prevent her angry thoughts from escaping like a swarm of enraged bees. Staring up at the large cross on the wall, she prayed to the Father, the Son, and the Holy Spirit, and added in the Blessed Mother for good measure.

Tell me what to do...tell me what to do...tell me what to do.

Disaster scenarios bubbled up in her mind. What if someone had broken into the house? What if a fire had sparked because of the old wiring? What if the girls had gotten sick, or left the gas stove on? What if the social worker had shown up?

She whipped herself into a state of agitation and despair, pounding her fist into her own pillow until she fell back on the bed, depleted. Not bothering to undress, she switched off the bedside lamp, and crawled under the covers, shivering for a long time before slipping into an uneasy sleep.

———

Connor walked in the door at seven the next morning, as the girls were having their breakfast. Isabella glared at him. At least, she thought, he had the grace to look sheepish.

She averted her gaze as he walked over to her, stopping to kiss Jayleen and Alexia on the top of their heads. When he moved behind her chair and wrapped his arms around her, she stiffened her shoulders against him, the muscles in her neck tightening. He was playing his games again. She resisted, shaking him off, but allowed him to kiss her cheek.

"Hey, Bella," he murmured in her ear. "I can walk the girls to school today. You sit and enjoy your coffee." He was mild, happy, like a shy boy trying to please.

"Don't bother," she said evenly, making her voice icy, indifferent.

Normally, she would have jumped up to get *him* a cup of coffee, too. Not today. She made a show of sipping from her cup, refusing to reveal even a hint of emotion because once she started, she knew she wouldn't stop.

What she wanted to do was make a scene: *Where the hell where you all night? You left them alone, you son of a bitch*! She wanted to throw dishes. Slap his sweet face. But she would not make a scene in front of the girls. They'd been through enough.

"Brought you something." Connor slipped into the chair next to her, smiling shyly. From his pocket, he slipped out a small box and set it down in front of her.

She shrugged.

He opened it. A silver ring with a tiny Claddagh symbol, a crowned heart held by two hands, lay on a piece of white cotton. She didn't ask where he had gotten it. She knew. Gil often got things from a friend who sold knock-off bags and jewelry on the streets of New York City.

Isabella hardened her heart, avoiding Connor's puppy dog look.

"I'm sorry," he wheedled. "I was just out with Gil. The girls were fine, right? No harm done." He glanced at his daughters. Jayleen smiled at him, but Alexia was expressionless, her eyes fixed on her cereal bowl.

"You should *not* have left them alone!" Isabella whispered. Then, summoning up her courage, she looked him in the eyes. "That woman next store probably saw you and me go out and called Child Protection Services again."

She saw his eyes go wide for a moment. Her words had hit their mark.

A moment later, when he asked anxiously if that was true, she almost lied. But his expression was so contrite, she shook her head.

"She didn't. Although it don't mean she won't," she chastised him. "If you wanted to go out, you should have waited 'til I came home."

She almost asked where he'd been all night but didn't, whether in fear of setting him off, or in fear of finding out what she didn't want to know.

Connor looked chastened. His expression turned serious and softly anguished. "You're right. I...I will from now on. I promise."

"Yeah, right." Isabella turned away and sipped her coffee. If she looked at him anymore, saw the hurt in his eyes, the sweetness in his lips, she'd soften.

"Come on, Bella. Forgive me?" He held out the ring. "Take my heart? Please?"

Isabella started to waver. She glanced up. His blue eyes were filled with longing. His soft smile curved up in hope. She covered her mouth and let out a sound between a groan and a sigh, caught between despair and the impulse to preserve what was left of their family.

"Oh, Connor!" She shook her head at him in disappointment but allowed him to slip the ring on her finger.

CHAPTER ELEVEN

In her next session with Isabella and Connor, Kimberley couldn't believe what she was hearing.

Connor was bragging about staying out all night, drinking with a cousin and friends. It was the first time either of them had even mentioned alcohol. Kimberley had assumed they were too poor and too busy to have time to bar hop. Obviously, she had assumed wrong.

"Everybody from Gil's crowd was there!" Connor's face split into a wide grin. Buzzed with energy from his big night on the town, he gestured enthusiastically. "We must've took up the whole bar. Gil was buying and we were doing these shots, see? First round, it was just the guys, right. Second round was fancy ones, Redheaded Sluts, for the ladies. Shit, those girls were just *hanging* all over Gil, especially Malena."

He glanced over at Isabella, who, Kimberley noticed, sat slightly apart from him, her eyes closed against his words, her thumb stroking her locket over and over.

"You remember Malena?" Connor went on. "She was always crazy. Well last night, to get his attention, you know what she does? She climbs right up on the bar and starts dancing, see? Like some exotic dancer, you know, but with all her clothes on."

He wiggled his body in a crude representation and barked out a laugh. Isabella winced.

"So Gil pretends he don't even notice." Connor leaned forward, excited, his eyebrows rising up and down, as though he's signaling the punchline to a joke. "Then, he gets her pretty good. Orders a Screaming Orgasm shot. Makes her drink it right up there on the bar. Everybody's screaming 'OR-GA-SM!' while she downs it." He let out a sigh of satisfaction and closed his eyes, his head tilted up. "Man, we got so hammered!"

Kimberley glanced over at Isabella to judge her reaction to all this. *She's trying to disappear. She's self-soothing.*

"So I'm hearing that you really enjoyed yourself last night," Kimberley said to Connor. "Is this something you do regularly?"

Connor snorted and shook his head. "I don't usually get the chance. I don't have the money, except when Gil's around. He knows I can't afford it. Do you know, he wouldn't let me pay for a thing last night?"

"Gil?" Kimberley interrupted.

"My cousin."

"He isn't around very often?"

Connor's expression turned wary. "He travels a lot." He shrugged, then glanced sharply at Isabella. "On business."

Kimberley nodded, checking to see Isabella's reaction. Still nothing. "And Isabella stays home with the girls when you party with Gil?"

Was it Kimberley's imagination or had the question hit a nerve? Isabella's eyes flew open, darting toward Connor, who returned it with that warning look Kimberley had noticed before.

"Yeah, well, I can't take the kids into a bar, now, can I?" Connor said. "That wouldn't be *responsible*, right?"

"No, of course not," Kimberley answered smoothly, struggling to hide her disapproval. She was not stupid; he had evaded her question. "But there are such things as babysitters, if you wanted to take Isabella with you."

"Oh, babysitters! Sure. Like a friend or her Ma coming over,"

Connor relaxed. He waved his arm expansively. "I mean, Isabella could've come, too, if she wanted. She knows most of those people. They were all from high school."

"Isabella, did you want to go last night?" Kimberley asked.

"Maybe," Isabella avoided looking at Kimberley. "If I'd even *known* about it."

"Yeah, well, it was definitely last minute," Connor explained calmly. "I mean, Gil just happened to run into one of the guys I work with and he mentioned it to me. Besides, Bella had her class."

Right there, Kimberley knew she had caught Connor in a lie.

———

"So, Bella was in class and you were out with your cousin," Kimberley said. "Then, who was watching the girls?"

Isabella gasped. But Connor was smoother, quickly explaining that he didn't go out until Bella came home.

"She was so tired, she just nodded off, right babe? So I went by myself."

Isabella still said nothing, stroking the locket more intensely.

"I'm sensing that last night is bothering you, Isabella," Kimberley persisted, recalling Jon's recent advice about clients unconsciously leading you to the heart of the problems, even as they resisted going there. "Do you want to explain what you're feeling?"

"Well." Isabella took a deep breath, then blurted out: "I don't really like it when he goes to see Gil alone. I think Connor's cousin should come over to the house to have dinner and play with the kids. It would have been nicer for *all* of us, instead of *some* of us staying at home alone."

Kimberley noted the anger in Isabella's response. It bothered her that Isabella was avoiding eye contact. "Did you have any idea Isabella felt that way, Connor?"

Connor bent his head sheepishly, as if he had just realized the error of his ways. "I hear you, Kim," he said, flashing a charming smile. "Guess I didn't know Isabella felt that way. But, you gotta understand. My cousin ain't that type of guy. He's single, he's young, he's a player, you know. Hanging out in a house full of kids? Just ain't his thing."

Shifting closer to Isabella, he put his arm around her. "It's not personal, Bella."

Isabella didn't shrink away, but neither did she snuggle with Connor as usual. Connor reached out and began to stroke her arm. He gazed at her with a devoted expression, attempting to reassure her.

Isabella closed her eyes, her stone-faced expression as impervious as a marble statue.

"When someone from your family comes over, we have always done a barbecue or something, right?" Connor persisted, moving closer to her. "I'm always there for it, right?" He looked over at Kimberley. "Her family's more kid-oriented, you know? In my family, we like a good drink. It's just not the same with kids around."

"I know what you're saying, Connor," Isabella said tensely, avoiding his gaze. "But I also get sick of the kids sometimes. I feel left out. And I don't go staying out all night with my girl-friends."

"But you're out at classes, in the adult world," Connor said. "And I'm home with the girls."

Isabella's mouth dropped open in surprise. "Yeah," she echoed. "Right, home with the girls."

It sounded almost like an accusation to Kimberley.

Connor sighed and hugged her.

Isabella didn't flinch, Kimberley observed. But she didn't soften either.

Isabella has her defenses. What's Connor's method of getting past them?

"When I do go out," Connor said. "I always come back home, right, babe?"

"Eventually," Isabella replied.

He squeezed her shoulder. "And I'm working, right, babe?"

"Yes."

"And there'll be work for the whole summer, right, babe?" he persisted. "Into the fall, probably. So that's all good."

Isabella nodded, shrugging her shoulders.

Connor drew Isabella against him. "So why be upset at the one night that I went out to have a good time?" He ducked his head, trying to get Isabella to meet his gaze. "I never said I was perfect. You knew that about me? I didn't lead on, did I?"

Isabella grimaced. "I know." She finally looked at him.

Connor kissed her forehead. "Forgive me?"

Isabella smiled ruefully. "I guess so."

Connor gazed at the therapist with a distinct look of triumph. "See? It's all good Kim. There's no problem here, just a misunderstanding."

A lot more going on here than just a misunderstanding, Kimberley thought.

"I bet even you and your husband, Ammon's his name, right? You have those, don't you?"

How did he know my husband's name?

Connor's grin, self-satisfied and superior, left no doubt that he was trying to show her that he was in charge. It confirmed her suspicions about the dynamic at work between this couple: Connor was the manipulator. Isabella was his enabler.

———

Kimberley had the same thought when Isabella called the next day to cancel Alexia's appointment.

I'm not putting up with this, she thought, dialing Isabella's house. She couldn't help feeling that Connor must be behind this, trying to sabotage her sessions with Alexia.

She left several messages, each one stronger than the last.

"Isabella, it's important to keep up the momentum of working with Alexia. It's the only way she will return to a normal situation. I am willing to come in special for you on Thursday at three p.m. If Alexia misses a session, I'm obligated to report it to the school psychologist. That's not going to please her. So call me back or call Emma at the desk to arrange to come in on Thursday. Let's make a healthy and proper choice for the girls' sake."

She wasn't surprised when Isabella texted her back to say she would come on Thursday. It would be a headache for Kimberley, coming in on her day off. But she wasn't about to let Connor sabotage his daughter's mental health.

CHAPTER TWELVE

"Mommy, look at what I did at school!" Paige practically jumped off the school bus, waving a piece of artwork in the air.

She flew into Kimberley's open arms, giggling and wrapping her legs around her mother's waist. They did their ritual nose rubbing and two kisses on each cheek.

Tony raced his tricycle in circles around them. "Let me see, let me see!"

"No, I'm showing Mommy. Not you!" Paige held the construction paper out of reach.

"Don't be mean to your brother," Kimberley set her daughter down. She took the crayoned drawing and praised its colors and design.

"It's a caterpillar, like the one in Eric Carle's book," Paige crowed. "Miss Bevett said it was the best one!"

"I wanna see!" Tony brushed his wheel against Paige's foot, who howled.

The two squabbled.

"Tony! You could have hurt your sister!" Kimberley called after them, as Paige chased her brother. "Say you're sorry!"

"Sor-ree!" Tony called out, showing no sign that he really was. But Kimberley was satisfied. Modeling correct behavior was the first step on the road to good manners, as her mother always said.

Inside, Kimberley found her father in the kitchen, spooning pureed squash into Jack's mouth.

"That's a good lad," Ian Wentworth cooed. "Tasty, eh? Wouldn't be caught dead eatin' this stuff, myself, mate, but you seem to like it." Ian glanced over at Kimberley, who was gathering her briefcase and shoulder bag. "Got everything?"

"I'm all set, Dad," Kimberley said, pulling on her jacket. "It's just two clients. They were sick on Tuesday, and I didn't want them to miss a whole week of therapy. Consistency is so important. I'll be back by five-thirty at the latest. Dinner's in the crock pot," she added, before heading out the door.

"Where are you going, Mommy?" Paige demanded as Kimberley walked to her car.

"The clinic, for a while."

"Your days are Mondays and Tuesdays, not Thursdays." Paige frowned at her mother.

"My clients had to switch days this week," Kimberley explained.

"I don't want you to go!" Paige pleaded, grabbing her hand. "You promised to teach me a new song on the piano!"

"Not today, Sweetie. Tomorrow."

"We have Brownie Troop tomorrow!"

"Then Saturday," Kimberley said briskly, kissing the top of her daughter's head. "Now I've got to run, or I'll be late."

But Paige wouldn't let go. She wanted to come. She wanted to have therapy in the toy room, as she called it, and play with the bear cards.

"They're not toys, they're therapy cards for work," Kimberley patiently explained for what must have been the hundredth time.

Tony ran to Kimberley and tugged on the hem of her coat. "Kiss, kiss!" he demanded. She knelt to receive a hug and a peck on the cheek.

"Everybody gets therapy but me!" Paige said in exasperation.

Kimberley smiled, knowing how Paige hated to be left out of anything. "I tell you what. We'll have a therapy session up in your room whenever you want. We can use your Go Fish cards."

"Then you have to buy me a new pack." Paige demanded. "The baby drooled on them and then Tony bit the corners off all the cards with blue fish! So he could tell what they are."

Kimberley arranged her features into mock horror. "What a catastrophe! I am not promising, but I'll try to find a pack at the drugstore on my way home. Okay?"

Paige's excited grin was all the reward Kimberley needed. She wished everyone's catastrophes were so easily solved.

———

As she greeted Alexia Mackenzie for her session some forty minutes later, Kimberley couldn't help but compare her client to her own daughter. Paige was only a year older and a grade higher, yet possessed far more confidence and enthusiasm than the painfully shy, emotionally closed child in front of her now.

As the therapist led the way upstairs to the child therapy room, she noticed that Alexia kept turning back to make sure her mother and sister were still in the waiting room below.

"It's all right," Kimberley reassured the girl. "They'll be right down there when we finish, or if you need your Mommy, we can call her. Okay?"

Without a word, Alexia walked listlessly to the toy shelf, looking for the Puppy game. It had become a ritual ice breaker. The last time, the youngster took out the board and arrange the puppies at different houses, always setting the puppy with the floppy ears in front of her. She wasn't interested in the game cards or actually playing a round. It was more as if she was arranging a doll house. When she was finished, she had sat back in her chair, fold her hands on her lap, and wait shyly until Kimberley spoke.

But today, the child only took out the puppy with the floppy ears and placed it in front of her. She sat mute and rigid in her chair.

"Are you having a bad day, sweetie?"

Alexia nodded, her bottom lip quivering. She reached out a finger to stroke the cardboard puppy. She wouldn't look up.

Kimberley fanned out her deck of bear cards, looking for one with a sad face, laying it in front of Alexia. "Is this sort of how you feel?"

Alexia said nothing.

Kimberley laid a second card down, one with a mad face. "Or more like this?"

Alexia nodded slowly, staring at the card of the angry bear.

"Is the anger here in your throat?" Kimberley laid her hand over her own throat, encouraging Alexia to do the same. "Can you feel it? Like a big lump of candy you can't swallow?"

Alexia nodded, then slipped her hand lower, over her heart.

"Is the anger in your chest?"

The child nodded more emphatically now.

"Want to let it out like I showed you, with a deep whoosh?" Kimberley demonstrated, and the child followed her lead. But her body seemed incapable of relaxing.

They did the whooshing sound a few more times.

"I hate school!" Alexia finally blurted out. "Everybody hates me."

Kimberley's first thought was to reassure Alexia that it wasn't true; to suggest that surely some of the children had to like her. But as a therapist, she needed to hold back her maternal urges and allow Alexia to lead her to the truth, however unpalatable it might be.

At her gentle urgings, the story came out slowly. A girl at school had thrown Alexia's drawing in the trash. Her teacher hadn't stuck up for her.

"She told me just go make another one." There was more than anger in Alexia's voice. Her cheeks were deeply flushed, and her jaw thrust forward.

There's that spark of defiance, Kimberley observed. *A tiny one to be sure, but a healthy spark all the same.*

"She told you to make another one," Kimberley echoed. "And ?"

"And I wouldn't!" Her voice rose in indignation, punctuated by hard, short puffs of breath. "And the teacher told me…that *I, I* was not being nice!"

"Oh, sweetie! I'm so sorry!" Kimberley empathized with Alexia's humiliation and the injustice of it all. "And how did that make you feel?"

Alexia shoved the bear cards away. They skittered across the table and fell to the floor. She folded her arms across her stomach and slumped back in her seat.

Go delicately, Kimberley. Go delicately.

"You feel sad and angry because the teacher didn't stand up for you?" Kimberley tried again, only to receive a stony silence in return.

"Did Carmen ever do that to you before?"

Again, no answer.

Kimberley selected two more cards, a pink girl bear with a smile and a yellow girl bear with a smile and laid them in front of Alexia. "How do you think you could get her to be friends with you?"

"She don't wanna be friends," Alexia shot back, looking away from the cards. "She broke all my pink crayons, too! I had six."

"Oh, my!" Kimberley struggled to hide her own anger. *I need to stay calm for Alexia.*

"She don't wanna be my friend," the child agreed. "Nobody wants to be my friend."

"There must be somebody," Kimberley suggested. "No friends on your street?"

"Daddy won't let me play with them. The boys threw rocks in our yard once. Daddy says we're not allowed to play with them."

"What about cousins?"

"We don't see them anymore," Alexia said, picking at the sleeve of her purple knit sweater. "Daddy don't like company."

That's a new wrinkle, Kimberley thought, making a note on her pad. *Something to bring up in the next family session.*

Using the bear cards, Kimberley gently encouraged Alexia to talk about the children in her class, so Kimberley could help her figure out how to make school better. Alexia chose mostly sad cards, and several 'mean ones' to stand in for Carmen, the girl who ruined her drawing, and another boy who sat at her table. Eventually, Alexia related a small chain of torments that included hair pulling, tripping in the hall, being cut off from the water fountain, and chased from the swings.

It was the first time Alexia had said much about school. Kimberley's heart ached for the child. She was going through a normal developmental stage, difficult for all children, but worse for Alexia, because she was so insecure in her attachments, and still grieving for her lost brother.

"Alexia, how would you like to play a different game?"

"Okay."

"Would you walk to the little shelf and get that playground puzzle?"

Alexia pushed back her chair. On her way to get the cards, she stooped down and picked up the bear cards that had fallen.

"Here, Miss Kimberley," she said, handing them over. Then, she leaned closer, staring at Kimberley's keychain.

"Who's this baby?" She pointed to the miniature photograph attached to the chain. "She's so tiny."

Kimberley realized at once what she was looking at. "That's my daughter. Her name is Gabrielle."

"She's even teeny-tinier than Lando."

"Yes. She is only just born in that picture."

"Her eyes are closed."

"Yes." Tears welled up in Kimberley's eyes. She blinked to hold them back.

Alexia stared for another moment, then gently touched the frame. "Could I visit her?"

"I wish you could." Kimberley's throat tightened. *We're getting into rough territory here, Alexia. But if that's where we need to go, let's go.* She took a deep breath for courage. "She's in heaven."

Alexia's mouth fell open a bit. She glanced up at Kimberley shyly. "Like us? Your baby went to heaven, too?"

"Yes, Alexia. My baby is in heaven, too."

"It's not fair," Alexia said, still gazing at the picture. "Why does Jesus take the nice babies? Why don't he send them back home?"

"It is unfair. A little bit like what happened to your picture today. It's hard to just accept unfair things without feeling angry or sad about them."

"I miss Lando. Mommy carries his picture in her locket." She ran her thumb over the Lucite block that held the photo.

"Would you like to keep a photo of your brother with you?"

Alexia looked up, eyes wide. She nodded, then swallowed hard. "Could I?"

"I have more of these key chains at home. I'll bring one for you. We could ask Emma downstairs to put Mommy's photo on the copy machine and make one for you."

Alexia's eyes shined. "Oh Miss Kimberley!" She threw her arms around the therapist and hugged her fiercely for a long time.

The dam holding back Alexia's emotions had opened a bit. For the rest of the session, the child began to talk about her brother in short, animated bursts. She skipped and hopped around the table, climbing on and off each chair in turn.

"I used to hide under the crib, and he'd look for me. His head would go this way, then that way. Side to side. I'd pop up, yell PEEK-A-BOO through the bars. He'd laugh. Then I'd hide again. He cried. *Mi hermanito*, I'd say and pop out. Then he laughed some more. Sometimes I took him out and put him on the floor, and he'd try to crawl to me." Giggling, she got down on her hands and knees to demonstrate.

Smiling, nodding, and clapping softly as Alexia's words tumbled out, Kimberley encouraged her to remember more. She recalled how Daddy would play with the trucks, rolling them a little to get Lando crawling after them; how Jayleen would hide in the closet, pop out and shout 'peek a boo' to make Lando laugh until he hiccupped.

What Alexia liked best was to climb into his crib at night and put her arms around him, pretending she was his Mommy, and he was her baby. She had done the same thing with Jayleen when she had slept in the crib.

"Lando cried a lot. He was Mama's sad baby. *Abuelita* says he was a 'sickly child.' When everybody else went to sleep, I climbed down and got under the covers with him." She wriggled into the chair next to Kimberley. "It was scary 'cause the bars make a noise and I thought Mama or Daddy would hear, but they didn't." Her face lit up. "Lando used to smile like crazy when I climbed in. I think he was crying' so I would play with him. He loved me because I would play with him. Sometimes I'd give him his bottle. Mama said I was his *mamacita*."

"It sure sounds like you were a wonderful big sister."

"Yeah, I miss him." She paused for a second. Her voice fell to a whisper, and her expression turned grave. "Nobody ever caught me, not even that night."

Kimberley knew they were entering delicate emotional territory. "Which night was that Alexia?"

"You know, the night God took Lando to his house in heaven."

Kimberley froze. She felt adrenaline starting to build and struggled to remain calm. If she betrayed her feelings, Alexia would panic and withdraw again.

"Alexia, were you in Lando's crib the night he died?

"Lando didn't die!" Alexia yelled indignantly. "He's in

heaven, and God won't send him back because I'm not praying hard enough yet!"

"What do you mean?" Kimberley struggled to remain composed at the startling declaration.

"I can't remember anymore." She stared down at her hands. Her little body seemed to cave in, and with it, all her emotions shut down as if she had shut the door to her soul.

"It's okay, Alexia," Kimberley soothed her. "You're not in trouble. It's great to see you have nice memories of your brother. It must have been so special. Were you sleeping in Lando's crib the night he died?"

"I keep telling you! He didn't die!" Alexia bolted up to stare angrily at Kimberley.

Oh! She doesn't understand! Of course!

"Alexia. Where do you think Lando is?"

"In heaven." The child's gaze was defiant. She stared up at Kimberley, her jaw set firmly, as if scolding her therapist.

"Right," Kimberley quickly agreed. "Like Gabrielle."

Alexia nodded.

This is not going to be easy.

"Well, then, let's talk about the night he went to heaven."

"I'm not allowed to talk about that." Alexia's face remained a blank, her voice devoid of emotion.

"Somebody told you not to talk about what happened that night?"

Alexia nodded, timidly.

"Who told you?"

She just shook her head.

Kimberley took a different tack. "Lando was sick. And Mama was, where?"

"At school."

"And Daddy was, where?"

"Downstairs."

"Okay," Kimberley said. "Daddy was downstairs. But he didn't come upstairs to help?"

Alexia tightened her lips. She wrapped her arms around herself.

"So you tried to comfort your little brother?"

Alexia nodded but avoided Kimberley's eyes.

"How did you comfort him?"

"He kept being noisy, so I played hide and seek with him. I hid under the crib, but he didn't care. He just kept screamin' and I kept trying to make him smile. Then I climbed inside and gave him my sippy cup. But he didn't want it."

"And then?"

"I gave him Floppy Dog. I was making Floppy Dog do flips." She tumbled her hands in a circle. "And then I heard the footsteps, so I crawled under the blankets at the bottom of the crib and acted like I was sleeping."

"And then what happened?" Kimberley prompted.

The child blankly stared at the cards laid out on the mat. She picked up one, a baby in a crib, and laid it in front of her.

"What did Daddy do?"

"Nothing." Alexia bowed her head for a long moment.

Kimberley watched her troubled face, absorbing the child's deep sadness as readily as she did her own children's. Kimberley knew she had to stand outside her client's confusion and angst in order to guide the child back to the present.

"And then what happened, Alexia?" she said gently.

The child's head came up, and she looked Kimberley in the eyes. "I fell asleep," she declared. "Lando stopped crying."

"So you both fell asleep, Sweetie?" she asked. "What happened when you woke up?"

The little girl didn't answer.

Kimberley's mind reeled. What Alexia was telling her was important information. She was possibly the first person to have found him dead.

"Maybe he went to Heaven because I stopped playing with him. Maybe God doesn't want me to be his sister?"

"Alexia, Sweetie, you had nothing to do with that."

Kimberley touched the child's hand gently. What a terrible secret this poor child had been carrying around for weeks now!

"Then why did he go away?" Her voice was barely audible.

"He was sick, Alexia. You said he was Mama's sick baby. That's why he went to heaven, not because you stopped playing with him. He loved you very much. You were his big sister. And you could never be replaced."

Alexia almost bolted from her chair.

"But Jesus didn't send him back!" Her expression was full of fury. "I asked him to. I prayed like Abuelita said to. I prayed for the miracle to happen. I told Jesus he could take me instead, that I would like it better in heaven than in stupid old school, but it didn't happen."

"Is that why you sleep in the crib?"

She nodded and said in a small voice, "Why won't he take me, too?" She hesitated, then added, "Do you think Lando has a new sister in Heaven?"

"Listen, Alexia. Jesus doesn't take people up to heaven unless they are very sick and can't get better. That's nobody's fault. And he can't send them back, because they are too fragile to live on earth. You and I and Jayleen and Daddy and Mommy are strong. But Lando wasn't. And my Gabriella wasn't. So Jesus takes them to be in heaven, where it's easier for them to be. That's what death is. It's not a bad thing. It's just what happens, usually when you get very old and have lived a long time. But sometimes, very fragile little babies die, too."

"Oh." She stuck her thumb in her mouth, sucking hard. She raised her dark sad eyes to Kimberley. "Are you sure that's why Jesus is keeping Lando? Not because of me?"

"Oh sweetie, I've never been so sure of anything in my life."

PART II

LOSS OF INNOCENCE

"Childhood, after all, is the first precious coin that poverty steals from a child."

—ANTHONY HOROWITZ, THE HOUSE OF SILK

CHAPTER THIRTEEN

Kimberley Mason followed the school guard down a long empty corridor on her way to the school psychologist's office. Her high heels clicked rhythmically, echoing loudly in the hushed silence as she passed closed door after closed door of classrooms. She wondered which one was Alexia's.

Why did she feel so nervous? If anything, she'd over-prepared for her first meeting with the team assigned to Alexia's case. Her briefcase held a concise progress report. She had a signed waiver from the parents authorizing her to discuss their sessions. Her boss had filled her in on handling official protocols and warned her against putting too many details in writing, which could be used in court against her or her clients.

Still, she never met anyone on the team and didn't know what to expect. She pushed open the door to the meeting room. Five pairs of eyes looked up expectantly as she announced herself.

"Great! Come right in." The woman nearest the door stood up, offering an outstretched hand and a warm smile. "I'm Lisa DeLaney, the school psychologist. Please have a seat. There's water and iced tea here. Help yourself to the cookies."

Kimberley slipped into the nearest chair, as the school psychologist introduced the others. "This is our principal, Dr.

Robert Cruz. Trish Sherman, Alexia's kindergarten teacher." The two educators nodded politely in turn. "Allison Moreau is our school district social worker." A young woman with long blond hair nodded in turn. "And finally, Dolores Fuentes is here on behalf of Child Protection Services."

Kimberley was startled. If Child Protection was here, did that mean that something else was going on?

Kimberley recognized her name. Her boss had mentioned her several times as a tough, passionate advocate whom he admired. She looked like no other social worker Kimberley had ever known. Dolores Fuentes had a regal bearing, and a face as finely sculpted as her short-cropped, salt-and-pepper hairstyle. From the red lacquered frames of her designer glasses to her vivid ensemble, a tropical print blouse under a rose-colored blazer, she looked more like a Miami celebrity than Newburgh social worker. Cool and composed, she radiated warmth and an electric intensity from her kohl-lined brown eyes.

The school psychologist gave a quick review of the incidents that had led to Alexia's intervention, noting that it was the first time she'd dealt with the Mackenzie family.

"I don't know much about the parents," added Lisa DeLaney. "Dr. Cruz?"

The principal stated that the father had attended this school district, this very elementary school, and the mother had also attended the local high school. "They've certainly shown a willingness to cooperate with Mrs. Delaney and with outside therapy. So that's a hopeful sign." He turned to Kimberley. "Mrs. Mason, maybe you can fill us in on how those sessions are going."

"Yes, of course," Kimberley said, opening her folder. "Do you want the report first, or the waiver form?"

"You can give me those later," said Lisa DeLaney. "Right now, we're just sharing information. Very informally."

Kimberley began with a review of how many sessions she'd had so far, adding that Alexia was making slow but definite progress in dealing with her grief. She mentioned the child's extreme attachment to her mother as a factor in her emotional withdrawal.

"It's not a particularly healthy attachment," she added, looking at the school psychologist. "Her mother relies on Alexia for comfort. That's something we're working on to change. I think Alexia's become overly protective of her mother. Every moment she was in school, she was worried about how her mother was doing without her."

"I got a feeling from talking to the mother that she was treating Alexia like an adult," the school psychologist said. "Does she realize that's inappropriate?"

"Yes, I think she's starting to understand, but it's a delicate situation. She doesn't seem to have any adults she can really turn to, so it's a matter of helping both of them to change that pattern."

"I'm curious," Dolores Fuentes interrupted. "How would you characterize the relationship between Alexia and her father?"

Kimberley thought a minute. "I'd say Jayleen, the younger sister, is very much Daddy's girl. I think Connor and Alexia have a more complicated relationship. It's pretty strained right now."

"Hmmm." Dolores Fuentes nodded thoughtfully. "What about trust?"

Kimberley was confused as to what the director of Child Protection was getting at. "I don't think Connor trusts many people. He can be a bit abrupt with her, impatient really. I think he's just having a really hard time coming to terms emotionally with the loss of his son."

"But why take it out on Alexia?"

That struck Kimberley as strange. "I wouldn't characterize it that way. Maybe, just that he's impatient with the slowness of the grieving process. His daughter and his wife aren't getting over it as quickly as he would like." She turned to the school psychologist. "The mother is really consumed by her grief, and Connor is avoiding his by trying to get right back to normal. That sets up a conflict and puts Alexia right in the middle."

Lisa DeLaney nodded in agreement. "Do you think that's connected to Alexia's meltdowns in class?"

Kimberley said she believed it did. "Aside from wanting to be home for her mother, I think it also had to do with Alexia's initial confusion about death. The adults kept talking about Lando being in heaven. So even though Alexia went to the funeral, she simply refused to believe her brother was dead."

Kimberley described how the child believed her brother was 'visiting Jesus in Heaven,' and her fears of God taking her mother and sister away.

"Now that we've cleared up some of her misunderstandings and reassured her that the rest of her family is healthy, Alexia seems to be slowly coming out of her chronic anxiety. At least she's calmer in our private sessions."

"I've seen a change in her," remarked the kindergarten teacher. "She's a little more focused now in class, but she's still acting weird with the other kids. It's like she's afraid of them. What's up with that?"

"She says she has no friends at all." Kimberley mentioned the bullying incident with the girl who threw her painting in the garbage.

"Oh, I remember that." The kindergarten teacher looked annoyed. "Carmen just wanted to see her painting, and Alexia started doing her don't-touch-me routine. So Carmen got mad, grabbed it and threw it in the wastebasket."

"I hadn't heard about this," said Dr. Cruz, turning to the teacher. "How did you handle it?"

"I fished it out and gave it back to her," Trish Sherman said defensively. "I made Carmen apologize and gave her a time out. But Alexia still had a tantrum, refused to touch it. She said it was dirty. It really wasn't. I mean, it was just paper refuse. I told her she could paint another picture, but she wouldn't." She turned to Kimberley, clearly frustrated. "What is it with her, that everything is dirty? She doesn't even want to hold hands when the children buddy-up to go to recess."

"She's afraid of getting sick like her brother did," Kimberley explained gently. "It's understandable when you think about it. She told me her brother had a bad cold the night he died. Although I don't think it had anything to do with his death," she added. "I believe it was a SIDS death."

"It's actually listed as a SUDS death," Fuentes corrected crisply. "The U is for 'unexplained,' with various factors that don't normally fit into a SIDs case. I'm not fully up to date on the investigation, but it's being looked into."

Kimberley was startled. She had no idea that the baby's death was being investigated. Another thing the Mackenzies hadn't shared.

Or did they even know?

A few minutes later, Dolores Fuentes opened a thick file and proceeded to land another series of bombshells on the proceedings.

Starting with the Mackenzie family, the Child Protection agent related a concise history of alcohol and domestic abuse stretching back several generations, which didn't surprise Kimberley until she mentioned that Connor's parents had been drug addicts.

"Connor Mackenzie and his siblings were in and out of foster care when they were small," Dolores Fuentes continued. She paused, looking up with a grim expression. "I worked on his case back then." She shook her head. "He was about four years old the first time we took them into protective custody."

Kimberley wasn't the only one to gasp.

Fuentes slipped out another paper, tracing her finger down a long list.

"Connor's father was incarcerated for petty theft, drugs, assault, breaking and entering, robbery, and a stabbing. He was just released from state prison. A maximum-security facility," she emphasized. "Connor's mother died of an overdose back when Connor was about ten." She went down a list of his siblings, each one either disappeared or dead from an overdose.

"Oh my God!" The words slipped from Kimberley's mouth.

"You were not aware of any of this, Mrs. Mason?" Fuentes frowned.

"No."

"It's not surprising," she added more gently. "There was no way Connor was going to tell you any of this on his own. But there's something else you should all be aware of, for the children's sake." She flipped through to another file, removing a sheet of paper. "Connor has paternal cousins in the area. Two are known drug dealers, in and out of jail. Others have been picked up on an assortment of petty charges all the way to grand larceny." She looked up and sighed.

Kimberley wrote the name Gil followed by a question mark in the margin of her notepad. *Was he one of the cousins the social worker was talking about?*

"These cousins, are they around the children?" asked the school psychologist.

"That we don't know," said Ms. Moreau. "The family says no."

"Mrs. Mason, do you have any information on that?" said the school psychologist.

Kimberley hesitated, still trying to process it all. She didn't know if she should mention Gil, then decided against it until she talked to her boss.

"Both parents have mentioned relatives, but I haven't sorted them out. I'll keep that in mind though."

"Good," Fuentes said. "I'm telling you, I feel so bad for these little ones. I was hoping Connor was going to turn out all right. Out of all of the siblings, he had the best chance. The fact that he lived with the maternal grandparents all through high school is probably why he finished. His sisters ran away, came back, ran away. Sad situation." She removed her glasses, wiping them precisely with a small blue cloth. "Until recently, Connor was doing okay. Pretty much off our radar, which, I can tell you, made me very happy."

"What about Alexia's mother?" asked the kindergarten teacher. "She seems very sweet."

Fuentes leaned back in her chair.

"Much different story there. Isabella Rodriguez grew up in New Windsor. Her father was a professional firefighter, well respected. Third generation Cuban-American. I know her mom, Beatriz, a terrific lady. Her parents were migrant workers, apple pickers at the orchards here. They all became citizens, and she became a nurse in the maternity ward at St. Luke's Hospital." She closed her eyes, gently shaking her head. "But everything changed when Orlando Rodriguez was killed responding to a warehouse fire."

"Isabella said they moved back to Newburgh when she was twelve," offered Kimberley. "She told me it was a very lonely time for her."

"I can believe that." Fuentes nodded thoughtfully at Kimberley. "The older sister graduated and took off for California. Isabella was kind of lost after that. The family lived in the HUD apartments. Are you familiar with them?"

Kimberley shook her head.

"Subsidized housing. The housing of last resort back then," Fuentes said, with a slight grimace. "That was the only thing the family could afford. Isabella met Connor when she was fifteen. He was working in an auto garage, doing boats on the side in the summer. Beatriz was devastated when Isabella got pregnant. She was the one who pushed her to finish her GED. She's the one paying for those night classes Isabella takes. I give both women a lot of credit for that."

Kimberley jotted down these last two bits of information to bring up at Isabella's next session.

"And of course, Connor and Isabella are on methadone. Voluntarily."

"Heroin? They were on heroin first?" Kimberley stammered.

"When was this?" asked the school psychologist.

"Right after their son was born. They voluntarily entered a

private drug treatment program, so there's no criminal case, as long as they stay clean." Fuentes leaned in, looking around the table. "That stays in this room."

"Was the baby born addicted?" the school psychologist asked, echoing what was in Kimberley's mind.

"Hard to say." Fuentes answered grimly. "He was born at home, so we have no medical reports or blood tests until he went in for his first wellness visit. I do know he was sickly. Not like his sisters. So I have to think it affected him in some way. I have to think, maybe, that was why they both entered the methadone program."

Kimberley was stunned. Pressing her pen hard on the page, she wrote:

Lando addicted?

––––––

Kimberley had hoped to find Jon back at the clinic when she returned from the meeting, but he was with a client. She went to the break room to eat the dinner she'd brought from home and a cup of strongly spiced chai tea before leading her afternoon support group.

Her mind was still reeling from the information she had received. It was like someone had stripped away everything she thought she knew about the Mackenzies, then turned it all upside down. Doubts began to creep into her mind. Did a suburban woman of her background really know enough to help someone like Connor? She had training. She had some experience. But at this point, was it enough? And yet, there was that drive to learn, to get better, and the confidence that she could bring something to the Mackenzies. And the willpower to prove herself capable of growing and learning enough to really make a difference in her client's lives.

Jon poked his head in.

"How'd it go today at the school?" he asked quietly.

She told him a bit of what happened.

"Jon, I felt like a fool."

"We all do that, sometimes." He put the kettle on for tea.

"It's normal?"

"Pretty much." He nodded. "The question is, what will you do with the information at your next meeting? And how does it affect how you see Connor and Isabella? Does it change your view of them? Stir up your biases or your feelings toward them?"

"I've got a problem with a baby that was born to an addict," she confessed. "How do I deal with that?"

Jon grimaced as he placed a tea bag in his mug. "Pray about it? That's what I do. Or if you're not into prayer, wrestle with it. On paper, on a voice recorder. The pros and cons. The biases, the judgments about them. It's something you have to learn to deal with early on, Kimberley. Your clients are who they are. They're going to lead you down blind alleys and use you to make themselves feel good in all sorts of ways."

Kimberley didn't like what Jon was telling her. "And how do I find the truth?"

"I don't know that it's your job to find the truth of your clients," Jon said. He poured the boiling water into his mug. "That's more a social worker's job, the police's job, maybe a judge's job. It's your job to help them see where they can be stronger, be healthier. To point out alternatives for better choices, especially where their children are concerned."

"That's it?" Kimberley said, a little stunned.

"That's a lot," Jon said.

Kimberley shook her head and took a big gulp of her tea. "That's not what I was taught in my training. We were supposed to help our clients find their true self, the one they had abandoned, so they could realign themselves in a positive way."

"Sure. That's the ideal," Jon said, giving a shrug. "But it's not always realistic with every client. Not in ten sessions. Sometimes not in a year of sessions." He stirred in a spoon of sugar, then lifted his mug. "I've got another client. If you want to talk more, let me know."

Kimberley watched him walk away, feeling more confused than before.

———

"You look like someone punched you in the stomach," said Kimberley's husband later that night. The kids had been tucked into bed and Ammon had finished grading a pop quiz, only to find Kimberley sitting in her favorite rocking chair in a darkened living room, staring vacantly out the front window.

"I *feel* like someone punched me in the stomach." Kimberley's voice sounded lost and far away, and her eyes were still riveted on the picture window.

"Something going on out there?"

"I'm spying on our neighbors."

Ammon snorted, thinking she was joking. When she didn't reply, he said, "Are you really?"

Kimberley looked up at him. "What do we really know about other people's lives?" Her expression was serious.

"I don't know. Not much, I guess. Unless you're mates. Or lovers."

Kimberley sighed, returning her gaze to the window. "Not even then, I bet."

Ammon sat down opposite her. "Hey, what's going on?"

"Life. Secrets. Some people have God-awful secrets."

Ammon sighed. He hated it when Kimberley was in one of her philosophical moods. "We don't have secrets. Unless you've robbed a bank lately and haven't told me."

His attempt at levity fell flat. Kimberley just shook her head. "That's the strange thing. If I had robbed a bank and got caught, I wouldn't have any secrets. It would all be down in black and white, in the newspapers, in criminal justice records. Anybody could find out."

"True," Ammon agreed cautiously. He had no idea where this was going.

"I could have found out. I just didn't think I had to dig around. I'm a therapist, not a detective."

"Is this about that meeting you went to?" He felt the familiar argument rising in his throat but checked it. He could see she wasn't really talking to him; just using him as a sounding board for something she was struggling with.

"I learned some things today that I *should* have known." Kimberley looked at him, anguish coloring her expression. "Although I don't know *how* I would have known. I just *felt* I should have known them."

"What kind of things?"

"Things I can't tell you because they're privileged information. The point is, I felt really, really stupid that the Child Protection social worker had to tell me about them." She lowered her face into her hands. "God, I must have looked like such a fool in front of the whole team."

"Hey," Ammon murmured. He touched his wife's knee, settling his hand there protectively. "Don't beat yourself up over it. You're still learning. You know how many mistakes I made when I first started teaching?"

Kimberley looked up and gave a mild smile at his attempt to make her feel better. Covering his hand with her own, she leaned over to kiss him. "Hey, you taste like strawberry ice cream."

"Want some?"

They kissed again, mouths parting this time as their kiss deepened. She stroked his fingers, making soft cooing sounds against his tongue. He massaged her knee, aroused by the sensation of heat warming his palm and spreading slowly through him.

"Yummy," she finally said. "Did you leave any for me?"

"You'll have to check the freezer," he teased, rising, tugging at her hand. He kissed her deeply, then lifted her, cradling her body against him. He whirled around the living room floor until he felt a familiar natural high, as though he had managed to defy the laws of physics, levitating far above Earth's gravitational field.

"The freezer will have to wait." Ammon carried her toward the staircase. "I'm in the mood for something better than ice cream."

CHAPTER FOURTEEN

Kimberley had taken Jon's advice to work through the disturbing revelations about her clients. She spent the drive to the clinic rehearsing what she'd say to Connor and Isabella.

"I'd like to bring up something that's been bothering me lately."

Too timid.

"At the meeting, the social worker told me you were on methadone."

Let's not blame it all on her.

"In every one's life, there are things we're not proud of. But in order to help you, it's important that you feel you can confide in me with the truth."

Too preachy.

"What the hell is wrong with both of you? Heroin? Methadone? Are you nuts?" Totally unprofessional and judgmental, although it was what she really wanted to say.

By the time she reached the clinic, Kimberley thought she had found just the right tone, the right words. But when Connor and Isabella had finally settled themselves on the couch and looked up at her with smiles as if nothing were wrong, the words popped out in an entirely different way.

"I'm having trouble understanding why, in all this time, you decided it wasn't important to tell me about your methadone treatments?"

By their reaction, she knew she'd hit the root of the problem. Connor whipped around and glared at Isabella, who shrank back into the seat.

"I didn't," she protested, shaking her head in denial.

"Then who?" he growled.

"Look, the point is not how I found out." Kimberley folded her arms and calmly gazed at Connor. "The point is that you weren't going to mention it. We can't establish trust by holding back important information."

"You talked to that goddamn social worker about us, didn't you!" Connor fixed Kimberley with an accusing stare. "God damn that bitch!" he said, his fingers tensing into a fist. "It has nothing to do with anything."

Kimberley slipped back into her therapist voice, taking back control. She was determined to keep the focus on the drug issue, not on Connor's paranoia about social workers or the system. They could revisit that issue another time.

"I can hear that you are very defensive about this, Connor. I can understand that many people would be defensive; wouldn't want to admit they had a drug problem at one point and had to be on maintenance. But your history of drug use has affected things. Including especially the way the legal system and the social services system see you."

"See?" Connor turned to Isabella. "Didn't I tell you, it doesn't matter what good things we do to make our lives better? They're only going to count the bad things against you. Not the good!"

"I think that the fact that you are on methadone is a very positive thing," Kimberley said. "You both get a lot of credit for that."

"Right," Connor muttered, folding his arms across his chest.

"But for our purposes, keeping secrets can be very harmful to the working relationship of a therapist and her clients." Kimberley paused to look at Isabella, addressing her directly,

"Keeping secrets can also be harmful to your family and your children."

"It's nobody's business," Connor muttered.

"Look, I can't help you unless I understand the full picture, can I?" Kimberley softened her voice a bit, noting Connor's blotchy complexion, which seemed to happen when was being threatened. "A little like, I imagine, it being easier to fix some-body's boat when you can see the maintenance history."

Connor shrugged. "Maybe."

"The whole point here is not to punish you or Isabella," Kimberley added. "It is to lay out a plan for getting your lives to work better, for your sake and the children's sake."

Connor opened his mouth as if to counter her argument, but then shut it, ramming himself stiffly against the couch.

Isabella was crying softly, tears streaming down her face. Always before, Connor had offered her a tissue. Now Kimberley had to gently remind him, and Connor only grudgingly passed her the box.

"I am not here to blame, or to preach, or to threaten. I just think it's time to talk about this, so that I hear your side, and understand what's really going on in your life." Kimberley waited a moment, until Isabella blew her nose and lifted her tear-stained face. "I'd like to understand how you began using drugs, and why and when you started the methadone. Would you like to start, Connor?"

The couple looked miserable. They looked like children being cornered by a parent for doing something bad. Connor sat abso-lutely rigid and stubbornly mute. It was Isabella who finally spoke.

"I knew we should have told her sooner," she said. She blew her nose loudly. "Remember, I said, Connor, what if she asks us about drugs. And you said she's not going to bring it up. And I said, even if she doesn't, she's going to find out, and then it will be worse than if we volunteered it. I said that to you."

Connor only shrugged his shoulders.

"I wanted to be upfront with you," Isabella scrunched up the tissue. "But Connor was afraid you wouldn't think we were good parents. Like Ms. Fuentes. That you'd be on her side, instead of ours."

Kimberley took a moment to process that, some of her disapproval draining out of her tight shoulders. "It's important that you think I'm on your side?"

They both looked up at her, as if the question were ludicrous.

"Yeah," said Isabella uncertainly. "Sure."

"So you're saying that you feared that if I knew about your drug history from the beginning, that I might label you as 'bad people' and not want to help you?" Kimberley continued. "Is that it?"

Connor gave a soft snort of acknowledgment. Isabella nodded eagerly.

"Well," Kimberley conceded cautiously. "You might have been right. Perhaps I would have looked at you differently from the beginning."

Connor nodded. "I told you," he murmured.

———

Isabella watched closely as Connor began telling Kimberley about his drug history. She could hear the street-smart sarcasm in his voice, a kind of bravado that came to him naturally. She saw him lean forward, like a panther going in for the kill, toying with the therapist's emotions.

He had pulled the same game with the social worker, but she had been like a brick wall. Dolores Fuentes had heard it all, seen it all, and had no shock left in her.

But Isabella could see that Connor's attitude was getting to Kimberley. And that hurt, because to Isabella, Kimberley had been the one person who seemed to be truly on their side. Who truly seemed to care.

And now judgment was clearly reflected in the therapist's

narrowed, green eyes, and her normally friendly face was rigid and tense.

"So like I said, I was smoking weed when I was Alexia's age," Connor said. "My dad gave us a joint when we were sick. It really makes you feel better. I mean, it is actually medicine, you know."

"But," interrupted Kimberley. "You did take heroin at some point."

"Not when I was five." Connor smirked.

"How old were you when you started taking other drugs?" Kimberley asked. Her voice was neutral, but Isabella detected an undercurrent of disapproval.

"I did ecstasy at parties or speed if I could get some—"

"What grade?"

"I don't know. Seventh maybe. Definitely eighth. After my Mom died. I suppose Ms. Rodriguez," he pronounced it 'Mizzz' to show contempt. "She let you in on all the dirt in my family."

Isabella hated it when Connor acted like this. She wanted to sink through the floor, bolt from the room, roll over and die. Kimberley wasn't the type to know about Connor's kind of family. She probably grew up in a perfect family, with the only drugs being aspirin, maybe. You could see that she ate healthy foods from her glowing skin tone and her slim figure. Just look at her clothes, Isabella thought. Not super trendy, but nice material, elegant, with a coordinating scarf and delicate silver earrings and bracelet.

Maybe Connor was right, maybe Kimberley was naive about the world they lived in. Maybe someone who grew up in a normal home could never understand. Maybe she couldn't really help them.

"And when you were living with your grandparents?" Kimberley was asking.

"I only did drugs at parties. Gramps didn't want it in the house."

"So that was good. You respected him," Kimberley said.

Isabella opened her eyes, surprised at her response and wondering what Connor would say to that.

"Sure I did. I told you, only at parties."

"Did you respect him out of love? Or fear?" Kimberley pressed.

Connor let out a snort. "The only person I was ever afraid of was the Bastard," he said levelly.

Kimberley looked at him for clarification.

"My father," Connor explained.

"Out of love for your grandfather, then," Kimberley said.

"I guess."

Isabella sensed that Kimberley was trying to take Connor into a dangerous place, a place of emotions. The only emotions Connor allowed himself to talk about were anger, resentment, or his love for her and the kids. She wondered how long it would take Connor to shut down.

"What did you think about your mother's addiction? And your brother's and sister's?"

"It was what it was," Connor said, smirking. "They were gonna do what they had to do, and I was gonna do what I had to do."

"Which included not to use drugs in your grandfather's house."

"Yeah."

"Would he have thrown you out?"

"No!" Connor bolted out of the couch. "You don't get it, do you? I didn't *need* to get high when I was with them."

Kimberley's face lit up. "Why not?"

"Because." He looked up at the ceiling, as if the answer were written up there. Then he shrugged. "Just because."

"Because of the boats?"

Connor looked clearly bewildered. "The boats?"

"You shared his love for the river and the boats?"

Connor glared back. Isabella knew he was upset because he

hadn't cowed the therapist. "What's your point?" He sat back down.

"I don't have a point, Connor. I'm just trying to understand." Kimberley's voice was calm, not judgmental. "I thought, wrongly now I can see, that people who are addicted always have to use drugs."

Isabella watched, holding her breath, wondering if maybe she could really trust this woman to stay on their side. Maybe Kimberley actually did have the power to make Connor see things differently.

"I don't understand what you want me to say," Connor said.

"I want you to hear yourself speak the truth, as you know it." Kimberley was looking at Connor with a gentle smile. "You know, I didn't grow up knowing my grandparents. They were all back in Australia. And so I don't quite have the connection you obviously did with your grandparents. You were much luckier than I was to have them so close. But it occurs to me that when they were alive, you respected their wishes and didn't do a lot of drugs, and certainly not in their house. I just wondered, when did that change?"

Connor didn't respond. He ran his fingers through his hair. It seemed to Isabella that he was trying to puzzle out what the therapist was getting at.

"I don't know," he finally said, the belligerence gone from his voice. "Grammy died when I was sixteen. Then it was just me and Gramps for a while. And he...well, he died later."

"Tell me about that day," Kimberley said.

Isabella of course knew the rest of the story. She waited to see if Connor would respond. How would he tell it? Would he try to shock Kimberley? Or would he say what he really felt about that day?

"We were working on the boat," Connor began. "I remember. I was replacing some of the boards on the deck that were rotting, and he was up in the pilot house."

"Is that a place?" the therapist asked.

Connor shook his head. "It's the pilot's cabin, where you sit to pilot the boat." He took a breath, as if he were inhaling a cigarette. "All of a sudden, I hear a thud. He just...he just keeled over." Connor's expression went blank. "He just fell. Then I climbed up to him, but when I got there... Well. You know."

The room filled with silence. Connor sagged against the couch, as if his bones had turned to jelly. He looked as vacant as if his mind had gone to another planet.

Isabella took over telling their story, talking directly to her lover in the hopes that it might have the power to pull Connor back to her.

"He had a heart attack, right babe? He was such a nice man, wasn't he Connor? He had this sad smile, sometimes, when he looked at you. I think he was real proud of you for trying to be good and finish school and all. And for loving the boats and the river just as much as he did."

She looked up at Kimberley. "I would watch them work on the big fishing boat in a warehouse down at the Newburgh marina. It's still in there. Connor's been trying to fix it up and sell it someday. Make a little money, maybe."

"How long did you know Connor's grandfather?"

"I met Connor maybe a year before his grandpa died, but I was fifteen and my mom wouldn't let me go out with Connor. So I'd go down to the river to watch them work. I wasn't there the day he died, but somebody told me about it. So I went to see Connor. To comfort him. I just turned sixteen. And after that, Connor went kind of crazy."

"Crazy?" Kimberley's voice was gentle.

"He needed somebody to love him," Isabella said. She reached out to touch Connor's knee. "I felt the two of us were orphans. You know? Both of us lost our dads, well, Connor his grandpa and me, my daddy."

Connor looked at Isabella and smiled.

"I had nothing," he said slipping his hand into hers. "Nothing. The Bastard was in jail. My mom was dead. My sisters gone. My oldest brother in jail. My other brother, who the hell knows!"

"I know *mi amor*," Isabella said. She lifted her free hand and stroked his hair, brushing it off his forehead. "I know."

Connor's blue eyes were soaking up Isabella. "You were there for me, Bella."

"I know," she said. "*Te adoro.*"

"I ran out of money," he told her. "Remember?"

"I know, I know," she crooned. "I know, *mi amor.*"

"If I had money, I wouldn't have worked for Gil. I wouldn't have driven that truck. I didn't know it was stolen. I swear, I didn't know. You know that."

Connor stroked her hair, and she luxuriated in the feel of his fingers moving gently against her scalp.

"He gave me the keys and said deliver this stuff to this guy up in Sullivan County, so I did. He was going to pay me three hundred dollars. That was a helluva lot of money."

Isabella gazed into his eyes, seeing that he was really talking about the truth now. He was finally beyond the games. "I know. I know you wouldn't have."

"But I was so glad for the money, I was so glad, I just took the keys and drove it, and then I got busted." He turned suddenly, startled, as if he had forgotten Kimberley was in the room with them. "I got caught with stolen property," he went on. "But I knew that I couldn't turn Gil in. He was my cousin. You don't turn family in. See? So I knew I'd have to go to trial. But I thought..." He turned back to Isabella. "I thought Gil's lawyer would get me off."

"I thought so too, *mi amor.*" Isabella held his hands. They were cold. She stroked his thumbs. "I thought so, too. I was praying for it."

"I mean, I didn't have any priors. It wasn't burglary. It wasn't armed robbery. So, I was in county jail for six months. Could have been worse. Could have had guns in the car, and they might have sent me upstate. And then Bella couldn't have come to see me." He stroked her cheek and when he smiled at her, Isabella felt as if she had entered a magic place, just for them. "You came to see me every week, even though you were pregnant with Alexia. With our little girl."

Connor's eyes were brimming with so much love, Isabella was overwhelmed with emotion and tears.

"I didn't ever mean to start shooting heroin."

"I know *mi amor*." Isabella turned to Kimberley, clutching Connor's hand. "He got jumped in jail. For cigarettes. For cigarettes!" The injustice of it made her chest ache. "He got a chair slammed over his back. He was in such pain. He went to the infirmary, and they gave him painkillers."

"Oxycodone," Connor said.

"But then, they sent you back to the cell, and it was still hurting him."

"That's when I started using heroin. It was easier to get."

Connor's thumb grazed Isabella's cheek. They had been fighting so much lately, and suddenly, at the worst moment of all, they were here remembering the past and falling back in love.

Crazy, Isabella thought. *The world was crazy, but I have Connor back. That's all that matters.*

———

"How long were you in jail?" Kimberley's question seemed to startle both Isabella and Connor back into the present.

"When I got out," Connor said, turning suddenly to talk to Kimberley. "Gil got me some more oxycodone." He looked up at Kimberley and smirked. "Know what those are? Opiates. The best painkillers. So I was fine for a while. I went to work for Jeff, and then we were doing okay. But then everything crashed again. I mean the economy, you know? End of 2008. And I had no work. And I couldn't get the oxy anymore, and so I started taking heroin again. It's cheaper, and it don't have as many side effects for me. I went back to doing jobs for Gil. It sounds crazy, but he was the only one offering enough to keep us going. I didn't want Isabella on welfare and having the social services people on our backs."

"I don't understand." Kimberley looked confused. "Aren't you on methadone, too, Isabella? Doesn't that mean you were using heroin, too, at one point?"

Isabella traded a knowing look with Connor. Kimberley was obviously very naive about the world. Isabella used the same tone of voice she would explaining something to the girls.

"When Connor was out of jail, he never used in front of me. Never. He used to go outside to the old boat shed. He did it in there, so the girls and I wouldn't see. But I saw how he'd come home in a really calm way; like he was floating. And once or twice, I saw him get sick. One time I was scared, but Gil came right over and brought him out of it okay. So, then we fixed up the other bedroom for Alexia. When it was too cold, he'd sometimes shoot up in the bathroom."

"How can you work and take heroin?" Kimberley looked confused again. "Doesn't it make you ill?"

"It wasn't like that," Isabella explained patiently, feeling superior at knowing more about life, in some ways, than her therapist did. "Most of the time, he was just mellow, coming down off the high. He could be twitchy sometimes, but he functioned okay. If Jeff called him, he always showed up and did a full day's work. And when he could scrape together the money, he was working on his grandpa's boat."

"But when did you start using heroin?" Kimberley asked.

"After she had Jayleen," Connor said. "She got, what do they call it again, post-something depression."

"Post-partum," Kimberley corrected. "I do know what that's like. Many women get it."

"With me, it was like I was always crying," Isabella said. "And I guess it sounds stupid, but I was always watching Connor and his friends get high and I got envious. It looked so peaceful..." She looked up at Connor and smiled, tracing the arc of his chin with her finger. "I wanted to feel happy again."

"I told you no, you shouldn't do it," Connor said firmly, grinning at her as if she were a child. "I told you, you wouldn't like it. It would leave scars on those pretty arms. And you needed to look after Alex and Jay."

Isabella sat back, taking in Connor's grin and wagging her finger at him in mock anger. "I was mad at you. I thought, I'm going to do it whether he wants me to or not. I was lonely. You got high and left me behind. He kept it on the top shelf of the medicine cabinet," she explained to Kimberley. "I waited till the kids were at my Mom's. My God, my hands were shaking so bad, I kept jabbing and missing, jabbing and missing."

"She ended up with bruises everywhere," Connor said, pulling her hand back into his. He rubbed his thumb against the soft skin below her wrist. "I was wondering where she was. So I went upstairs, and when I saw her with the needle and all the little pricks where the blood oozed through on her poor arm, I almost cried. The way she was going, she was going to collapse her vein, so I did it for her."

Kimberley had a pained look on her face. "You were trying in your own way to keep her safe?"

"Yeah," Connor said, his voice tender. "Yeah, I was. I mean, I know now it wasn't the best thing for me to be using in front of Isabella, but it was what it was. If I had it to do over, I might not let her do it."

"It was my choice, *mi amor*," Isabella murmured, feeling happy that they were finally connecting again. "I wanted to know what you felt. I wanted to be with you. You were far away from me, and I wanted to be sharing it with you."

They were quiet for a long moment, and in that space, Isabella felt herself come back fully into the present again. She wiped her eyes, now wet with tears. *So many choices. So much regret.*

"If I hadn't been pregnant, it wouldn't have mattered," she told Kimberley. "But I did get pregnant. For a while, I kept thinking that my baby wouldn't be affected, you know? I know it sounds stupid now, but that's the way you start to think when you're using. You think, somehow, we're immune. Our baby is immune. But it's not that way."

She buried her face in Connor's chest, sobbing as images of Lando sick and in withdrawal, his tiny body convulsing, flooded her mind.

Connor rocked Isabella slowly. "It is what it is," he murmured. "It is what it is."

"You had Lando at home?" Kimberley asked. "Wasn't that dangerous?"

Something in the timber of Kimberley's voice ignited Isabella's maternal instincts on full attack mode. "If you're saying we didn't care about the baby enough to have him in the hospital, you're wrong," she retorted. "My mother's plenty experienced with withdrawal babies. She knows more than the doctors do. I was already off heroin and on methadone months before I delivered Lando. We went to a doctor my Mom trusted. He got us into rehab. Lando had a few withdrawal symptoms, but we tried to do the right thing."

She stared coldly at Kimberley, whose mouth was slightly open. "We're not monsters."

"I didn't say you were," Kimberley replied. "But I do have to ask. If Connor was smoking marijuana at a young age for medicinal purposes, is that something you use for your children?"

"No!" said Isabella and Connor in unison.

"I loved my baby," Isabella said fiercely to drive home the point. "We're good parents. We do the best we can. Connor and I would never intentionally hurt any of our kids. Would we?" She glanced up at Connor for support.

Kimberley started to say something. Connor turned away, as if to listen to Kimberley. Isabella had a sinking feeling that he was avoiding her question.

"Would we?" she prompted again, nudging him, giving him a chance to defend them.

But he pretended not to hear.

CHAPTER FIFTEEN

Kimberly set her windshield wipers to the highest setting as the drizzle that had started on her drive home intensified into a sudden downpour. Traffic on Route 84 was light, but the windows blurred from the pelting rain. Intermittent gusts of wind buffeted her car, and trucks kicked up torrents of water, forcing her to slow down.

A burst of jazz signaled a call coming in on her cell phone. It was probably just Ammon calling to see if she was on her way. She let it ring while carefully pulling onto the shoulder of the highway. By the time she was able to pick up, the call had already gone through to voice mail. She was just thumbing through her menu to see if he'd sent a text, when it rang again.

"Hello."

"Is this Kimberley?" a breathless voice demanded. "It's Isabella! We just got a letter from Child Protection. They're investigating us!"

"Okay, Isabella. Calm down. What does—?"

"Connor just stormed out of the house. I'm worried." Isabella's voice broke with a sob, then rose in desperation. "I don't know what to do!"

"We'll figure it out. Okay?" Kimberley said, gripping the phone. A passing truck threw up a spray of heavy water against her car door. The sky lit up with a streak of lightning. The cell phone crackled with static.

"Can't you do something?" Isabella pleaded. "Can't you get them to leave us alone." She began to sob, speaking in Spanish.

"I can tell that this has you really worried Isabella, but I need you to focus and calm down," Kimberley said, using a grounding technique to keep her client's panic contained. "I need you to speak English so I can understand what you're saying. Can you do this for me?"

"Okay, okay," Isabella said. "But I don't know what to do. I don't know why they have it in for us."

"Isabella, let's take it one step at a time without jumping to conclusions," Kimberley persisted, keeping her voice neutral. The frantic beat of the wiper blades was annoying. She flicked them off. "Is there something specific you would like me to do?"

"I don't know!" Isabella moaned. "I tried calling, but they're closed."

"Who's closed?" The car rocked violently, hit by another gust from a passing truck. Kimberley involuntarily pressed harder on the brake, bracing herself. "I can't... Listen, I'm in my car and it's pouring, and I'm pulled over on the high—"

"Connor wants us to take the kids and go away somewhere. Georgia, maybe," Isabella interrupted. "He's really upset."

"Tell him not to do that, Isabella. It will only make things worse."

"I did tell him. That's when he took off. He always does that. Just takes off and—"

"Where are the girls?" Kimberley interrupted.

"They're fine. They're right here with me."

"And you're at home?"

"Yes. Can you come over?" Isabella sounded as fragile as one of her children.

There was no way she could drive all the way back to Newburgh, Kimberley thought, struggling between her desire to get home and her concern for Isabella and the girls. "When did this all happen?"

"Just now. When we got home from your session, we just piled the mail on the kitchen table. Connor didn't go through it until just a little while ago. That's when he found the letter." Her voice rose to a wail.

"I can't come now," Kimberley insisted. "Besides, there's nothing I can really do until tomorrow."

"Okay, tomorrow." Isabella pleaded. "Could I bring the letter to the clinic to show you?"

"I'm not at the clinic tomorrow."

"But couldn't you come anyway?" She sounded frantic, her voice rising in pitch. "Just to help us? Couldn't you call them, call Dolores Fuentes or whoever's there and ask them what it means? What will happen?"

Kimberley leaned back against the head rest, suddenly exhausted. She stared at the fat drops splatting against the blurry windshield.

"If I call," Isabella said. "I just don't think I can deal with it by myself. I just don't think I can ask the right questions."

The rain was letting up a little. Kimberley breathed deeply, working her shoulders to remove the tension.

"This is what we'll do, Isabella. I'll call you tomorrow morning, after I find out if I can make it into the office." Kimberly's mind switched into list mode. "I have to get a babysitter or call the daycare and see if they can take Jack."

"Oh." Isabelle sounded startled. "I didn't realize you had a baby."

"Yes, I do." Kimberley glanced at the dashboard clock. It was already after nine-thirty. "Right now, I have to get home. And I will call you tomorrow morning. Around ten. Okay, Isabella? Will you be alright until then?"

"I guess so," Isabella said softly.

"All right then. Hopefully, Connor will cool down and come back in a bit. In the meantime, try to get some rest. Make sure the kids get to bed. Can you do that?"

"Yes," Isabella replied. "Yes, I can do that. And Kimberley? Thanks. I'm glad you're on our side."

———

Ammon was just hanging up the phone when Kimberley came in the front door.

"Hey, I was trying to get you," he said, by way of greeting. "Your cell phone dead?"

"No." Kimberley said. "But I got a call from a client on the way home." She laid her pocketbook on the kitchen counter. "I had to pull off the road to take it."

"No worries," Ammon said, moving toward her. "It was only that your mum called. She and your dad are going to lunch after their photography club tomorrow. She wanted you and Jack to join them."

"Oh, I forgot." Kimberley threw back her head and sighed. There went one potential babysitter. "I'll have to call them back tomorrow morning. I'm too exhausted now."

"Did you get milk?"

"Milk?" She groaned. "Oh no. I forgot! Let me go and..."

"Not the end of the world." Ammon chuckled. "We got that packaged stuff in the pantry. Maybe the kids won't notice the difference."

"Paige will. She can always tell."

Ammon put his arms around Kimberley. "Had a bad day?"

"Not terrible." Kimberley snuggled against him. "But not terrific, especially with the storm on the way home, and the trucks whipping by, flinging water on the car. It was a bit terrifying."

"Poor Kimmy." Ammon hugged her and began to sway back

and forth. "Well, you're all right now, my brave girl. You're home and safe."

Kimberley smiled, breathing in the familiar scent of his after-shave and wool sweater. "Exactly where I want to be."

———

"Normally, Mrs. Mason, we'd love to have Jack," said the daycare manager over the phone. "But I've got two staff members out sick, and we're already overwhelmed. I hope you understand."

"Of course," Kimberley lied, gripping the cord. At least the daycare manager couldn't see how upset she was. "We'll see you tomorrow, as usual."

"Thanks for understanding." The line went dead.

Kimberley looked over at Jack. He was so cute, in his soft blue corduroy coveralls and striped shirt, as he lay on his back under the bars of the baby gym. She watched him grab at the blue stuffed octopus that dangled above him, gurgling with pleasure each time he made the toy sway. Kimberley knelt down beside him and shook one of the dangling rattles.

"Hear that Jack? Do you like that?"

The baby squealed with pleasure and she scooped him into her arms. "God, I love you, my little man," she cooed, hugging him tightly. "But Mommy's going to have to take you into work with me today." She rubbed her nose gently against his, then kissed it. "It'll only be for an hour, at the most. But then we'll go have lunch with Grammy and Grandpa. You'll like that, won't you. Won't you?"

She wished she could just spend the morning playing with Jack. This was the part she loved best at this age, the cuddling and cooing, the sweet sound of his chortle, and the ritual of gentle baby talk between them.

"But we have to go," she said, rousing herself into action.

She decided not to tell Ammon about taking Jack to

Newburgh. But even as she strapped him into the car seat, and carefully stowed his playpen and diaper bag away, she began to second-guess herself. She was getting into a bad habit of keeping things from Ammon ever since she took this job. Still, why upset him over nothing.

———

Kimberley was surprised to see Connor in the parking lot. He was alone, leaning against a battered and rusty white truck. He held a large envelope in one hand, his other shoved deep in the pocket of his dark gray parka. His head was tilted back, watching the seagulls sail overhead, his mouth open, his expression dreamy. He didn't look like the panicked man Isabella had described last night. Which made Kimberley wonder whether her trip here had been necessary.

Heaving himself away from the car, Connor raised a hand to Kimberley as she got out of the driver's side. When she opened the back door to unhook Jack, he lumbered over.

"Guess you couldn't find a babysitter."

"No. It didn't work out."

He nodded, hovering next to her as she scooped Jack into her arms. "I know how that goes."

He was much taller than she realized; taller even than Ammon. She grabbed the diaper bag and flung it over her shoulder.

"Anything else?" he asked.

"Just the playpen," she said. "It's in the back."

"I'll get it." He strode to the back of the Subaru and lifted the hatch door.

Kimberly pointed out the rectangular zippered carry bag which held the folded-up playpen.

Connor pulled it out. "Your car could use a wash," he commented, lowering the hatch.

Kimberley laughed as she headed for the clinic, holding Jack.

"Sure could. I drove home in that rainstorm last night. The trucks kicked up a lot of mud."

"Yeah, I know what you mean." His boots crunched against the gravel lot, as he hoisted the bag over his shoulder.

"Hey there, buddy," Connor said, as he followed her. "Cute kid. What's his name?"

"Jack."

"Hey, Jack. You're a smiley baby." He chuckled.

"Is Isabella inside already?" Kimberley asked.

"She's home with Jayleen. She got a cold. Didn't want Child Protection arresting us for neglect." The words were bitter.

"Okay. I'm sorry Jayleen is sick." Kimberley kept her voice neutral. That meant she would be alone with Connor, uncertain as to how he would react without Isabella to mitigate his moods. "I just have to stop by the desk for a moment. Maybe you could go on ahead and take the playpen up?"

"Sure. Is the door open?"

"No. Here's my keys." She fumbled in her pocket and produced her key ring, holding up the office door key. "This one. Thank you, Connor. I'll only be a minute."

She watched Connor start up the stairs, then stopped by the reception desk.

"Hello Jack," Emma Wu cooed. Then she leaned toward Kimberley. "Is everything all right? You want me to see if Jon can sit in with you?"

Kimberley bit her lip, not sure. "No. He's here though, right?"

"In his office." She picked up the phone. "I can ring him now."

Kimberley hesitated. "No, I'll manage. Hmm. Just let him know that I'm here, though."

———

Connor already had the playpen set up next to Kimberley's desk.

"Why, thank you, Connor. That was nice of you to set it up."

Lowering Jack inside, she arranged some toys around him and popped a silicone teether into his mouth.

"Didn't think I knew how?" His tone was light, but the smile was as defiant. "We have one of these. Bought it second hand. I'm sure yours is new."

"Connor. Have a seat." Kimberley pulled out her desk chair and sat down to face him.

He remained standing, hands deep in his pockets, staring at her baby. With his jaw thrust forward, his eyes seemed to reflect anger, or maybe resentment.

"I was not trying to put you down," she continued calmly. "It was really nice of you to set up the playpen for me. That's all. It was a compliment. Do you understand?"

Connor nodded, shifting his weight. His jaw relaxed.

"I know you are an experienced father," she complimented him. "I know how much work that entails. I have three kids just like you and Isabella."

"I *had* three kids." He slapped the envelope down on the desk. "If these bastards take away my daughters, I won't have any."

Kimberley gazed at him, gauging how to deescalate his resentment and paranoia. "Why don't you sit down while I read this, Connor?" She removed a thin sheaf of papers from the envelope.

Connor stood a moment longer. Then he dragged the rocking chair in front of the desk, his expression pensive. Stretching his long legs out in front of him, he began to rock slowly, staring down at his muddy work boots.

Kimberley read the formal letter from Dolores Fuentes at Child Protection Services, stating that they were investigating allegations of child abuse of Alexia and Jayleen Mackenzie. A short list of what they were investigating included drug use by the parents; possible abuse or neglect of all types; the counseling progress, adjustment to grief and loss; and the general wellbeing of the children. But there was nothing describing specific allegations.

"Connor, would you know what allegations of child abuse they are talking about here?"

"I thought maybe you'd know."

"Me?" Kimberley was startled at his accusatory tone. "You think I told the social worker that you were abusing the children?"

"Yeah." He stopped rocking and shrugged. "At the school meeting. Maybe you told them then?"

Kimberley looked at Connor's sullen expression, a cross between suspicion and defeat.

"Connor, listen to me. These allegations did not come from me. Do you understand that at this moment I have no reason to believe that the girls are being abused or neglected by you and Isabella?"

His eyes flickered away. Then, he nodded.

"Okay. I'm sorry I…it's just hard to trust outside people, you know?"

"I understand."

Connor hung his head for a moment. "Listen, Kimberley. You…you've been really good. I mean, the girls like you." He began to move his hands in tiny circular motions, as if he were playing with an invisible string. "I guess, well, Isabella says I haven't been so nice to you sometimes."

"I understand. Thanks for saying it." Kimberley smiled, touched by the awkward apology.

He looked up at her. "Isabella wants you to call that…that… social worker and ask her who's been saying this stuff against us."

"I can call right now, if you want." Kimberley sighed. "But if they have no written permission from you, they are not obligated to tell me. Do you want to talk to Dolores Fuentes yourself?"

"No way!"

"Even just to say that you would like her to explain the investigation to me?"

He shrugged, then nodded reluctantly.

"I'll try calling now." She picked up the phone and dialed the number on the top of the letter. A secretary answered, and after a short wait connected her to the social worker.

"I have Connor Mackenzie right here," Kimberley said, after explaining the situation. "He's very distressed and wants to know what exactly you are investigating and what the nature of the allegations are against him. I can put him on the phone to acknowledge that he would like you to give the information to me," she added, looking over at Connor with a nod. She handed the phone across the desk.

Connor took it reluctantly. "This is Connor," he said, sotto voice. His expression was wary, and he held the phone away from his ear, as though it might give off a shock. "Yeah, well, I'll sign one of those. But just tell Kimberley what we have to do, is all I'm asking." He listened for another moment, then handed the phone back to Kimberley. Settling into the chair, he rocked slowly.

His expression was tense and watchful, his hands worrying an invisible string, as Kimberley talked to the social worker and scribbled a few notes.

After a few more questions, she felt she had gotten all she could under the circumstances. "Thank you for your time, Ms. Fuentes. I appreciate it." Kimberley hung up the phone.

She noticed that Connor was staring at Jack in the playpen. The sight of him, sleeping peacefully, only made her feel worse for Connor's situation.

"She said because of the baby's death, it was partly a routine investigation," Kimberley began. "Apparently, the EMTs smelled marijuana in the house, although they didn't find anything. They also said you shoved one of the investigators and were screaming at them."

"I was upset!" Connor's face was anguished. "Anyone would have been upset. My baby was dead! Okay, granted, I pushed the guy away, but he was like, ripping Lando right out of Bella's arms and she was screaming. I couldn't just stand there and do nothing."

"She said," Kimberley glanced at her notes. "That you also gave the investigator from the medical examiner's office a hard time when he came to investigate."

"He was asking questions like we were some kind of murderers! I was pissed off."

"Okay," Kimberley said. "So the night Lando died, you were shocked, angry and sad, and you were upset at the EMTs taking the baby away. And you were upset that the medical examiner made you feel like a bad parent. Is that right?"

"They were like, the baby's dead and we have to take him to the morgue. I was like, Christ, can't you get him to breathe? Can't you do something?"

Kimberley was trying to listen calmly, but her mind flew back to her own past, to the moment she was turning Gabrielle's tiny, fragile body over to the doctor. She had wanted to scream then, even though her doctor had been completely gentle and respectful of how difficult it was to let go. But if someone had forced the baby from her arms? She would have probably tried to rip their heads off, too.

"I understand, Connor. But I'm wondering if there was something more to it than you're being angry at the EMT. Were you smoking marijuana in the house that night?"

"My neighbor's kids. They smoke it all the time in the backyard. The smell comes in through our windows." He looked straight at Kimberley. "I'm telling you the truth. I reported them a couple of times. That's another reason their mother hates us. Listen, we're trying to do the right things here. We go to methadone. I have a steady job now. Isabella is in college to get a good job. The kids are safe and clean and fed. It's just Alex is all weirded out about Lando, but you're helping her, right? Her teacher says she's doing better."

He leaned forward, and Kimberley saw real anguish in his eyes.

"You say you want to help us, Kimberley," he pleaded quietly. "Couldn't you just write a letter? Tell them we've been coming to counseling, and getting our lives together, and yeah, we were really upset that night, but we're trying to do the right thing, here."

For the first time since she'd met Connor, she saw that all his defenses were down. That he was truly trying to do the right thing. And that was enough for her.

"Yes, Connor," Kimberley said. "Yes, I can do that."

CHAPTER SIXTEEN

Alexia stood on a kitchen chair by the stove, watching the kettle heat up. Steam came out of the broken spout. That meant the water was hot enough to make peach tea.

She turned off the gas burner. She slipped on an oven mitt to lift the kettle. It was heavy, even with both hands. She bit her bottom lip in fierce concentration, trying not to splash as she poured hot water into the horsey mug for Jayleen, who was sick upstairs. She filled the pink heart mug for Mama, who was sleeping on the couch. Then, her arms tiring, she poured the last of the water into her yellow daisy mug, a present from *Abuelita*.

She replaced the kettle, then leaned way over to reach the honey jar at the back of the counter. She stirred a spoonful of sweetness into each mug.

Scrambling off the chair, she lifted Jayleen's mug and carried it all the way upstairs, proud not to have spilled a drop. Her sister was asleep, snoring softly, so Alexia left the tea on the dresser.

Flying down the stairs, she took the last two steps in one big jump, stretching out her arms like her favorite cartoon ballerina. Then she retrieved the other mugs, one at a time, setting each on the coffee table. Her mother was curled up with a pillow on the couch.

"Mama? I have some tea for you." She tugged gently on her mother's sleeve. "Mama?"

Her mother's eyes fluttered open. "Oh, *Miha*. Thank you." Struggling up, she reached for the mug.

"It's hot, Mama. Don't burn your lips."

"*Te adora, miha*," her mother said, giving her a sleepy smile. "What would I do without you?" She took a sip. "Ummm! It's good. Ummm."

Alexia nodded happily. "Mama, can you watch *Angelina, the Ballerina* with me?"

"Oh, okay. What time is it?" She glanced at her watch. "Wow, three-thirty. I really slept. After this, though, I have to get dinner."

Alexia slipped in the DVD and settled on the couch, snuggling against her mother's warm side. This was what she liked, to have Mama all to herself. Whenever Mama sipped her tea, Alexia took a sip. Whenever Mama laughed at the funny parts, Alexia did, too. Whenever Angelina the Ballerina danced, Alexia told Mama, "I want to be a ballerina."

"One day when I get my job, then you can take dance lessons," Mama promised.

The episode was only halfway over when Alexia heard the jiggle of the kitchen door handle. That meant Daddy was home.

"Hey Bella? Bella!" Daddy called out as he opened the door.

Alexia closed her eyes. Maybe Daddy would go right upstairs and not bother them.

But he came into the living room, waving an envelope. "I got her to write the letter."

"Great." Her mother smiled, stood up, then wobbled.

Alarmed, Alexia jumped up and put her arms around her mother to stop her from falling.

Her father hurried over, concerned. "What's up, Bella? You sick, too?"

"I don't know. I feel woozy, that's all. I fell asleep."

"Get off your mother." Daddy waved Alexia away. He placed his palm on her mother's forehead. "You don't have a fever, babe," he said, kissing her cheek. "Maybe you're coming down with what Jayleen has?"

"Maybe." Mama kissed him back. "Tell me what happened."

Daddy looked over at Alexia. "Go check on your sister."

Alexia glared at him. Daddy came home and ruined everything. "Can't I finish watching?"

"Go check on Jayleen." He gave her a look that meant 'do it now'."

Alexia swiped her mug off the table. A splash of tea fell on the floor. She didn't care. The dark anger was hurting her chest again, but she didn't dare talk back to Daddy. She started up the stairs.

"We'll watch it later, *Miha*," her mother called after her.

But Alexia knew she wouldn't. There was dinner, and then Mama had to study, and then bedtime.

All the way up the stairs, Alexia felt the anger filling her chest. She knew Daddy was listening, so she stomped loudly and made a point of slamming her door. She didn't care if she woke Jayleen. She put her mug down and picked up Floppy Dog from her sister's bed. Jayleen didn't move. Worried, Alexia leaned over her sister and listened a moment to make sure she was still breathing.

"Come on, Floppy," she whispered. "Let's listen to what they're saying. But we have to be really, really quiet, so Daddy don't hear us."

Alexia nudged the door open, so as not to make it creak, then tiptoed out to the landing. She held her breath in case Daddy heard her. She was getting good at this. She sat down on the top step, out of sight, and hugged Floppy Dog tightly.

Her parents' voices drifted up to her.

"So you were right. She's got a baby." That was Daddy's voice. "And get this. It's a boy. Same age as Lando." He sounded angry. "A few months older, maybe."

"Wow!" That was Mama.

"Wow is right. Should have seen the clothes the kid was wearing. All brand new. Fancy. And the play pen. Christ, all brand new and in a special sleeve and everything. I could tell she was fuckin' surprised I knew how to set it up. Huh! I showed her."

Alexia realized Daddy was talking about Miss Kimberley.

"You were nice to her, though. Right?"

"Shit yeah. Whaddaya think? I helped her with the kid's stuff. I wanted her to write the letter, right? She wrote it up in front of me. Gave me this copy for our records."

"So why are you upset, Connor? Didn't she say the right things?"

"Yeah, but that's not the point. She didn't tell us she had a baby boy, she just said she had kids. How do you think that makes me feel? We're spilling our guts out to her, and she's asking us all kinds of personal shit, and she's not sharing anything."

"But that's not... She's a professional." Mama sounded upset. "She's supposed to...my teachers tell us, you're supposed to keep a professional distance."

"That's bullshit. The reason she didn't tell us is, she thinks she's better than us."

"Mio Dios! You're so suspicious. Maybe she thought we'd be upset if we knew she had a baby boy, when ours was dead. D'you ever think of that?"

"Bullshit." Daddy used bad words all the time. "She didn't tell us she had a baby because she doesn't trust us."

The moment Alexia heard those words, her dark anger went away. A warm, happy feeling settled in her tummy. She hugged Floppy Dog tighter, rubbing her cheeks against the velvety ears.

Miss Kimberley had told her that she was special. Now she knew it was true. Miss Kimberley showed her all the photos on her key ring and told her all about her kids: Paige, the girl just like her only older, and Tony, who was three like Jayleen, and baby Jack, who was like Lando, and the poor baby girl with the closed eyes, who was in Heaven, too.

Alexia smiled.

"*I know a see-cret...*" she whispered sing-song into Floppy's ear. *"Even Mama and Daddy don't know. Her baby's in heaven, just like my Lando."*

She was quiet a moment, listening to Daddy's words float up the stairs.

"She probably goes home thinking, glad I'm not those people. My baby's healthy and all, not like those drug-addicted Mackenzies."

"God, Connor. Don't talk like that."

"They're all alike. Just out to collect a nice fat paycheck by poking their noses into other people's business. I'm telling you, she *ain't* our friend."

Alexia shook her head. Daddy was wrong. Miss Kimberley *was* her friend.

"Cross my heart and hope to die," she whispered into Floppy Dog's ear, as she traced an X across her heart. "I won't never tell about Miss Kimberley's baby in Heaven. Not even if Daddy asks me."

CHAPTER SEVENTEEN

"Mommy! Mommy!"

Kimberley glanced up from the backyard garden bed where she was planting a second row of pink and white pansies on the area they had made into a memorial garden for Gabrielle. Jack was snoozing in his stroller, bundled up in his baby blue blanket against the chill April breeze.

"Look what Daddy brought home!" Paige cried, dragging a huge cardboard box across the patchy lawn, which was still brown in spots with a few fading circles of dirty snow under the stand of pines near the fence. She settled the box into place, fussing as she removed its canvas cover.

"Cockroach Hotel! Isn't that a funny name, Mom?"

"Ugh!" Kimberley shuddered, swallowing back bile as she stared at a Plexiglas box inside the cardboard one. Dozens of the odious creatures were scurrying along clear tunnels connecting multiple compartments.

"Not too close," she told her daughter. "And keep it away from Jack."

"Oh, Mommy. They won't hurt you." Paige leaned closer, peering into the box from various angles. She brushed back the straight brown hair from her face. "It's a science experiment. Daddy keeps it in the lab at school."

"Uh-huh." Kimberley eyed it warily. "You're sure they can't get out?"

"It's totally sealed," Paige explained calmly, turning the box around. "See? There are two little screen vents for them to breathe, one here and one there, but Daddy said the cockroaches can't squeeze through them."

"I don't trust it." Kimberley edged back from the contraption. "There is no way *that thing* is going near the house."

Ammon jogged over, carrying Tony on his shoulders. He stood over Kimberley, looking down with an amused expression.

"What do you think of our cockroach farm?"

Kimberley squinted up at him. "Couldn't this have stayed at school?"

"I thought the kids would enjoy watching the critters," he said, smiling down on her. "I can show them some of the neuro-robotic stuff we're experimenting with. Something to do, since we couldn't get away this week."

His words stung Kimberley. Ammon had been looking forward to visiting friends again near Disney World over the break. But since she had no vacation time at the new clinic, they'd had to cancel. Ammon had tried to make the best of it, planning day trips to the Museum of Natural History in New York City and the Discovery Science Center at Liberty Island on her days off, but she knew he was disappointed.

"I'm sorry we couldn't go," she said reflexively. She picked up the hose and started to spray water around the newly planted flowers.

"No worries. Sometimes things just don't work out, is all," he said, eyeing her with a quizzical expression. "Down you go, mate," he added, lifting Tony off his shoulders and setting him beside his sister.

"You're not going to keep that here?" Kimberley said, gesturing to the Plexiglas box.

"Thought it could stay in the garage this week."

"The garage?" Kimberley shuddered. "I don't want cockroaches running through my house."

"Our house," Ammon corrected mildly. "They need to be warm."

"I could keep them in my room," Paige suggested.

"My room!" Tony cried.

"Nobody's room!" Kimberley said sharply. "They can stay in the woodshed."

"The woodshed is fine," Ammon said blandly, avoiding her eyes. "Don't jostle it, Tony."

He flopped down next to the children, patiently explaining the habits of cockroaches and the experiments his students conducted with them, as the children peppered him with questions. It might have made for a lovely scene, Kimberley thought, except that it was cockroaches.

Turning back to her pansies, Kimberley turned off the hose. She grabbed her trowel and stabbed it deeply into the soil, annoyed at Ammon.

He knows I have a bug phobia. How could he even joke about keeping them in the garage?

Just last week, when she'd told him she'd killed two cockroaches in the clinic's bathroom, Ammon had warned her that the insects could crawl into her handbag or briefcase, hitch a ride with her, and infest their home.

Now, he was the one bringing them home, treating them almost like a pet. It was really too much!

Her resentment grew with each pansy she planted. Ripping open a bag of fancy-fringed tulip bulbs, she took her frustrations out on the soil as she punched out eighteen perfectly spaced holes in front of the mountain laurel shrubs.

She had just finished patting down the dirt covering the last bulbs when she heard squeals of laughter. She turned to see Paige riding on Ammon's back, who was bucking like a bronco. Tony clung to his father's neck, trying to wrestle him to the ground.

Jack looked on with his bright blue eyes wide open, his mouth open in delight.

Normally, Kimberley would have joined in the fun. But today, the rough housing only heightened her annoyance.

"Ammon, be careful of Jack!"

Her husband looked up. Clearly annoyed, he shook his head slowly, then resumed his horseplay. The children paid no attention to her outburst, which only made Kimberley feel worse. How could she stay mad at Ammon when he was so good with the kids? But her pride, her disgust with his bugs, and her aching knees, wouldn't let her apologize.

She stood up slowly and peeled off her garden gloves. As she did, her eyes drifted to the bottom of their driveway. That same white truck with the rusted back panel was parked just across the street, at the Andersons, her elderly neighbors. Probably a repairman.

"I'm going inside to start lunch," she announced. Gathering her tools and the empty flats, she marched off toward the garage, jaw clenched, and heart steeled against her family's laughter.

———

The answering machine in the kitchen was blinking. Kimberley washed her hands under the kitchen faucet. She pressed the button to hear her messages, then wiped off on a fresh kitchen towel as she listened on speaker phone.

"Hi Sis. It's Charlotte. I found the sweetest sweater for Jack. I thought I'd pop over tonight to drop off those CDs I borrowed from Ammon. Let me know!"

"Ammon! it's Mark! Up for a little racquetball action on Friday? Call me back."

"Hello Mrs. Mason. It's Emma Wu at the clinic. Just wanted to update you for tomorrow's agenda. You have a cancellation for four p.m. Also, you might want to check your office answering machine. Child Protection called several times today and left messages. I told them you wouldn't be in until tomorrow."

Kimberley's stomach knotted. It had to be about the Mackenzies.

Frowning, she dialed the clinic's main number, then punched in her personal code to retrieve her messages. She held the phone to her ear while she gathered sandwich ingredients and baby food from the refrigerator.

"You have five new messages," said the automated voice.

Five! Someone must be having a meltdown.

With one hand, she plunked jars of peanut butter, jelly, and mustard on the kitchen counter as she listened to the first message from her boss, Jon. He wanted her to stop by his office before starting work.

"Just great!" Kimberley complained, as she lined up slices of wheat bread in two rows along the Formica counter. Now, she'd have to leave a half-hour early.

The next message was from a new patient, who gave a breathless, rambling account of why she had to cancel tomorrow's session. The anxiety in the woman's voice fed into Kimberley's own deteriorating mood. She began layering ham, cheese, and bologna as she waited for message three.

"This is Dolores Fuentes office at Child Protection Services," said a crisp, unfamiliar voice. "Ms. Rodriguez would like to follow up on your recent letter on behalf of your clients." She left a number where Kimberley could reach her.

A second message followed, just as crisp and just as nondescript.

Well, it didn't sound all that urgent. It could wait until tomorrow. Kimberley relaxed a little, and began to spread peanut butter for Tony's sandwich as the last message began:

"Hello?" The soft voice sounded hesitant. She couldn't quite place it. "Hello, Kimberley?"

Kimberley put down the butter knife.

"I guess you're not in. It's, uh, Isabella. Isabella Rodriguez?

Please, uh, Kimberley, if you get this message before our session tomorrow, could you call me at home? We had a registered letter."

There was a long pause. A door slammed, followed by the sound of someone crying in the background. Kimberley put her hand over her heart, worried as Isabella's faint voice continued.

"Child Protection Services says we got to come in for a hearing. A hearing. I...I guess we can talk about it tomorrow. I guess...I guess it can wait until then. Just wanted to let you know."

Kimberley rooted through her purse for her cell phone, then thumbed Isabella's cell phone number, waiting tensely while it rang and rang and rang. Finally, the call went through to voice mail.

"Isabella? This is Kimberley Mason. I got your message." She was just leaving her cell phone number, when the back door slammed, and the house filled with the sound of her family's voices. "I will see you tomorrow, at the regular time, and we can talk about it then. Don't worry," she finished, "We'll figure something out."

———

Starting the day with a visit to her boss made Kimberley feel as if she were a student checking in with the principal before class. Maybe he just wanted an update on the parenting support group.

The door to Jon's office was slightly ajar. Kimberley could just see his profile, facing away from her. She knocked softly on the door frame. "Jon?"

"Come on in."

Pushing open the door, she stepped into the room. "Hi Jon, you wanted—"

She stopped when she saw Dolores Fuentes from Child Protection Services. A bulging leather briefcase sat on the floor by her feet.

"Oh! Sorry!" Kimberley was flustered. "Emma didn't say you had someone with you. I'll come back later."

"No, no. Come in. Sit down." Jon gestured toward a free chair. "Close the door. The reason I asked you to pop by early was because Dolores wanted to discuss something of a thorny issue that concerns your clients. And since it concerns a legal issue, I thought I should sit in."

"Oh. I see." Kimberley glanced at the social worker, feeling as if she'd been ambushed. What was going on?

"I'll get right to the point, Mrs. Mason," Dolores began. "We had an interview with Isabella Rodriguez and Connor Mackenzie last week at their house and it didn't go very well. I thought we could discuss their situation in more detail. From our recent phone call, I hope I'm under the correct impression that you had a release to share relevant information."

The case worker sounded scrupulously formal, which put Kimberley instantly on her guard. What other bombs was she going to drop today to make Kimberley look like a total novice?

"Well, I do have a release for discussing it with the school team," Kimberley said, trying not to sound defensive. "I know you sat in on that meeting. But technically, you aren't part of the team. So, Jon, wouldn't I have to get an additional release to talk to Ms. Fuente?"

"Absolutely," Jon said.

"Wait a minute," Dolores interrupted. "That day you called my office, I assumed you had a release from the couple to talk that day. And then there was the letter you wrote."

"What letter was that?" Jon asked.

"Just one that explained what they were feeling the night their son died," Kimberley felt trapped. "And to reiterate that they've come to all their sessions and made sure Alexia has come to all of hers."

"And you had their written consent to write that letter to the Child Protection Agency?" Jon said.

"Yes." Kimberley glanced over at him. "It's in the file, their request for me to write a letter on their behalf. He signed it in the office. But it was a one-time consent."

"I don't understand," Jon said. "Why one time? That's unusual."

"Because he and Isabella were in a panic. They couldn't process the information in the letter. They needed, in a sense, someone to be able to explain what was happening in a way that made them feel safe."

"Hmmm." Jon frowned.

Kimberley could see that he was troubled by something, but since he wasn't forthcoming, she decided to defend herself. "In all honesty, I doubt Connor would sign another consent form to have me talk to Ms. Fuentes."

"Why not?" Jon asked, surprised.

"Let's just say he doesn't, well—" Kimberley hesitated. "That he doesn't trust authority figures."

"Oh, hell, let's be honest," Dolores interrupted, with a smile that bordered on a grimace. "He doesn't trust me, specifically."

Kimberley was shocked at the social worker's candor.

"Why?" Jon echoed.

"I was the case worker who placed Connor and the other Mackenzie children in foster care." She glanced at Kimberley. "Of course, I was also the one who helped his grandparents finally get custody of Connor, but I don't get much credit for that part."

Jon turned to the social worker. "So that's why you thought Kimberley had their consent to discuss the case with you?"

Dolores nodded. "No harm done, Jon. If it is a one-time consent, then—" She shrugged. "That's all I can do for now."

"I understand they have a meeting with you on Friday," Kimberley said to the social worker.

"Yes." Dolores sighed. "That's what I was hoping we could discuss." She shrugged, clearly exasperated. "So all I can say is this: things are starting to move very quickly in this case. If at any point in your sessions with the family, you suspect Connor

Mackenzie is a possible threat to his remaining children, well." She leaned in, her penetrating gaze sending a warning chill down Kimberley's spine. "If you feel they are being exposed to *any* kind of abuse or neglect or possible threat, if you have evidence that he is using drugs in the home, you must report it to us, immediately."

Kimberley was furious. *This woman is accusing me of not doing my job properly!*

"I know the law," she managed to say. But the social worker was already standing up to leave.

———

She watched as Jon rose and led Dolores Fuentes to the door, shaking her hand and holding it for a few moments as he murmured something too soft for Kimberley to hear.

"What did she mean?" Kimberley asked when Jon closed the door again. "I wish you had told me that she was the reason for the meeting."

"Kimberley, as your boss, I think you are doing a fantastic job." Jon gave her a puzzled look. "As your mentor, I just wanted to be on hand for what I thought was a routine matter of making sure you had gotten the proper consent forms. When she told me you had written a letter on behalf of your clients, I assumed that your clients had signed a release form for you to talk with her further about the case."

"Connor was adamant on that point. He was only giving consent for the one-time purpose of me writing the letter," Kimberley replied. "That's okay, isn't it?"

Jon sighed and sat back down, tapping the tips of his fingers together, almost as in prayer. "Were you pressured into writing that letter?" He peered intently at Kimberley.

"No! I mean..." Kimberley felt flustered. "Isabella asked me over the phone. They were both very upset. They felt they were being misjudged for being agitated right after their son died. And that no one was giving them credit for trying to do the right thing. After hearing how they were treated by the medical examiner's staff, I mean, they didn't even allow them a proper goodbye with their baby before they—"

"Wasn't that the day that you were here by yourself with Connor?" Jon interrupted. "That day you asked Emma to tell me you were here?"

"Uhmm, yes," Kimberley agreed reluctantly.

"And that's why you came in on your day off, to write the letter?" Jon persisted, leaning forward in his chair.

"Yes." Kimberley winced, feeling somehow like a student sent down to the principal's office.

"And only the father signed the consent form? Not the mother?"

"Yes." Kimberley closed her eyes, slightly nauseated. "They were both supposed to come, but…in the end, only the father."

"Dolores said that you called her office, with the father on the phone giving her verbal consent to talk to you about the case," Jon persisted quietly.

Kimberley felt faint, as if the world had spun out beneath her feet. "That was a mistake?"

Jon nodded.

"How bad a mistake?"

He shrugged. "It gave the wrong impression to Child Protection."

"That I wasn't following the rules?"

"No. They thought you had the proper authorization to discuss the case with them, when, as it turns out, you only had one party's. If the couple was having problems, say, and Isabella wanted to make a complaint against you for not getting her consent, it might be a problem."

Kimberley breathed in deeply to calm the shame that washed over her. "I'm sorry."

"That's not ideal, but that's not what I'm really concerned about." Jon once again tapped his fingertips together. A sign,

Kimberley realized, that he was deeply troubled. "I'm concerned that you are over-identifying with your clients because your baby also died."

"No." Kimberley rallied herself. "Objectively, I do think they were being misjudged. There are so many emotions that happen when a baby, any child, dies. And there was a distinct lack of respect for the family's grief, from what I heard."

"But you only heard it from your clients' side."

"Well, yes. But—"

"The point is not that you should or shouldn't have written a letter," Jon said. "The point is, under what circumstances you should have written the letter. What you don't want to happen is being manipulated by your clients, whether because you feel intimidated..." He paused, waiting for her reaction.

Kimberley shook her head and began to object.

"Or you felt obligated." Jon finished.

Kimberley indicated she hadn't.

"Or," he persisted. "You were taking on the couple's loss as your own?"

There was some truth to that, Kimberley realized. She sat back wearily, closing her eyes for a moment to mentally relive Isabella's phone call and Connor's visit. She had not felt manipulated. Moreover, Isabella's panic during the rainy night phone call had triggered her outrage and anger, as if Gabrielle's death was happening all over to her again.

"Yes. To the last." She sighed. Jon's kind face, filled with concern and sympathy, cooled her feelings of hot shame. "How should I have handled it?"

"Just take it as a lesson," Jon said, "This is how easy it is to lose control of the situation."

CHAPTER EIGHTEEN

"It's too bad Paige got sick," said Kimberley, as she and Ammon drove to the high school for the annual science fair. "She really wanted to go."

"I know." Ammon took his eyes off the road for a quick glance at his wife. "You look good." His voice was gentle and low. "That a new dress?"

Kimberley smiled at the compliment, letting her hand rest on his thigh. "I wore it at Easter."

"Sorry. I should remember these things." Briefly, he touched her hand, his thumb grazing hers. "That color, what is it? Teal? Aqua? It makes you glow!"

"Thank you!" Kimberley said, feeling immensely content. She leaned back against the headrest. "Thank goodness for Charlotte. With Mom and Dad away, I wouldn't have been able to find a babysitter on short notice."

"It feels like we're on a date," Ammon said.

"Uhm-hmmm," Kimberley murmured, stroking her thumb against his thigh. They sat like that for the twenty minutes it took to reach the high school.

"Lots of people here tonight," he said as he slowed down behind a line of cars heading into the school's long driveway.

"That's what I like to see."

Kimberley felt as if she were floating on a cloud of content-ment, happy to have Ammon all to herself. It didn't happen often.

She imagined them driving home later that night, perhaps kissing under the stars. Perhaps he would carry her up the stairs, into their bedroom, and . . . her fantasy was interrupted as he pulled into his reserved parking spot in the teacher's lot.

The night air was cool, with a hint of the coming spring in the waning evening light. Ammon took Kimberley's hand in his to help her out of the car. Turning toward the gym's double doors, they fell into step, matching their gait, their joined hands swinging.

Inside, rows and rows of long tables filled the vast space, each filled with science projects. As they moved down the rows, Ammon continued to hold her hand. Something he couldn't have done if the kids had been with them. She admired the easy way he had of stopping here and there to encourage his students with a word of advice or praise. So many of the students, colleagues and parents lit up when he greeted them, illustrating how well-liked and admired he was. Each time he introduced her as 'Mrs. Kimberley Mason', she could feel his pride in having her as his wife.

At one point, he turned to gaze into her eyes. "You're a stun-ner," he whispered in her ear. Kimberley giggled like a schoolgirl.

As the buzz of voices built to a crescendo, Kimberley felt exhilarated, thoroughly caught up in the excitement of the evening.

"Kimberley, I want you to meet someone," Ammon said, leading her over to a section where a model of the full-sized bios-phere that usually sat in the courtyard had been set up. A tall man with a blond, close-cropped beard and crew cut, and wire-rimmed glasses was fiddling with a monitor.

"Frank, hi!" Ammon hailed him. "Everything looks great!"

Frank glanced up, then grinned broadly. "Ammon! You made it! I was worried you weren't going to find a parking space!"

Ammon laughed, then introduced Kimberley.

While she only vaguely remembered Frank, she pretended otherwise, flashing a warm smile. "Of course. Nice to see you again!"

They shook hands. But Frank was looking around the room. "Oh, Ammon wanted you to meet my wife, Nancy. Let me introduce you. Ammon, can you check out this sensor? I'm not sure it's working."

Kimberley thought she saw Ammon wink at Frank as she was whisked away quickly toward the refreshments table, staffed by several women and students. Frank leaned over the table to tap the shoulder of a dark-haired woman in a navy-blue pant suit, who was scooping coffee into a large urn.

"Nancy? Hon?" The woman looked up. She was older than Kimberley, as Frank was older than Ammon by a good ten years.

"This is Kimberley Mason. You know, Ammon's wife."

"Oh, hi! Yes, I remember you." Nancy smiled. "Could you help with the refreshment table? That would be great!"

Kimberley's heart sank. It was the last thing she wanted, but she felt unable to refuse.

———

Manning the coffee station was not the way Kimberley had envisioned her evening out with Ammon. She had done it many times. But tonight she felt annoyed by the whole situation. She knew how political things could get at the school. Spouses were expected to pitch in. But Ammon should have warned her.

Grumpily, she arranged the coffee station, trying different configurations to keep the stacks of featherweight cups from tumbling onto the floor, setting out packets of creamers and sugars, and arranging stirrers in cups. Frank's wife was lining up paper plates of homemade brownies, cookies, and store-bought miniature muffins on the long cafeteria tables. Another woman, who Kimberley recognized as the PTA treasurer, was counting dollar bills and coins into a gray metal money box for doling out change.

"Anything else?" Kimberley asked, when she reported back to Nancy.

"Oh, if you can just help take money for a little while until Sheila Trevor comes back with the coffee, that'll be great."

"Looks like a big crowd," Kimberley said, moving behind the long cafeteria table that doubles as a counter.

"It really is this year," Nancy said, using her fingernail to slit open the cellophane wrapping on an enormous box of assorted Keebler cookies, the kind sold in discount warehouse stores. "So Frank was telling me that you are a child therapist, too." She doled out cookies onto paper plates. "I work for The Family Place in Middletown. Brand new clinic. We specialize in kids who have emotional situations and disabilities. You know, working with school districts to place them in Special Ed programs, and testing."

"Oh!" Kimberley smiled politely. "That's interesting. I'm actually a family therapist. I just started working part-time for a center in Newburgh. I'm running a parenting support group there, through the Family Court System. It's going pretty well."

Nancy glanced up, her hands full of cookies, to give Kimberley a puzzled stare. "But you are looking to join a new group, right? That's what Frank told me."

"Why would he think that?"

"Uh," Nancy hesitated. "Ammon said you were looking to get out of there. It's a risky area. I can't blame you. I told him we still have a few slots open."

Embarrassed at the woman's frank stare, Kimberley mouth fell open as she wrestled with how she should answer. All she felt was the sting of anger.

"I guess Ammon forgot to mention it, with all the excitement of the science fair and all." She tried to sound upbeat. "Husbands," she joked. "Always looking out for us."

Kimberley was stuck for more than an hour before she could sneak away to find Ammon. He was busy judging the ninth graders, while Frank judged the seniors. The winners were announced at nine p.m. It took another hour for the two men to clear their display tables and return the equipment to the labs. By the time he was ready to leave, Ammon was in a buoyant mood, happy that his two juniors had won the biosphere prize.

"I'm sure they'll do well on the state level next month," he crowed. "That's going to look great on their college resumes next year."

Kimberley said nothing. She was tired. A migraine was forming at the tender base of her skull. Mentally, she was playing out different conversations, trying to figure out the most diplomatic way of confronting him about Nancy Cray. But finally, she couldn't hold it inside anymore.

"Ammon, why did you go behind my back with Frank Cray's wife?"

"What?" Now Ammon sounded annoyed. "Frank mentioned it one day. It came up casually. I thought maybe it would be something you'd be interested in."

"I just started with Jon's clinic. Why would I leave now?"

"I just thought…"

"I told you I was going to stay!" Kim's voice was sharp, accusatory.

"And I told you," Ammon's voice got low as he moved closer. "It's not safe."

Kimberly stood up. "But to go behind my back, Ammon!" she cried. "That's not like you."

Ammon spun around, glancing to see if anyone had overheard his wife's outburst. He hated scenes. Angrily, he headed toward the double doors.

Kimberley's heels clicked loudly on the gymnasium's polished floors as she hurried to catch up with him. She could tell by his posture and his gait that he was angry with her. He always held his tension in his shoulders, his head thrust forward, as though he was going to lead a charge. Although she couldn't see his face, she could picture his expression, his strong chin jutting out, his mouth tight, jaws chewing over his embarrassment.

"Ammon!"

He didn't break stride.

"Ammon, wait up!" Kimberley walked faster, willing him to stop. She imagined him turning around, holding out his arms to enfold her, their apologies tumbling out in between fevered kisses and hugs.

But it didn't happen that way. She broke into a trot, worried that he might just drive away and leave her in the parking lot to find her own way home. With every step, the fear of being abandoned built up until she nearly spit at him with the full force of her escalating anxiety.

Horrified, and remorseful at what she had almost done, she slowed down, finally catching up with him as he inserted his key into the car door.

"Are you over your snit?" he said stiffly, without glancing in her direction.

Her mouth fell open. He'd never been so rude, so cutting! All her indignation returned. "You're treating me like a baby."

Ammon yanked open the car door. "Maybe it's because you're acting like one."

Both of them settled into their seats without a word, only the individual slams of their doors and clicks of their seat belts punctuating the angry silence.

Ammon started the engine.

"You ruined our night out," Kimberley finally said.

"Why? Because I tried to find you a safer job?"

"I am safe," Kimberley insisted.

"Who knows when one of your court-ordered clients might come into the clinic with a grudge and a gun? You don't think about that."

"That hasn't happened," Kimberley insisted sulkily, folding her arms across her stomach.

"But it could," Ammon retorted, craning his neck to see as he backed out of the parking spot.

"Well, anything could happen!" She turned to look at him. "That could happen in any clinic in the best of neighborhoods. It could happen in your school."

He was quiet.

For a long while, neither one said anything. Now and then, the passing headlights illuminated the couple's faces: stony, expressionless.

Ammon was thinking that Kimberley was too stubborn to ever admit that he was right. Maybe he had been wrong to push her. But he wasn't ready to admit it.

Kimberley was thinking that she didn't need Ammon's interference in her career, just when it was getting started. She knew he did it out of love, but it felt patronizing. She just didn't know how to say that without insulting him further.

"I've never, ever, interfered with your decisions about where to teach and how to teach," she said quietly.

"Not the same thing."

"Why isn't it the same thing?" she countered angrily. "What gives you the right to tell me where I can and can't work?"

"Because, I have the responsibility to keep my family safe," Ammon answered quietly.

"This is the twenty-first century," she began. "I am not some outback wife who needs her husband's blessing every time—"

"Don't lecture me!"

Kimberley froze, pressing her hands together tightly. She felt like she might explode.

"All right," she said quietly.

"All right." Ammon said.

They didn't speak for the rest of the ride home.

CHAPTER NINETEEN

At the next family session, Isabella and Connor discussed their completed 'homework', a list of their five year goals: Isabella's college graduation, a job as a nutritionist; buying a truck, and Connor starting his own boating business.

"Tell me more about your plans," Kimberley said. "Isabella said you've been restoring your grandfather's boat little by little."

"Little by little, that's the truth," Connor explained. He fidgeted with the brim of his baseball cap, embroidered with 'Newburgh Riverfront'. "It's a Hudson Valley Riverboat, made in Esopus. It got wrecked in a storm, and the insurance totaled it. But I bought it back from salvage for three hundred bucks."

"How much work is there left to do?" Kimberley asked. She knew nothing about boats, but this was the first time Connor really seemed enthusiastic about a project.

"A lot of work." Connor said. "Don't have the money to fix it all at once. Jeff lets me have the leftovers from doing his boats. Varnish, paint, you know."

"Jeff is his boss," added Isabella.

"That seems generous of him," Kimberley said.

"Well, yeah," Connor said. "He used to work for Gramps

before he got his own boat. Said he'd love to see the Queen Adele back on the river on day."

"It's named for Connor's grandma," Isabella volunteered.

"Is it in your backyard?"

"Too big." Connor seemed amused at the question. "It's in a warehouse Gramps use to own down at the landing. Been there ever since he died."

"He's down there every free minute," Isabella said, smiling at Connor. "He swaps work for the space. But I think he mostly likes to sit way up in the pilot house and pretend—"

Connor cut her off. "I think about things up there. I plan things."

"How much is a boat like that worth?" Kimberley asked, trying to steer the conversation back into positive territory.

Connor didn't know the answer, but he was sure about one thing: he would never sell it.

"So you would restore it in order to use it as a business?" Kimberley said, realizing she'd pushed him in the wrong direction.

"Yeah, that's it," Connor said, leaning back against the couch. "My own business. I always wanted that. Then I'd be captain and hire losers like me to work on my boat."

"You're not a loser," insisted Isabella, touching his hand.

Connor shook it off. "Sometimes it just feels like that."

Kimberley asked if he had written a goal plan.

"Just a list," Connor said, pulling out a piece of folded paper from his back pocket. He began to tick off the items he had already done.

Kimberley had no idea what the items were, but she nodded enthusiastically. "Would you like to talk about what else needs to happen? Do you have a business plan?"

Connor shook his head. "Just a list."

"Well, okay. It may just a list now. But it could be a business plan." Kimberley tried to explain about estimating, pricing each phase out, coming up with a budget.

Connor's lips moved slightly as he read through the list. His enthusiasm seemed to slip away. Slowly, he folded the paper again, meticulously redoubling the creases, then slipped it back into his wallet. He sat, deflated, staring blankly into space.

Kimberley's heart sank, trying to figure out a way to summon back his original enthusiasm. "Connor, what's wrong?" She felt that somehow, she had stepped over an invisible line, putting herself on the wrong side of what had started out as a positive session.

"Nothin'," he said, shrugging again. "I guess I could do that. Make a plan." He didn't sound enthusiastic.

Kimberley realized, with a sinking feeling, that his mind was now firmly shut against her and the entire idea of a plan. Somehow, she had lost him completely.

———

Connor was in a dark mood when he parked his old white Ford F-150 in front of the warehouse and fitted his key into the padlock. The weather-beaten side door stuck, resisting his efforts until he wrestled it open. The hinges were creaking and rusty, despite his liberal use of WD-40.

The boat filled about a quarter of the warehouse. She sat high, resting on makeshift skids, her underbelly exposed, half painted white. He craned his head to look at her: the good old Queen Adele, named after his great-grandmother.

Normally, when Connor looked up at the captain's station, it appeared through the filter of his childhood. The Queen Adele sat high above the sparkling river, his Gramps waving from the pilot house, then setting his cap firmly as he steered the big riverboat away from the dock. As a boy, he usually visited the dock with his Gramma, but on rare occasions, his own mother had held him up and encouraged him to wave as Gramps sailed off with his group of paying fishermen.

For the most part, when Connor thought about the boat, he

pictured it already finished, looming big and bright and magical against the clear steel-blue river. Not today. He tried to conjure it up, closing his eyes, willing the picture to come into focus; but saw only vague, dark shapes. When he opened his eyes, Connor saw it for the first time as the half-restored, sad relic it had become.

Slowly he walked around the boat, considering it from every angle. His brain catalogued every ding, every rough edge, every rusted and stained fitting, every bit of peeling paint and rot.

For the first time he was sober enough to recognize that he was fooling himself. He didn't have the money to repair the engine, which was still sitting under a tarp near his apple tree in the backyard, where he tinkered with it now and then. He couldn't imagine what it would cost to replace the section of rotting floor-boards on the port side of the deck, or to restore or replace the steering apparatus and other auxiliaries that were on his list. Hell, there wasn't even a gangway; just an old aluminum ladder propped up against the hull.

Connor gulped down a sob.

Climbing onto the boat, he turned and gazed around the main deck. His idea of replacing the old benches inside the outer perimeter, by picking them up cheap at auctions and second-hand shops to refurbish, seemed too expensive now. His hope of finding a partner to finance the restoration had already died. Even his cousin Gil had been lukewarm about the idea, although happy to store his drug shipments in the Queen Adele in anticipation of selling them on the street. Connor liked the rental money Gil threw his way for that, but it wouldn't be enough to restore the boat. No, he could see that now.

He roamed the first deck, then climbed up to the weather deck and pilot house on the top of the boat. Taking his wallet out, Connor unfolded the list carefully. Removing a pencil from behind his ear, he began to make calculations in the margins in cramped, tiny letters. Losing track of time, he hunched over the paper until his neck ached.

At some point, it all became too much. He stared at the list in misery. He stared down at the deck below.

What a fool he was!

He'd been crazy to think he could ever pull it off, not that he didn't know how. He did. But he admitted, for the first time, that he hadn't made much progress in these last five years. Why would he think the next five would be any different?

For some reason, he remembered the only time his father came down to the warehouse to see him work on the Queen Adele. Heard the scorn in The Bastard's laughter:

Look at it. What a wreck. You're dreaming', Connor. Nobody's gonna wanna ride on old riverboat, even if you did fix 'er up. You're just pissin' your money away.

The memory brought anger, then shame. How much money had he pissed away on repairs so far? His hands began to shake.

I need my meds.

He clamored down from the pilot house, noting the scarred balustrades and the windows in need of caulking. How had the boat even gotten to this state? That hurricane that swamped the boat, banged it around, smacked it up against docks and other debris. It had been totaled, and the insurance company paid out the money, which ended up paying for hospital bills. Connor asked the company if he could buy the salvage for a couple of hundred dollars, and begged Gramps' partners to house the damaged boat in the warehouse. They humored him when he said he would fix her up himself.

If Gramps hadn't died, it would have been possible. But all his knowledge had disappeared with him.

Feeling hopeless, Connor made his way to the engine room. The jitters had returned. Anxiety formed a hard knot in the base of his skull, threatening to bloom into a full-blown panic attack. Laying his hand against his chest, he could feel his heart pumping erratically. He felt twitchy, sick to his stomach, and a little bit faint, his blood sugar dropping through the floor. Shakily, he managed to reach the small area behind a locker, where his gramps had installed a closet, with an old-fashioned safe inside.

Connor could hardly think. He was on automatic pilot, now. He stared at the dial, then shook his head as if trying to dislodge the combination from some dark corner of his depressed brain. He spun the dial for a while, hoping the motions would summon the correct numbers.

Goddamn it! He squeezed his eyes tight, wanting to bawl his head off, but needing to open the f-ing door so he could get his meds. That's what he called them. Not Gil's merchandise, but *his* meds.

He tried again, spinning the dial backwards and forwards, willing the numbers to come to the fore. And then, suddenly, in a burst of relief, the combination was on his tongue, guiding his hand until he could swing open the little door wide.

Dozens of cardboard cartons were stacked inside. He took one out and opened it, removing a slim box of pills. Prying open the flap, he removed a foil-backed card, and began popping out tablets, gulping them down dry. He shoved the remainder of the card inside the high neck of his work boots, then tossed the carton back inside the safe, slamming the door and spinning the dial this way and that for good measure.

His cousin would be pissed if he took too many. Connor knew that, but it was just too tempting. He needed the meds. And wasn't he taking all the risk, hiding them here in the boat, in the warehouse?

Oh, sure his cousin said no one would get caught. But he had said that the last time, too, when it had all gone wrong. And when push came to shove, Connor knew that all bets were off. Everyone was on their own. Maybe even his family. This child protection hearing was going to change everything. Would Isabella stick up for him? Would that shrink stick up for him? Connor didn't think so.

Looking around him, Connor could see the future clearly now.

It would take ten years to finish the boat, at the rate he was going. Maybe the shrink was right. She had mentioned selling it.

He wondered if he knew anybody who was interested in buying the boat as is? Somebody who might fix it up themselves. What would he even charge? He didn't know. Not much. He needed enough of a stake to get far away.

But where would he go? His brain reeled with different scenarios. He tried to remember who he knew in the South; who he could contact in Rehoboth Beach; in Florida, maybe. There was that guy who ran tuna boats out of the Keys. What was his name? The three brothers who had a marina on the Gulf near Galveston had said if he was ever in the area...

Connor was dizzy. His vision was blurred. He began to sway, sinking down against the wall onto the stripped deck. He was blissing out now. Mercifully, 'the meds' were starting to kick in. A warm, drowsy feeling overtook him little by little. He blinked, trying to keep his eyes open. But it was useless. They closed.

Connor nodded off, arms dangling at his side, head lolling, legs splayed out, dead to the world for the next few hours.

CHAPTER TWENTY

It had been a particularly harrowing double shift at the Neonatal Intensive Care Unit for Beatriz Rodriguez. She decided to splurge on something hot and nourishing. A bowl of chicken soup, she thought, would go nicely with the sliced chicken breast on whole wheat sandwich she'd brought from home.

The hospital cafeteria was quiet at eleven in the morning. Too early for lunch, too late for breakfast. Only two tables were occupied: two residents in scrubs, and a janitor that Beatriz recognized from the maternity wing. Choosing a table in the far corner near a window, she set her insulated lunch bag down, removed her sweater and placed it on the back of the chair.

For a moment, she stared out the window, her eyes unfocused on the river view outside, as she replayed the events that had unfolded at four a.m. as the tiny infant in her ward began to fail and she was rushed into surgery. The awful moment when the team understood that the surgeons, those miracle workers, had been unable to save their four-pound, three-ounce patient; and the final devastating call to the morgue. Through it all, Beatriz had stuffed all her emotions inside until she was could finally find refuge in a bathroom, where she retched and cried away the pent-up agony of it all.

Taking a deep breath, she drew up her shoulders, pasted a smile on her face, and headed to the hot lunch station.

"Hey, Beatriz," said Robbie, one of the regular cafeteria workers. "What can I get you today?"

"I am in need of some Jewish penicillin," Beatriz said. "Chicken soup, please."

"It's chicken and rice today." The older man smiled, dipping his ladle into the steaming metal stock pot. "Rough shift? You look exhausted."

"No more than usual." Beatriz didn't believe in burdening someone else with a sorrow they couldn't do anything about. "Come on, reach down in there for those carrots," she teased. "You know I like my veggies."

"Sure thing," Bobby said, filling the bowl. He placed it on her tray. "Anything else?"

"Not today," Beatriz said. She enquired after his mother.

"Trying to keep the diabetes under control, but it's not easy for her. Sweet tooth." Bobby shook his head in exasperation. "How do you tell an eighty-year-old woman what to do? Not easy."

"No, it's never easy. Ahhh," she sighed, thinking of her own mother, who had died so many years ago. "Take care, Bobby. Give my love to your mother."

"I will. You be well."

Grabbing an apple and an orange, Beatriz headed to the cashier to pay. When she returned, Kathy Herrero was already sitting at the table, buttering a bagel.

"What'd you get this time, cousin?" Kathy greeted her. "Soup?"

"Chicken and rice," Beatriz said, sliding the tray over toward her cousin.

"Oooh, and everything nice," Kathy answered, inhaling the aroma. "Smells good. I had the minestrone last night."

"Working a double today?" Beatriz said.

"Nah," Kathy answered. "Going home at two. I took off to see Jaina's concert tonight. She's playing with the jazz band."

"That's good. It being her last year. You need to be there." Beatriz took a sip of her soup. The warmth of the liquid settled her upset stomach. She stretched her shoulders, then hunched them up around her neck.

"Back bothering you again, Bea?"

"Ah, the usual." Beatriz shrugged and took another sip of soup. Then she unzipped her lunch bag, reaching for her sandwich. The two cousins ate in silence for a moment, both of them looking troubled.

"We lost a baby last night," Beatriz finally said, this time speaking in Spanish. "Intraventricular hemorrhage."

"Mio Dios." Kathy made the sign of the cross. "How were the parents?"

"Devastated. Who wouldn't be? Even when you're prepared, well..." Beatriz let the rest of the sentence hang in the air. She shrugged again and wiped away a tear forming in the corner of her eye. "Just four pounds. Breaks your heart."

Kathy reached over and enfolded Beatriz in a hug.

"I'm okay," Beatriz said, moving away, unwilling to indulge another flood of tears and bile. "Any news from Manny about Lando's autopsy yet?"

Kathy gave her a funny look. "Well, sort of," she said unenthusiastically.

Beatriz didn't like the sound of that. "He said he heard something."

"They sent out the stomach contents," Kathy replied. She laid her hand over Bea's wrist. "Manny said it means they found something in the blood tests. Something not normal. So they sent out the stomach contents to be further tested."

"Okay." Bea gripped her cousin's hand. "Okay. It could mean something. Could mean nothing."

"Could mean nothing," Kathy agreed. "Gonna take weeks before they get it back, he said."

"Weeks?" Beatriz echoed.

"Or months, even."

The cousins squeezed each other's hands. Months, Beatriz thought. It could take months to find out what happened to her grandson. There would not be a finalized death certificate. No way to put this all behind them, not for months. Manny would know. He'd been a denier, an assistant to the pathologist in the County Medical Examiner's office, for ten years.

"Okay," Beatriz said again, attempting to regain her composure. Her hand shook as she tried to take another spoonful of soup.

Kathy took a bite of her bagel. For a few minutes, they were silent, staring out the window at the river scene below.

"So that means it wasn't SIDs," Beatriz finally said in a quiet, far away voice.

"Probably not," Kathy agreed.

Beatriz nodded. "I kind of thought so, from the beginning."

"I know." Kathy nodded. "I remember you said that."

"Manny said that too."

"Yeah." Kathy nodded again. "That's what he thought."

Beatriz nodded again. She wasn't going to let this shake her, not in front of Kathy.

Haven't you always known it wasn't SIDs. Lando was born addicted.

And she knew exactly who to blame for that—his father. Connor had gotten Isabella hooked on heroin. Thankfully, Isabella had been clean when Alexia and Jayleen were born, but even then, Connor had probably passed along his gene for drug addiction to the girls, too.

"I went to see a lawyer," Beatriz said. "I'm petitioning the court to adopt the girls."

Kathy nodded. "Okay. You're really doing it."

"I'm really doing it," Beatriz said.

"It's the right thing to do," Kathy said. "Connor is the problem. We all know that."

Oh yes, Beatriz agreed.
Everything was that boy's fault.

———

"Daddy? Daddy?" Alexia reached out one hand and shook her father's shoulders gently, jumping back in case he swatted her away. "Daddy?"

Connor was slumped on the couch, head down on his knees, his arms flopped at his side. He'd been that way since he came home. Mama had tried to wake him, but she gave up and left for her class.

Alexia reached over again and shook his shoulder. "Daddy, can Jayleen watch TV?"

She glanced over at her sister, who was rolling Matchbox cars around the painted streets on Lando's play mat.

"Jayleen wants to watch her show, Daddy." She jiggled his shoulder again.

Daddy lifted his head a little, turning his face toward Alexia. "Uuuh?"

"Jayleen wants to see Sesame Street, Daddy."

She studied Daddy's face. His eyelids fluttered, like he was trying to open them. Drool leaked out of his open mouth. One eye suddenly opened. Alexia flinched, tensing her body, ready to spring away.

"Whaaaa?" he moaned.

"Can Jayleen watch TV?"

"Ooo-kay," Daddy mumbled. Then he closed his eye. His head dropped back onto his knees.

Alexia grabbed the remote. Finding the right channel, she glanced over at Jayleen, gesturing to come and join her on the couch.

Her sister stood up but didn't move. She stared at Daddy. "He's gonna fall over again."

"Yeah." Alexia sighed. "Come on. Help me."

The girls sprang into action. Jayleen dragged the coffee table away. Alexia positioned her shoulder against Daddy's side, intending to push him over onto the couch. It was hard. Daddy was big. When she did this wrong, he ended up on the floor.

But this time, he tumbled over slowly, his head and shoulders landing on the cushions.

"Help me with his feet, Jayleen."

The two girls dragged and pushed and pulled until they got Daddy's legs up onto the sofa. When his arm flopped back onto the floor, they giggled softly. Scrambling up onto the couch, they cuddled close, wedged into the remaining space to enjoy Sesame Street.

They shouted and sang along with the Muppets, counting numbers and wiggling to the beat of the songs.

"I wish Rosita and Elmo and Big Bird could come to play at our house," Jayleen said.

"I don't think they'd like our house very much." Alexia glanced over at Daddy. "I bet their Daddy doesn't get sick all the time."

"Yeah," Jayleen agreed. "Maybe they'd come to Abuelita's house?"

"Yeah. Abuelita's house is nicer."

They sang and called out their counting numbers with the Muppets until a loud knock on the front door made them freeze.

Nobody who knew them ever used the front door. Only strangers.

"Sshhh!" Alexia wrapped her arms around her sister. "If we don't answer, maybe they'll go away."

Jayleen nodded.

The knocking grew louder.

Daddy groaned.

Now, whoever it was at the door banged again, hard and insistent.

"Daddy," Alexia whispered, shaking her father's leg. "Daddy! Someone's at the front door."

Daddy groaned again. His legs twitched. His arm flopped around.

"Should I let him in?" Alexia shook her father's leg again. "Daddy!"

"Noooo," Daddy groaned, slapping her hand away.

The banging suddenly stopped. Alexia and Jayleen gripped each other, hardly daring to breathe, their eyes glued to the television screen. After a few minutes, their hearts stopped racing and their panic subsided as they watched the gentle adventures of Grover.

The banging began again, this time at the back door.

Alexia froze. Had she locked it when Mama left for her class?

"Connor!" a deep, angry voice yelled over the sound of banging. "Connor, you prick! Open up!"

The girls froze, gripping each other. Jayleen buried her face into Alexia's side.

Where was Daddy's cell phone? Should she call Mama? Call Abuelita at work? Alexia couldn't stop her body from trembling. She couldn't move. She could barely swallow.

Hail Mary, full of Grace. Hail Mary, full of Grace. She prayed hard, the words whirling through her mind as she shielded Jayleen against her.

"Connor! I know you're in there!"

The banging got louder. Daddy groaned again, his whole body twitching and jerking.

They heard a smashing sound, like glass breaking. The back door had a row of three small windows next to it. It was the bad man. He must be trying to get in. Alexia sat up, but Jayleen held her back. She shook her father again but got no response.

"Stay here," Alexia whispered, pushing her sister away.

"No, no!" wailed Jayleen.

"Sshhh!" Alexia leapt from the couch, anger more than courage propelling her toward the kitchen.

Hail Mary, Hail Mary, Hail Mary.

An arm in a gray sleeve poked through the broken pane,

groping toward the lock on the back door. But the dead bolt, Alexia could see, was in place. He couldn't get in. For now.

She grabbed a small paring knife from the table, gripping it in her fist as she marched to the door.

Hail Mary, full of Grace... Protect us now and in the hour of our need.

Alexia stabbed the tip into the intruder's hand. She heard a sharp scream, felt the hand jerk away. She stabbed once more, harder now. Blood spurted. The hand, with the knife still stuck to it, jerked back through the window.

The intruder screamed bad words. Each word was punctuated by a bang that made the door shudder.

"Shut up out there!" someone else yelled; one of the neighbors, maybe. "I'm calling the cops!"

A face appeared at the tiny pane. She recognized the gray beard, the shaggy eyebrows, and the ice-cold blue eyes that looked at her with hatred. She knew those eyes. This was the man her daddy called The Bastard. The one who showed up here the night Lando went to heaven. The one who stood there and watched her at the funeral.

"My Daddy's calling the cops on you right now!" she yelled bravely. "Go away! Or they'll come and put you back in jail!"

The man scowled, cursed, then disappeared.

Alexia trembled for a moment, as the adrenaline and courage drained from her body. Then she crumpled to the floor, sobbing softly.

Jayleen found her there a few minutes later, and gently led her older sister past their still-comatose father, up to bed.

CHAPTER TWENTY-ONE

Isabella looked around at Kimberley's office, wondering where to sit. She was pissed that Connor had begged off today. And she could see that the therapist was annoyed, too, especially with her vague excuse.

She didn't dare tell her what he really said. That Kimberley was making everything worse. That he didn't trust her not to turn them in.

Isabella hesitated, not wanting to sit on the couch. That was *their* spot. She decided on the rocking chair, testing it gingerly, moving back and forth a bit before settling into the padded cushion.

Kimberley was silent, waiting behind her desk.

Isabella closed her eyes and leaned her head against the chair's back.

"I like rocking chairs," she mused, allowing the tight muscles in her shoulders and back to relax slightly. "But it feels strange," she added, smiling up uncertainly at Kimberley for a moment. "Being here without Connor, I mean."

"Uhm." Kimberley nodded. "How so? Can you describe it?"

"The whole point was to get *family* counseling, right? So,

now, it's just me here. Like, it's me who's supposed to make everything better, all by myself, without any help from..."

She stopped, realizing that she was complaining, something Connor hated. He could complain about others. But if she complained about him? Oh, no. But what the hell, she thought resentfully. He was home getting high, and she had the right to complain, although not too much.

"What happened that he couldn't make it? Especially since he asked me specially to meet with him over the letter."

There was a sharp undertone to Kimberley's question that made Isabella cringe. She could make a reasonable excuse for Connor. He couldn't get time off from work. Except that wasn't true. He was home sick, which was kind of true. She shrugged and resumed rocking.

"Isabella, where is Connor?" Kimberley repeated.

"He's changed." Isabella sighed deeply, mulling over Connor's aloof and secretive behavior the last few days. She picked at a loose thread in the hem of her pink sweater, working to slice it between her perfectly polished fingernails. "He's, you know, just always in a bad mood. Always argues. Every little thing gets him going."

"Is he abusive?" Kimberley asked.

"No, not at all," Isabella countered, sounding annoyed. She snapped the thread off. "Just... He just don't want to deal with anything. He don't want to talk about nothing. I mean, anything." She could picture Connor, his evasive gestures, the way he flicked the remote over her head whenever she tried talking to him, his stony expression like a teenager who just wants his parents to disappear. She hated the way he looked at her, like *she* was the enemy. Something he had only started doing since Lando died.

"I don't know how to motivate him anymore," Isabella added, gazing up at Kimberley.

"Motivate him?" Kimberley leaned forward. "How do you mean?"

Isabella sat up, smoothing the hem of her sweater. "He used to fix stuff around the house. Mow the grass. Trim the hedges. Paint the shed. Find toys for the girls in yard sales, and like that, and fix 'em up." She looked over at Kimberley. "But now he just seems sad all the time. . . It's like he doesn't care about us. Or maybe, like he has no hopes anymore."

"Tell me what happened since we talked about your goals," Kimberley said.

Isabella shrugged again. Rocking in the chair was soothing. It always reminded her of those happy times breastfeeding her babies. Without Connor here, she felt less inhibited. More like she was talking to a girlfriend, not a therapist. Sometimes, she pretended Kimberley was her girlfriend.

"So, did you talk more about your goals from last week?"

She ignored the question. "When we first met," she began. "We'd go down to the waterfront and watch the boats. We couldn't afford the restaurants, but we would walk around and just talk. And Connor would point out the boats and say which ones he'd have in his fleet, you know. Like one for people who wanted to go dancing and hear music on a river cruise. And, like a sailboat, a big one, for people who wanted to have more of a sailboat experience. One for guys who wanted to go fishing."

Isabella stopped talking, lost in the memories of those days, remembering the weight of Connor's arm around her shoulder. He had looked so cool in his black leather jacket and in her mind, she wore her favorite turquoise sweater, the one Connor said made him think of the sea.

"And?" Kimberley prompted.

Isabella felt herself drifting away into the past. She was sleepy, from the methadone she had taken this morning. It was easier to go deep into her memories than to stay in the present, where there was so much pain. If only she could just drift away.

"Isabella?" Kimberley's voice was sharp. "Isabella, are you hearing me?"

Isabella shook herself, hearing a ringing in her head. "Yeah, yeah. No, I was just—sorry Kimberley. I had my methadone this morning and I'm a little sleepy. But I was thinking, just now, how different it all was then. Connor had friends. He hung out with his buddies from school. And there was his best friend, this guy Zoom. I don't know his real name, but he and Connor used to go fishing and they'd take his grandfather's boat out, not the big boat, the little skiff. And they'd take me out too, sometimes on the river. It was nice. We'd catch some fish, then go home and fry 'em up, and have supper together. Sometimes, four or five friends all for dinner. It was nice. It was, like, a real family."

She shook her head and seemed to drift off again.

"Then what happened?" Kimberley's voice brought her back.

"After he got out of jail, nobody came around anymore. Not even Zoom. I don't know why. I don't know if he pushed them away or they just didn't want to have anything to do with him. It bothered him for a while, but then it just seemed to make him be like, *muy concentrado*. So focused, so goal oriented, you know. He was gonna fix up his grandfather's boat. We'd take Alexia to the warehouse where he kept the boat and help Connor. Little Alex, she was so cute. I got her these cute overalls with a 'Daddy's Girl' sweatshirt."

Isabella laughed thinking about it. It was so vivid.

"It was really fun," she said. "I gave her one of my cake scrapers, you know, so she could help us without hurting the finish. That's when we started calling her Alex. Connor wanted a boy, you know, to help him sail the boats and run the company, like he did with his Grandpa. And when we had Lando, he was like, me and my boy are gonna work the boats!" Her voice rose in happiness, then stuck in her throat.

"Only…only now," she whispered, sinking back into the dark hole of despair. "Now, all our dreams are dying."

———

Kimberley's heart was breaking just listening to Isabella's story. She could see Isabella's deep vulnerability and sense her growing despair. She could understand it viscerally. After all, she and Ammon seemed to be growing apart these days in ways she would have never foreseen.

"People can grow apart," she said quietly. "Sometimes, when tragedy happens, you have to make new plans. Or adjust your—"

"In my family," Isabella blurted out, sitting up straight. "You worked like a dog to make your dreams come true." Her eyes widened with a flash of anger. "Especially when there was a tragedy."

"Like your mother did?"

Isabella ignored the question, rocking angrily back and forth. "There was a time when he'd get high from trying to make his dream come true. There was a time when Connor would get high on me!"

"But he doesn't now?"

"No."

"Why not?"

Isabella laughed suddenly. The whole thing struck her as a huge, sick joke.

"Maybe the methadone is smothering both our dreams!" she blurted out. "Only a few weeks ago, he comes home all excited because he got a job for the whole season. And now, he seems like he's down on everything. I mean, fixing up that boat is gonna take so much money. And all these other guys are already established. So he just works for them, mostly under the table." She clapped her hand against her mouth, looking guilty. "Ooooh. I shouldn't have said—"

"It's all right, that stays with me." Kimberley gave her a reassuring smile.

"Okay, well." Isabella nodded. "The truth is, he wants to leave. Now he says he wants to sell the boat—I don't know who the hell would buy it—and move down to the coast somewhere. Myrtle Beach. The Cayman Islands. Florida. Georgia. He's all over the place. It's crazy. But he keeps talking about it more and more, 'specially now, with all the trouble from Social Services. He keeps talking about a fresh start."

"What do you think?"

"It's not going to be any better there. It's gonna be worse!" A harsh, bitter laugh came up from deep inside her chest, deep inside her heart.

"How will it be worse?" Kimberley pressed her.

She sat up and glared at Kimberley.

"You're a mother. You know. Here at least, I have a support system. My mother, friends, my cousins, to watch the kids, you know. I got my classes. I'm working on *my dream*. And *there,* wherever *there* is, we'll have no house, no car, no family." Isabella felt the anger rising now, overwhelming her chest with the heat of bitter frustration. "No friends! No money. God only knows if there will be any classes or if I'd have the money to even go."

"And what would happen if you didn't go?"

"Are you telling me I shouldn't go?" Isabella stared at her blankly. "I'm trying to hold my family together here," she finally said, her eyes narrowing with suspicion.

"At some point, you have to ask yourself if the toxic situation you have is worth holding together," Kimberley said.

"Yes, it is," Isabella said. "You know it is. My girls need a father."

"But what kind of a father?"

"Their father," Isabella said angrily. "I know what it's like to lose a father. I lost my father. It was awful. We'll lose the house, everything."

"That could happen if Connor doesn't get help," Kimberley said gently.

Isabella made a strangled sound.

"What if he overdoses?" the therapist pressed on. "It could happen."

Tears welled up in her dark eyes and Isabella began to cry. She bent her head down to her chest, as if she could protect her heart from disintegrating, sobbing in great gulps. When she finally looked up, feeling hopeless, she saw that only a few minutes had passed on the big clock.

"Show me the letter," Kimberley said quietly, holding Isabella's gaze with sympathy.

Isabella reluctantly held it out to her.

Kimberley opened it and read the contents. Connor and Isabella were to report to a hearing in Family Court.

"He says he won't go." Isabella could barely get the words out between involuntary sobs. "What would happen if he don't show up?"

"It would not be good for you or Connor to not show up." Kimberley reached over to offer her a box of tissues.

Isabella pulled a few out and blew her nose. With a second tissue, she wiped her eyes. She tried to compose herself, tried to stay in the present, but began to drift again until she realized that Kimberley was holding her hand with a steady, gentle pressure. Isabella grasped the therapist's hand and squeezed it.

"I need Connor to stay here," she pleaded, as if the therapist might hold the key to keeping her family together. "At least until I get my degree. See, after next year, I can apply for a scholarship that would pay for me to go full time. And Jayleen will be in kindergarten and they can both stay after school instead of day care. And then I can really get somewhere. But I need to know how to keep him happy here." She squeezed Kimberley's hand again. "How do I do that, when we get these letters from Child Protection that just make Connor want to run away from it all?"

She searched the therapist's eyes, desperate for the answer.

"Maybe, we need to reframe the question," Kimberley said gently. "Maybe the real question is, how do you achieve your dreams and goals no matter what Connor does?"

Isabella just stared at her. It wasn't the answer she wanted to hear.

———

Alexia was sorting through a box of crayons in the waiting room when something made her look up.

Mama was coming down the stairs. Even from across the room, Alexia could tell by her mother's slumped shoulders and slow, deliberate steps that something was wrong. She glanced over at Jayleen, but her sister was engrossed in a game with two other children.

Mama sighed heavily, flopping down in the nearest chair. "Your turn, Alexia."

Alexia closed her coloring book and started to put the crayons back in the box.

"Hurry up," Mama said crossly, snatching a magazine from the pile on the table. "Miss Kimberley is waiting."

Mama sounded mad. *What did I do wrong?*

Alexia stood up quickly, expecting Mama to walk her upstairs like she always did. But Mama just sat, staring at the magazine. Alexia swallowed hard. Would she have to go by herself? Was she being punished for something?

The heavy feeling spread through her tummy. It was a long way to the stairs. Alexia took a couple of steps, then stopped.

What if I forget where to go?

What if I can't find Miss Kimberley?

Alexia glanced back. Mama had her blank face on, staring into space, the magazine spread open on her lap. Oh, no! She was disappearing again. Alexia darted back, wrapping her arms around her mother's knees. Sometimes that was the only thing that brought Mama back. The magazine slid to the floor.

"Get off me!" Mama scolded, pushing her away. "She's waiting."

Alexia stood up, stung by the rejection. Slowly, she walked

across the room, keeping her eyes trained on her blue sneakers. As she reached the big front desk, a black man came down the stairs two at a time. That made her stop.

He looked as tall and skinny and dark as Delard Robey, who lived across the street. But he wasn't like Delard at all. Delard wore black sneakers and baggy gray sweats, with a red band holding back his braided hair. This man wore a brown jacket and tan pants. His hair was short. The strangest part was his shoes: they were shiny black. They made her think of Mr. Cruz, the school principal. He was the only man she ever saw wear a jacket and shiny black shoes every day.

"Can I help you find your way?" the man said, as he came around the desk. He squatted down to her level.

Alexia stared down at the bare floor floorboards and shook her head. Daddy had warned her to stay away from black men on the street. *Don't trust them. They are not one of us. That goes for cops, teachers, principals, and social workers, too.*

"Is your mother or father here?" the man asked.

His voice was kind, but his question worried Alexia. She tried to peek up at him without raising her head. The best thing was to say nothing. She didn't want to get Mama into trouble. Her feet twitched. Should she try to slip past him or go back? She didn't know.

"Alexia! Up here!"

Miss Kimberley stood at the top of the stairs, pretty in a blue flowered dress. She was smiling like one of the angels in Abuelita's Bible.

"Oh Miss Kimberley!" Alexia cried in relief. She flew past the stranger and up the stairs until she reached out to clasp her therapist's warm, outstretched hand, feeling safe for the moment.

PART III

PROTECTING INNOCENCE

"Speak up for those who cannot speak for themselves."

- PROVERBS 30:8

CHAPTER TWENTY-TWO

Once in the familiar children's therapy room, Alexia had calmed down. She felt completely safe now. She patted her chest, showing off a pink, plastic locket. "Miss Kimberley. Look at what Mama bought me in the dollar store!"

"Ooh! Pretty," Kimberley said, squatting down to the child's level, smoothing her dress around her knees.

"It's just like Mama's," Alexia exclaimed, opening the locket. "See? There's a picture of Lando inside, and one of Jayleen, too. And it's all mine."

"Did Mama give it to you?" Kimberley said.

"Abuelita did." Alexia stroked the photo of Lando with her finger.

"Who is Abuelita?"

Alexia stared up in surprise. "You know, an *abuela*. Grandma."

"Ah," Kimberley said. "Thank you for teaching me the Spanish word."

"You don't know any Spanish?" Alexia clucked her tongue and gave her a pitying smile. "You can always ask me," she said proudly, patting her heart. "I know Spanish real good, and English, too. Daddy don't know any Spanish."

Alexia ran to the table. "Where's the Lost Puppies game?" Alexia looked around the table, which was covered with a variety of toys. "And how come no therapy cards today?"

"I thought we'd do a special session today," Kimberley explained, taking a seat at the table. "We're going to use all these toys to tell stories and do some work."

"Hmmmm," Alexia stared for a moment, holding onto her locket with the very same soothing motion that her mother used. "Where'd you get these toys from? I never saw them in the toy box."

"These are my children's toys." She motioned for Alexia to join her.

The child climbed onto her favorite chair. She kneeled to get better look at the toys. "Are these all theirs?"

"Yes." Kimberley felt a sting of regret. Perhaps she was making the child feel bad by comparison.

But that wasn't what was bothering Alexia. "Are you going to give them back?"

"Of course."

"Or your children would be mad, right? If you gave their toys away?"

"Yes, I think they would be very upset. I just borrowed them for today."

Alexia reached out to pull the dollhouse closer. "Wow. Whose is this? Is this Paige's."

Kimberley was impressed that Alexia remembered her daughter's name. "Yes. But everyone plays with the house and the bus and all the people. Would you like to start our play therapy with the house?"

"Okay." Alexia smiled and pulled the doll house closer. "We have this in school. But I never get to play with it all by myself."

For the next forty minutes, Kimberley used the toys to set up various scenarios, allowing Alexia to practice her communication and assertiveness skills. In one scenario, Kimberley encouraged Alexia to talk about her home life. Alexia moved the dolls around to show how she helped her mother dust and sweep and wash the windows. She liked handing her mother the wooden pins and clothes from the laundry basket to hang on the line outside. Kimberley learned that she and Jayleen and Lando had all shared the same room.

"This doll house has more rooms than we have in our whole real house," Alexia said, wistfully.

Kimberley used the toy bus as a setting for different role-playing games: How do you handle the kids on the bus? What do you think of the people on the bus? She used Tony's matchbook cars and his play mat printed with city streets to talk about Alexia's neighborhood.

Kimberley noticed that Alexia was emotionally very timid in public settings. She seemed to view the world around her as a dangerous one.

"Daddy says, when you're on the street, no talking to strangers," Alexia said, moving her plastic people to wait for the bus.

"What if you met somebody nice? Made a new friend?" Kimberley suggested.

Alexia shook her head.

Kimberley moved on to another play scenario, using Tony's collection of toy vehicles. She had been careful to include public vehicles, from a garbage truck to a telephone repair cherry picker. There was also a set of plastic men, including a fireman, policeman, and a soldier.

Kimberley took a white wooly sheep from Paige's farm set and set it inside a plastic barn.

"What would happen if the barn caught fire?" she asked Alexia. "Who would you call?"

Alexia quickly chose a fire truck and put the fireman on top. "That's my Papi," Alexia said. "He was a fireman."

"Right, so what do you know about firemen?"

"Mommy said he's a hero. He died in a fire, helping to put it out."

"Firemen do protect us," Kimberley agreed. "They are very brave."

"Yeah, but, why do they have to die?"

"They don't all die. Some are trapped in the wrong place and can't get out. Maybe that's what happened to your Grandpa."

Alexia nodded as she rolled the truck over to the barn. She put the figurine on the ground and pretended to squirt water on the fire.

"The fire's out," she announced, removing the toy sheep and hugging it to her. "Now you're safe, Lamby Pie. I won't let anything hurt you."

"How did that make you feel?" Kimberley asked. "Did you like being able to rescue the sheep?"

Alexia nodded. "Uh-huh."

"Do you think that's how all fire fighters feel when they help somebody?"

Alexia nodded again.

Kimberley picked up a police car and a giraffe. "Let's pretend the giraffe is lost, and he's running toward the police car for help. How would the policeman help?"

"That's dumb! The giraffe would not do that."

"Why not?"

"The giraffe would run *away* from the cop's car. The giraffe ain't supposed to be in the city. The cops would put the dumb giraffe in jail!"

From her sarcastic tone, Kimberley got the impression that the child was trying to teach her something.

"But the police are also there to help people, just like fire fighters." She rolled the police car toward Alexia, who shrank back slightly.

"No, no, no." Alexia shook her head firmly. "Cops chase people and put them in jail. They are not like my Papi. They come in your house and look for stuff to put you in jail. Everybody knows that, Miss Kimberley."

"But couldn't they be called to rescue people, or stop someone from hurting another person?" Kimberley moved the police doll closer.

The child kept shaking her head, insistent. "No, no, no!"

"So what should the giraffe do? The police are coming."

Alexia hesitated, them scooped up the giraffe and tucked him under her arm. "Hide till they go away."

"I see." Kimberley kept the doll where it was. Casually, she rolled the police car an inch back and forth. "Who told you about police officers?"

"Daddy."

Kimberley rolled the car to the far end of the table. "And what does Daddy say?"

Alexia shook her head. She picked up the lamb and nuzzled it against the giraffe. "Lamby pie and Giraffe like each other."

"Could Lamby Pie tell me what Daddy says about policemen?"

Alexia held up the lamb. For a long moment, she said nothing. "He says the cops don't like us. If they come, we have to hide 'cause they always make problems. They pretend they want to be our friends, but all they really do is put people in jail."

"I see." Kimberley picked up the police doll. "Have you ever seen a real policeman?"

Alexia looked up. "Yes."

"What did they do?"

"Once, when we were in Daddy's car, they flashed their lights, and made us stop, and Mama was scared, and Daddy told us not to say nothing. They looked inside the front of the car, and they opened the trunk, and it was really cold and Lando was crying, and they gave us a ticket 'cause we didn't have a car seat. It was no fair, 'cause the seat broke, and all's we were doing was taking Lando to the doctor."

Kimberley nodded, patiently. "Any other time?"

"Cops came the night my brother died," Alexia added, in a small voice. "They looked all over the house. They had cameras and they took pictures of everything. Daddy said they were looking for stuff to pin it on one of us."

Kimberley was startled by that phrase. *Pin it on one of us.*" It sounded like something Connor might say. And if so, it was a terribly inappropriate thing to tell a little child.

"Is that what Daddy told you?"

"I heard him say it to Mama." She looked away, then added in a whisper. "Sometimes I listen, and they don't know."

"I see. And sometimes, do you get confused by what you hear?"

Alexia nodded. Her eyes were brimming with tears.

———

Kimberley moved her chair closer to Alexia. What could she say to this child? That her father was paranoid? That her parents were addicts, and that's why they worried about being arrested? That everything she'd been taught about strangers and social workers and policemen was distorted?

Then again, what did Kimberley know about Newburgh and how it worked? She lived in a suburban neighborhood where the police were called when there was a break-in. Not a city where many residents were torn between calling the police and fearing the police.

"Not all police officers are out to arrest people," Kimberley said, hoping to reassure Alexia. "In fact, my neighbor is a police officer, Officer Danny. He mostly helps people. When people break down in their cars, he goes to help them until a tow truck comes. One time, he was called to help capture a deer that got loose in a shopping mall."

Alexia looked up. "What did he do?"

"He kept people away until the animal doctor came to give the deer a tranquilizer to put him to sleep, so they could carry it back to the woods."

Alexia considered that. "Like the giraffe?"

Kimberley picked up the giraffe and swooped it through the air, as she often did to make Jack laugh. "Help, help! The giraffe just escaped from the zoo! Someone left the gate open. Oh no! Alexia, call 911 to get some help!"

Alexia picked up Paige's pink play cell phone. "911. Get over here! We gots a giraffe in the street!" she cried, entering the spirit of the game. "Send the police and, and a doctor. Right away!"

"Okay, now Alexia." Kimberley rolled the police car nearer. "Let's bring over the nice police officer to help us put the giraffe back in the zoo. She's a scared giraffe, because she loves to be in the zoo."

"How's he going to catch him, Miss Kimberley?"

"Okay," Kimberley agreed. "Let's say that they catch the giraffe with a rope, like a cowboy would. What could we use for rope?"

Alexia took a rubber band off the table. "Can he use this?"

"Oooh, very good. Okay, let's lasso him. And then the animal doctor could give her a needle to calm her down."

Abruptly, Alexia pushed back her chair from the table. "No needles." Her face was grave. Her complexion paled.

"All right. No needles," Kimberley said quietly. "Alexia, why no needles?" Had the child seen her parents shoot up heroin?

"Makes you sick," the child mumbled.

"I see. It makes who sick?"

Alexia wouldn't answer. She was frozen, her deep brown eyes fixed on some point in space, her hands tucked under her lap.

"Did you see someone use a needle?"

Alexia nodded.

"Who was it?"

Alexia shook her head.

Kimberley was trembling. She didn't want to put words in the child's mouth, but she wanted to know what Alexia saw, or thought she saw.

"You can't tell me who it was?"

The child shook her head again, more firmly.

"Was it Mommy?"

Alexia shook her head.

"Was it Daddy?"

Alexia shivered, looking down at the floor. She popped her thumb in her mouth, sucking hard, then nodded.

"It was Daddy?" Kimberley repeated.

Alexia nodded again, peeking up at Kimberley.

"When was this, Alexia?"

"Lots of times," Alexia finally whispered.

Kimberley nodded, smiling. "Is he diabetic? Do you know what that is?"

Alexia shook her head.

"It's when someone can't process the sugar in the food we eat. They need to take a needle of insulin to help the body regulate their insulin levels. Then they feel better."

Alexia thought a moment. Then she shook her head. "He don't feel better after," she declared. "He goes all sleepy. I can't wake him up. I shake him and shake him, and he still won't wake up. He talks, but it don't make sense."

Kimberley felt lightheaded at the information she was being told. How could the child be right? Connor was in methadone treatment. You couldn't do both, could you? "Was this a long time ago, Alexia?"

The child shook her head.

"Is Mommy home when he takes his needles?"

Alexia shook her head again.

"He does it when Mommy's at class?"

Alexia nodded. Her dark eyes shone with trust and solemnity.

Kimberley felt that trust keenly, understanding that the fate of Alexia's world hung on her next question.

"When was the last time you saw him so sleepy you couldn't wake him up, honey?"

"Last night." Alexia's lower lip quivered. "When the bad man came and tried to get in the house."

"What bad man?"

The tears flowed now. "The Bastard," she moaned.

Connor's father, Kimberley recalled. She put her arms around Alexia, soothing her.

"It's all right, sweetie. It's all right." She kept patting Alexia's back as the child calmed down.

"Has the bad man ever come to your house before?" she finally asked.

Alexia nodded. "The night Lando died."

———

Kimberley stared at the form on her desk: LDSS-2221A New York State Office of Children and Family Services, Report of Suspected Child Abuse or Maltreatment.

Down at the bottom of the long form of blanks to be filled, under the subset titled Basis of Suspicions, the very last line stated:

PARENT'S DRUG/ALCOHOL MISUSE

There was no doubt in her mind that as soon as she reported it, it would put into motion everything that Isabella and Connor had feared from the beginning of their session.

And yet, what choice did she have? Her responsibility was clear-cut. But still she sat there, too paralyzed to pick up the phone and report what she knew.

She put it off throughout the day. Even when she went to the kitchen to heat up her leftovers for dinner, she couldn't bring herself to call.

I have to speak to Jon first, she rationalized. *I have to make sure I fill it out correctly.*

A persistent anxiety lodged like an annoying lump between her shoulder blades throughout her packed schedule. The questions it raised made her wonder about all her clients. Did they tell her the truth, or hide the truth? Did they tell her only what they thought she wanted to hear? During her other sessions, she kept studying her clients for signs that they were hiding something. No matter how she tried to shake the feeling, every session was tainted by the knowledge that she had no way of judging the veracity of her clients' stories.

———

Kimberley buzzed Jon, asking for a meeting before she left for home. It was just after nine by the time she stood outside his office, a thread of light spilling from underneath his closed door. The night receptionist was gone, the waiting room deserted. Only one other therapist was working upstairs.

Hesitating for a moment, she finally knocked on Jon's door.

One look at her face, and his calm demeanor and welcoming smile changed to one of concern as he ushered her inside. She sat stiffly in the wing chair, facing a framed photograph of a particularly beautiful bend of the Hudson River strewn with a trio of sailboats. It usually had the power to lull her in a meditative mood, but today it was a symbol of her clients' dreams. Dreams that were going to be dashed to pieces because of her duty.

Without a word, Jon listened quietly to Kimberley's account of what Alexia had told her about needles, and the night Lando had died.

"What do I do?" Kimberley burst out, trembling with the anxiety that had been building all night. "Do I report this? Do I confront them first? Do I make sure I heard, or rather, interpreted Alexia's comments correctly?"

"The first thing is to think about this calmly," Jon said.

"Focus on what you know." He lifted his hand, raising his thumb. "One, you know the child has seen needles in the house, perhaps on the night her brother died, and last night. Two, unless the father is diabetic, the assumption is he was using it to inject heroin or some variation. Those are the exact facts to report."

"I know Jon, I know," Kimberley said quietly. She nodded, still in shock over the repercussions of what she had to report. "Then why do I feel like a traitor to the whole family?"

Jon sighed. "I know exactly how you feel."

"You do?"

"I've been through this myself. Similar situations." He removed his glasses and wiped his eyes. "It felt like a betrayal on some level. On the other hand, it's the right thing to do in the long run. I would just focus on what to tell Child Protective Services right now."

"But once I do, I lose any chance at helping the family stay together," Kimberley said. "It's what Connor feared all along; that I'd be just another person judging him at his worst." She looked up at Jon, filled with remorse. "What if I am the one jumping to conclusions here? Don't I need to give him a chance to defend himself."

"That's not your concern here, Kimberley. The concern is what you are obligated to do professionally, legally, and morally for the girls."

"But how do I know that I wasn't putting ideas into Alexia's head? Or that she might have confused past incidents with later ones? Or…or?" She looked up at Jon, the responsibility of what she had to do pressing on her chest so hard that she felt a panic attack coming on. "Will they take the children away?" She pressed her hand over her heart. "I couldn't bear it!"

"I know this is emotionally difficult for you, Kimberley," Jon said, his voice dropping into a soothing tone. "Just stick to the proper regulations." Reaching over to the phone, he held the receiver out to Kimberley. "Do you want to me to dial the hotline number? From then, you have forty-eight hours to send in the written report."

For a moment, Kimberley couldn't move. Finally, she reached out, hand shaking, and grasped the receiver from Jon's hand. A shiver shot up the length of her spine, as she waited for someone to answer on the other end.

Once I do this, there is no going back.

CHAPTER TWENTY-THREE

Connor could barely keep himself seated at the kitchen table. The only thing that was keeping him from exploding was playing with the piece of clothesline, tying a Buntline Hitch, an Alpine Butterfly Loop, and finally a Carrick Bend. Gramps had taught him all the boating knots, along with the history of his seafaring ancestors, the MacNeil clan of the Bara Islands in Scotland.

To my mind, the Carrick Bend's the bonniest of all the boating knots, Connor. A true Celtic knot, with no beginning and no end. When you tie this knot, think of the MacNeil clan. Though they were banished off the islands and scattered to the four corners of the earth itself, their souls will come to help a true MacNeil. And that, you are, Connor. That you are.

Connor tied the Carrick Bend with great care, praying for his Gramps to keep him strong through this ordeal, as social worker Dolores Fuentes with her clipboard and questions hunted for whatever the hell she was looking for; looking through the girl's room, checking pantry shelves, medicine cabinet, and bedroom drawers. He'd leaned against the back door, this time fashioning a Bowline on a Bight, imagining it around the social worker's neck as she rummaged through his outdoor shed.

He knew she wouldn't find anything. He'd hidden everything

in Gramp's boat, inside the paint cans. They wouldn't find a trace of needles, heroin, or even the oxycodone he'd been taking. He was smarter than Fuentes. Smarter than Isabella. He never told her anything about Gil or their business. Never left any traces. As far as she was concerned, Connor wasn't using at all. Not in the house, not anywhere.

Fuentes walked toward him. She was dressed in a black pants suit, and the heels of her carefully polished pumps, he noted with satisfaction, were sinking into the soft spring mud of his yard. She scowled as she faced him, with a no-nonsense look.

Connor smirked, then held open the back door to let her back into the kitchen, where Isabella was drinking a cup of herbal tea.

Fuentes planted herself in front of Isabella, but she was staring at Connor as he came inside.

"I've had a report that you are using in front of the children."

God, a cigarette would taste good right now. Connor could almost taste the smoke, filling his mouth, lingering in his nose. He didn't say a word in his defense. He didn't have to. Isabella was already protesting, unable to hold in her emotions. She was like a tiger protecting her cubs, pushing her chair back, lashing out.

"He doesn't use at all!" she insisted, standing up. "We're on methadone. Here's the records. We go faithfully. How could he be shooting up?"

Fuentes scribbled something down on her clipboard. Then she looked straight at Connor, giving him that calm, cool stare that really ticked him off.

Connor held her eyes with cold, icy detachment. He shook his head slowly, folding his arms. He was not about to confess anything.

How stupid do you think I am, Mizz bitch? I been at this almost as long as you have.

But still, it bugged him. Who reported him? One of Alex's teachers? The school psychologist? Or was it Little Miss Kimberley?

"I have it that your daughter has seen you shoot up in front of her," Fuentes said.

"What!" Isabella screeched, her cheeks turning mottled white with anger. "Who's making these accusations? Absolutely not true. Not true!"

Connor just kept shaking his head. *Had to be the therapy bitch. Putting words in Alex's mouth.*

"*Maldito!*" Isabella was arguing, her speech starting to deteriorate into Spanglish. "My daughter, sometimes, *una estúpida.* She mixes things up in her head. Did you know that she thought if she prayed hard enough, she could bring her brother back from the dead?" she added, exasperated. She smacked her hand down on the table, leaning in toward Fuentes. "Did you have that in your report?"

Connor let Isabella rant on, concentrating on tying a chain splice. The less he said, the better. The more he tamped down his emotions into nothingness, the better. Isabella obviously was on his side. Let her go on arguing his case for him.

But he could tell Fuentes wasn't buying it. She looked at him with a disgusted expression.

"Connor, I need a statement from you about this. Did you shoot heroin in front of the kids?"

Connor stared about an inch past the social worker's left ear, knowing she hated to be ignored.

"I don't shoot heroin," he said calmly, locking his gaze with Isabella's, who had gone white with fright, or maybe it was rage. "I'm on methadone." And he could say that with a clear conscious. He hadn't had to use heroin since he started getting the pills from Gil. True, sometimes he crushed them up, melted and shot them up. But it wasn't technically heroin. All he had to do was stay calm, deny, and let Isabella protect him, until the bitch gave up and went back to her office.

"What a rotten day!" Isabella sighed as she tied her apron behind her back. The social worker was long gone, but she was still unnerved. She ran the hot water, and began washing, rinsing and stacking the dinner plates.

She didn't like it when Connor had deliberately avoided her questions about using. All through supper, the question hung in the air, although they wouldn't speak about it in front of the girls. She was worried that he would take out his anger on Alexia, but he hadn't.

But now, after sending the girls upstairs to bed early, he had worked himself into a full-out foul mood. Hunched over the kitchen table, his blue flannel shirt sleeves pushed past his elbows, he groused nonstop about living in Newburgh. Chain smoking, he barely finished one cigarette before he was using it to light another. In between deep drags, he chugged from his second bottle of beer.

"I'm going to get Little Miss Kimberley back."

"You don't know if it was her," Isabella said. "It could be her teacher. I never liked that teacher."

"Don't care who it was. I'm so ready to pull the pin on this place. Move where nobody knows us," he said. "Just blow up this shit hole. Kachoom! Start new."

"Blow up the house?" Isabella shrieked. "What are you talking about?"

Connor rolled his eyes. "I meant *sell* it. Whadja think? I was gonna actually blow it up?"

"We can't *sell* the house, Connor. Not without your sister signing the papers." Isabella grabbed the pan she'd used to fry hamburgers and dipped it in the soapy water. "Your grandpa shouldn't have put this house in both your names."

She looked over at Connor.

"Screw the house," he said, stabbing his cigarette butt in the overflowing metal ashtray, grinding it out slowly. "With all this shit that's coming down on us, Isabella, we gotta stay ahead of these motherfuckers. They're trying to destroy us."

"We can't just leave," Isabella protested.

"Why not?" Connor ran his hands through his hair, then over his forehead, using his knuckle to rub his eyes. "We should just stick around because I can't find my stupid sister and make her sign a paper?"

"Maybe one of your cousin's could find her." She squirted more soap on a burnt spot.

"Yeah, if Gil wanted to, he *could* find her. But I ain't asking him to. Besides, I'd have to give her half the money."

"Half's better than nothing," Isabella muttered under her breath, as she poured all her frustrations into her cleaning.

"You scrubbing a hole right through that pan?" Connor banged his empty beer bottle on the table.

Isabella flinched. Angrily, she hit the water spigot to rinse off the pan.

"What's up with you?" Connor asked. "And don't give me the 'nothing-smile'."

She blinked back the tears, afraid that if she looked at him she'd start bawling. "I'm scared, Connor," she said, her back still turned to him. "If we can't sell the house, where would we live?"

"Rent it out, maybe?" Connor asked. "Might work. Yeah. Get a monthly check sent to us. Then I find a job down south. Nice weather. I work on boats. Gil knows this guy down in—"

"You're not going to do that!" Isabella said, slamming the pan on the counter.

Connor turned to stare at her. "What up with *you?*"

Isabella gave him a warning look. "Shhh, Alexia can hear us."

"Fuck that. It's her fault we're in this mess."

"Her fault?" Isabella was stunned.

"Time she got woke to the fact that life sucks a big one. We stay here, she's gonna find that out in a hurry."

"Connor! Don't say that." She hated when he started talking crap like his cousins.

"Listen, the way I see it," Connor said, pausing to light another cigarette. "We're either out of here or those bitches are going to take away our kids. I told you it was a bad idea to see that shrink."

Isabella turned back to the sink, the tears stinging her eyes. "*Un podrido cosa decir,*" she muttered angrily. *A rotten thing to say.*

"Don't speak that Spanish shit," Connor snapped. "You know I hate that."

That was the last straw. Isabella started to weep. The tears spilled out of her, and she bent her head down, blindly holding her hands under the faucet.

"Are you crying?" Connor said softly.

She nodded, gulping down her tears, unable to speak.

Connor scraped back his chair. "Tell you what," he said softly, coming up behind her. He turned off the water. Wrapping his arms around Isabella's waist, he leaned his cheek against her hair. "I'll go down first, find a job, then let you and the girls know where to meet me. It's a good plan. We'll be okay, my little mamacita."

His voice was soothing, sweet. But his words shocked Isabella. It was the first time he'd ever talked about splitting up. Her heart beat faster. Her throat went dry. Her knees started to buckle.

He's going to leave us behind. He's going to ditch us.

CHAPTER TWENTY-FOUR

Kimberley welcomed everyone to the Thursday night parenting support group. She really loved the mix of clients, which included a teenaged single mom who was trying to finish high school, several couples with preteens who had been through juvenile court, an elderly couple raising a two-year-old grandson, and a widowed postman struggling to care for his three young girls.

"Tonight's topic is about positive reinforcement," Kimberley said, writing the phrase on the large whiteboard in the waiting room. "Last week we talked about—"

At that moment, the front door opened. To her surprise, Connor walked in. She stared, expecting to see him followed by Isabella and their two girls. But Connor was alone as he shut the door behind him.

"Welcome, Connor," Kimberley said, gesturing him to enter. "Are you here for the Parenting Program? We were just getting started."

He stared at her, then took a seat in the back.

Unsettled by his unexpected appearance, Kimberley forced herself to launch into a discussion about the previous week's theme: earlier bedtime strategies to cut down on behavior problems and promote good sleep and study habits. "Anyone want share how you used these ideas this week?"

The teen mom jiggled her son on her lap. "I been using my phone to remind me to start supper early," she said. The baby was no longer having meltdowns from being hungry, she was happy to report, and she was using alarms for everything from bath time to bedtime. "He hears it go off, and he's asking me what's it time for next?"

"I'm so glad it's working for you," Kimberley said. "What about you, Mrs. Jordan?"

The grandmother admitted that earlier bedtimes meant she didn't get to see her grandson anymore, since she worked a late shift at the mall. "I can't even put the TV on now, or I'll wake him up!"

The conversation rotated around the room with personal stories. Everyone had something to contribute, except Connor. He sat there with a surly expression, his eyes fixed on her, swaying slightly in his chair by the door.

Determined not to appear rattled, Kimberley brought the conversation around to positive reinforcement, outlining ways to 'catch your child doing something good' and 'praising the heck out of it,' as her boss liked to put it. She played a short video on the subject, wrapping up at eight o'clock by handing each parent a printout and chart to use at home.

"Hope to see you back next week," Kimberley said.

As always, she chatted with some of the parents as they headed out the door. But she couldn't avoid Connor's unnerving stare.

At last, only he was left. But he didn't rise to leave. A cloud of tiny flies swarmed near the door. Reluctantly, she shut it.

"What a surprise, Connor," Kimberley said quietly. "I hope you got something useful out of tonight."

Connor shrugged. "Wanted to see what else you did here."

"Well, what did you think?" Kimberley leaned against the

door frame, looking down at him. He seemed his usual guarded self, yet strangely calm.

He shrugged again. "Nothing I didn't already know."

"Really?" Kimberley said politely, thinking that there was a great deal he probably didn't know about parenting. "Well, I wish you had brought Isabella and the girls."

"They're home." He stood up, leaning toward her, making her want to shrink back. He was a great deal taller than she was. His eyes narrowed. "And I'm not."

"What do you mean?"

"They kicked me out," Connor said bluntly.

"Kicked you out?" she echoed, bewildered. "I thought you owned the house."

"I do." His voice was devoid of emotion, almost unnaturally so.

"Then...?"

"Social Services came today. Miss Fuentes told me there was a complaint." He took another step closer, resting his hand on the wall next to her, just above her head. "I wondered if it came from you?"

"What kind of complaint?" Kimberley pressed the small of her back against the wall, bracing for...for what, she wasn't sure.

"Using. In front of my kids." He brought his other arm down behind her back, essentially pinning her against the wall. "My daughter tell you that?" He glared at her with those cold, blue eyes. She could smell beer and garlic on his breath.

"Connor, I'm..."

"On my side? I don't think so."

"It's time for you to leave now." She squirmed as he pressed in closer, his arms still closing her in. "My boss will be down any minute."

Connor moved back. "Okay." Suddenly, his entire demeanor switched from menacing to polite. "No problem, Kimberley. If that's the way it's going to be, then, that's the way we'll play the game."

He removed his hands, held them up, and stepped back.

"No problem," he said, nodding pleasantly. "My truck's parked out back. Next to your Subaru. The blue Forrester, right? With the 'baby on board' sign?"

Something in the way he said it, the way he emphasized "*baby on board*", frightened Kimberley. She opened the door, and stepped back, as Connor shoved his hands in his hoody pockets, and stepped into the night.

It took her a few minutes to calm down. Trembling with anger and shame, she knew the report she had filed so many weeks ago had just come back to haunt her.

———

Kimberley locked the front door of the clinic, her thoughts still reeling. She had lied twice to Connor, once about the complaint, once about her boss being still here. Jon was home, and she wondered if she should call him. Thinking better of it, she headed to her office to type up a short report of the meeting. It took her ten minutes to collect her thoughts, and another twenty to finally finish. After resetting the alarm, she let herself out the back door, and was in her car by a quarter to nine.

With any luck, she'd be home in time to have a nice cup of cocoa with Ammon while he was grading papers.

But luck was not with her. She had barely reached the end of the driveway when the car wheel began to thump. Pulling into the road, the thump got louder.

A flat tire! Damn!

The streets were deserted. The streetlamp in front of the clinic was not working, and the moon was obscured by clouds.

Kimberley wasn't sure she could change the tire herself, especially in the dark. She certainly didn't want to call Ammon; he would have to leave the kids alone. No sense bothering her Dad. Flipping on the interior light, she dug around in the glove compartment for the card from the dealer's road service. She had just punched in the number for the service, when she glanced up to see a glow, like the red tip of a cigarette, coming toward her.

Whoever it was, was barely visible. Reflexively, she locked the doors. The car service answered, and she described where she was and what had happened. "How long would it take for someone to get here?"

"Twenty minutes to half an hour," the service assured her.

Sighing, she switched off her phone, then turned on her car radio for some music to keep her company.

The cigarette glowed brighter, the silhouette of its owner emerging more fully as it neared the passenger side. A tapping at the passenger window startled her.

"Need help?" The voice was male. A face loomed in the window, the features unrecognizable.

"I've got a service coming, thanks," she called, barely able to get even those few words out, because she was tight with fear. "I'm fine."

"Hey, whaddaya know. It's Miss Kimberley. What's wrong, Miss Kimberley? Car trouble?"

For a split second, Kimberley was too stunned to say anything. Then she recognized the voice. It was Connor's.

What the hell was he doing here?

He tapped on the window again, and she rolled it down reluctantly.

Connor leaned his chin on the open window and gazed at her levelly. "Well, Miss Kimberley. I don't have any place to go. I figure I'll sleep here in my truck tonight, since Child Protection said I'd have a better chance if I left. So here I am."

"I'm sorry," Kimberley said. All kinds of alarm bells were going off in her head. "I really am. Do you? Do you need a place to..."

"To stay?" He snorted. "Why? You offering your place?"

She could hardly breathe.

"I didn't think so," he said, continuing to stare at her, his chin still resting on the open window of the car. "Maybe you could open up the clinic so I could sleep on the couch?"

"I, I'm sorry, Connor." Unnerved by his stare, Kimberley stumbled over her words: she just locked up and didn't know how to deactivate the alarm.

He sighed deeply. "Sure," Connor said evenly, shaking his head. "No problem, Kimberley. No problem at all. I just figured maybe you could help me. That's all."

"I would if I could," Kimberley said defensively.

"Sure you would." His voice was bitter. His words mocked her intentions. He straightened up. "Well, see you around."

Kimberley slid the window closed, feeling torn between her natural desire to help and her instinct to protect herself. She prayed for the car repair service to come soon.

She expected Connor to walk away. Instead, he leaned against a nearby tree, smoking his cigarette. *What have I done to him?* On impulse, she rolled down her window. "Connor?"

"Something wrong, Kimberley?" Connor asked, looking amused.

"I, uh. . ." Kimberley hesitated, as he walked over and leaned into the window again, a wisp of smoke from his cigarette wafting into her car. "I thought you had a cousin. Gil. Can you stay with him?"

Connor started to laugh silently, the smoke leaking from his lips. "Worried about me, huh? Or just feelin' guilty, 'cause you screwed me. What a great therapist you are! Gil's away on business. He'll be back tomorrow." He shrugged, twisting his mouth in a grimace as he took another drag off his cigarette. "In the meantime, here I am. But the other question is, why are you still here? I know you got a *home* to go to."

Kimberley sighed. "Listen, Connor. I know there's a homeless shelter near here."

"No way." Connor shook his head. "That place is full of batshit crazy motherfuckers, off their heads mental or whacked out. No, I ain't going near there. I'll sleep in my car tonight. Safer."

"Is that why you came by tonight?" Kimberley asked, suddenly sympathetic.

Connor shrugged. "Go home, Miss Kimberley."

"I can't."

He just stared at her.

"I have a flat tire. I'm waiting for the roadside service to come."

"Oh yeah?" His jaw was working, as if he were deciding something. "I can change a flat for you."

"Oh, that's okay, I'll just—"

"Pop the hatch."

"It's not necessary," she began, but he was already headed to the back of her car.

"Got a flashlight?"

She sighed. Reluctantly, she activated the hatch. Hopping out of the car, she yanked the rear door open to grab a flashlight from the back seat.

"Where's your jack?" Connor asked, as she handed him the flashlight. "Underneath?"

"They're on their way," Kimberley said, flustered at the way he was taking over. The darkness, the late hour, the fact that no one else was around and the service still hadn't showed up, made her nervous.

Without a word, Connor reached in and hauled out the folded stroller.

She took it from him and laid it carefully on the sidewalk. He casually tossed Jack's diaper bag on top of it, which annoyed her.

"I'll take my briefcase out, thank you!" she said sharply.

"No problem, *Miss* Kimberley." Connor backed away, holding up his hands. His voice was tinged with sarcasm.

She pulled out her briefcase, stowing it safely in the back seat. By the time she returned, Connor was already lifting out the spare tire.

"Donut tire, huh?" Connor remarked, raising it up in appraisal. "Car this new, they should have thrown in a real one."

Kimberley said nothing as he pulled out the tools. She shone the flashlight on the tire. Connor grunted and cursed, straining against the wrench, his breath coming in explosive puffs until he finally loosened each lug nut, spinning them off their screws and sending each one pinging into the hubcap. As he jacked up the car, Kimberley noticed that his work boots, reflected in the light, looked badly worn on the soles. The laces were frayed, Kimberley noticed, and one of the seams was split. For a moment, she felt sympathy for him.

Connor said nothing while replacing the wheel with the donut. Soon, he had the ruined tire and tools back and tools back in the well and was stowing the stroller and diaper bag back in the cargo area.

Kimberley called to cancel the repair service, only to find out the mechanic hadn't even left yet.

She turned to Connor. "Thank you for everything," she said quietly.

"Yeah." He lit another cigarette and drew in the smoke deeply, making the tip glow red against the night. "The service never showed. Good thing I was here."

"Yes." She reached for her purse, thinking to give him some money for his trouble. She held out a twenty.

He eyed it for a moment, then took it, tucking it in his pocket without a word, before retreating into the darkness.

———

The next morning, Kimberley stared at her mechanic, trying to make sense of what he was telling her.

"See here?" He pointed to the tire that Connor had replaced. "There's a slit in the back wall. Two places. Here and here. Somebody with a sharp, long knife, from the look of it."

"Oh, God," she whispered, breathing hard. Kimberly shivered. "I don't understand. Who would do this?"

The mechanic shrugged. "Don't know what to tell you, Mrs. Mason. You got an enemy? Cause this looks deliberate, to my way of thinking." He scratched his head. "Don't see many like this."

Kimberley looked at him, uncomprehending. "I just don't know what to think."

"I can replace it right now, but I'm thinking that you might want to take this back with you, to report to the police. Your husband know about this?"

"Not yet," Kimberley said.

But when he does, he's gonna hit the roof.

CHAPTER TWENTY-FIVE

On her way home from the car repair garage, Kimberley picked up Jack at the day care. "Come on my little man," she said, hugging him and kissing him.

Jack giggled, then grabbed for her hair.

Gently, she undid his grip, then popped him in his car seat, and stowed the bag in the back. They were home in a half hour.

As she brought him inside, Jack started to cry.

"What is it baby? Pewee! You need a change." She bore him upstairs, leaving the diaper bag in the hallway. It wasn't until she had returned downstairs and popped him into his playpen that she began to go through his diaper bag to replenish juice boxes, diapers, and more.

That's when she found the note. Strange, she thought. It was written on torn notebook paper, not the normal daycare stationary.

When I see you with your little boy I get really mad. I think, so why do you have a nice helthy boy and my baby is dead? Life ain't fair is it? There you are in your nice house with your nice car and everything, so why are you butting into my family's business? Making my little girl tell lies about her daddy. That ain't right. I knew you weren't on our side.

Leave my family alone. Or you will be sorry.

She was trembling. If she called Ammon, he would insist she call the police. Insist she resign. She didn't want to resign. But she did want to protect her family.

And what were the pros and cons of going to the police?

She'd call her big sister for some legal advice.

She texted Charlotte, then called her Mom on the phone. "Please come over Mum. I need your help. Something's happened and I need somebody to help me think through this."

"Of course. But your Dad isn't here. He's at his photo club meeting. Should I...?"

"No. I... I'd rather it was just you and Charlotte."

"Oh, I see. Women problems."

"Sort of," Kimberley answered.

"I'll be over in two shakes of a lamb's tail," Lee said. "Just you sit tight, darling girl."

———

Charlotte and Mum arrived just a few minutes apart. Kimberley sat them at the kitchen table and poured the coffee with a trembling hand, as they peppered her with questions.

She unfolded the note she had found in Jack's bag, smoothed it out, and wordlessly passed it to her mother, who in turn handed it to Charlotte.

"Is he dangerous?" Mum asked.

"Dangerous?" Kimberley echoed.

"You know, enough to hurt the baby," Mum insisted. "To hurt you, or the kids."

"I don't think so, but when people feel desperate. . ."

"How the hell did he even get this into Jack's bag?"

"I've been racking my brain to figure out how he could have done that," Kimberley admitted. "I think it might have been when he helped me with a flat tire. I had the diaper bag in my car last night."

"Has Ammon seen this?" Mum asked.

"Not yet."

"Or your boss?" Charlotte asked.

"I just found it. When I came home." Kimberley dropped her head, her lower lip trembling.

"It's alright, darling." Mum reached out and took Kimberly's hand. "We're here for you."

Charlotte scanned the note again. "He says something about when he sees you with your baby. Where could he have seen you with Jack? You don't take him to the office, right?"

"Not usually, only once. It was months ago. I met him in the parking lot. He helped me set up Jack's playpen." As she continued with the details, she realized how stupid she had been.

"Could he have put the letter in then?"

"No, I would have found it sooner, don't you think?"

"Does his kids go to your day care?"

"No, of course not. It's in Rock Hill. His girls go to a day care program in Newburgh."

"Do you know what his car looks like? The license plate number?"

"He said he has a truck. I've never seen it. I've only ever seen them walking to the clinic. But I..." she hesitated, suddenly remembering and then telling Charlotte about the white truck she spotted parked across from her house. "It was only a couple of times in the last two weeks."

"So we have a possible case of stalking," Charlotte said crisply. She reached into her briefcase, pulled out a notebook.

Kimberley felt trapped, agonized, and embarrassed by her sister's onslaught of questions. Had she ever mentioned the name of the day care? Had she ever talked about her children to her clients?

"Yes," Kimberley said. "I did. I don't think I said the name of the day care. But… Oh my God, Charlotte! I just can't be sure. Of course…"

"What?"

Kimberley put her hand over her mouth, suddenly remembering something. "At the first session, Connor mentioned Ammon's name. I remember thinking that was strange. But he could have looked me up online."

"Kimberley, you could have a maniac on your hands. The letter. The tire." Charlotte stood up. "Let's just go to the police right now."

———

Ammon was jubilant as he drove home that night from the school board meeting. His proposed class for advanced students in biotechnology, which he had planned and advocated for over the last two years, had finally been approved. He felt like celebrating.

But the house was dark when he pulled in the driveway. He glanced at his watch. It was after ten o'clock. Kimberley must have gone to bed already. Deflated, he realized his news would have to wait until tomorrow.

Quietly, he moved through the house, loosening his tie, stowing his briefcase in the closet, removing his shoes on the mat by the door. After checking the locks on the back door and the cellar, he tiptoed up the stairs, and stopping in each of the kids' bedrooms to kiss the top of their heads. Wishing he could wake them, he lingered a few moments, watching them sleep with a deep sense of satisfaction. He and Kimmy had done well, providing them with a safe, nurturing home. It was a very different life than he had had growing up on the sheep ranch in New South Wales, where chaos was the hallmark of his father's late-night, drunken rampages.

Reaching the master bedroom, Ammon walked to the dresser. He removed his Seiko watch, setting it gently in the inlaid wooden tray Kimberley had bought him on their first Christmas together. The expandable wristband was beginning to sag. He made a mental note to stop at the repair kiosk on their next trip to the mall. A scrap of paper lay on the dresser. He glanced at it, holding it up to his face to make out the writing in the dark. Kimmy had a habit of leaving notes for him about the next day's agenda. He moved to the window, holding it up to catch the sliver of moonlight streaming through a gap in the curtains. Then he read the words and burst out with a curse that woke his wife.

"Ammon?"

"Where did this come from, Kim?"

"What, what…?"

He stood over her, his hand shaking, his chest tightening with a cold rush of anger and betrayal. "This is a threatening note, my girl. Who sent it to you?"

Kimberley sat up, obviously bewildered.

"It's from the SIDs case isn't it?" He could barely keep his voice low, his anger threatening to explode. "Isn't it?"

"Yes," Kimberley blurted out. "Yes, it's from Connor. I…"

"I'm calling the police *right now*!"

"No, Ammon!"

"What do you mean 'no'? What the hell is wrong with you, Kimberley Mason? Have you lost your mind? This is going to be put to rest right now."

"I already reported him to the police."

Her words were like a switch, calming Ammon enough for him to take a deep breath. It took a moment or two more before his chest relaxed and his anger lowered a notch or two.

"When?" he finally asked, waving the note.

"Around noon. Charlotte went with me. We filled out a report."

Ammon stared at the paper in his hand. "Didn't they want this as evidence?" He wondered for the first time if Kimberley was lying just to appease him.

"No, they didn't take it. Should they have?" She stared up at him. "I guess they should have. They told me to hold onto it."

He stared at Kimberley, the moonlight falling across her bare shoulder. Her confusion and guilty tone left a sour taste in the back of his throat. He wanted to believe her, but his gut instinct didn't agree. He couldn't help his harsh answer.

"That sounds like bullshit to me."

Kimberley's eyes widened in alarm. Ammon seldom used curse words. She realized that he didn't trust her.

"You can ask Charlotte."

"And who stayed with the kids?" he countered.

"Mum…"

"Bloody hell," Ammon sat on the bed. "You called them, but not me."

His accusation lingered in the air.

"I'm sorry, I, they came right away. I had just found it, and my sister's a lawyer. I wanted legal advice."

"Great!"

"And I didn't want to bother you at school," she trailed off lamely. "I knew it was a big day for you. And you had the meeting tonight. Did they approve your new class?"

He said nothing.

She knew he felt totally betrayed.

"Please believe me, it's going to be all right," Kimberley said, easing toward him.

He stopped her with a hand on her shoulder, studying her face for a moment. "Oh, it *is* going to be all right, my girl. One way or another."

"Ammon, let's talk about this in the morning, when—"

"No, we're going to talk about this now. This has got to end. You either quit the case—"

"I can't just quit today."

He gripped her shoulder tighter. "I told you I would support your career as long as it didn't affect the family. Didn't hurt the kids. This," he shook the paper hard, "is way beyond our agreement."

Kimberley gasped. "Ammon, I will look for a new job. But I can't just…"

"You have to choose," he insisted, giving her a shake. "It's us…or them."

Kimberley stared at him, moonlight revealing his grim expression. His grip conveyed a tightly coiled, barely contained rage. For the first time, she was frightened of him.

"*I* would never give you that kind of ultimatum," she whispered.

"*I* would never put you and the kids in this position."

"You're hurting my arm, Ammon."

He released his grip immediately, pulling his body back. "Sorry." He looked shocked. "I'm sorry."

Everything was out of control, she thought. Connor. Ammon. Herself. Everything about the case flashed through her mind, revealing how completely naïve she'd acted from the very beginning. The policeman who had taken her statement had reassured her that she wasn't the only mental health worker who was threatened by clients. Telling Ammon that would only make things worse.

Ammon's voice cut through her guilt-fogged brain. "When you get your priorities in order, then we'll talk." He stood up and headed for the door.

"Ammon!" she cried, reaching for him. "Don't leave."

His sigh was harsh as he turned and studied her again. "Oh, Bloody Christ, Kimmy! Don't you know me by now?" he said wearily. "I'm just headed downstairs for a whiskey and a smoke."

She listened to his footsteps moving down the steps and felt ashamed. She'd never lied to Ammon before this case. Calling her sister before him, she now realized, had been a huge betrayal. She'd put the kids in danger. And she'd painted herself into a real corner. She couldn't tell him that she'd found the note in Jack's bag. He'd kill Connor for sure. And then he'd end up in jail. And then their life would fall apart...and...and it would all be her fault.

Oh dear God, she prayed, clasping her hands together. *Help me fix this. Help me put this right, if I can.*

She fell back against the pillows. For the first time in her married life, she felt utterly lost and completely alone.

CHAPTER TWENTY-SIX

In the days after filing the police report, Ammon and Kimberley were barely talking to one another.

Vowing to keep no more secrets from him, she sat down with him and confessed to every mistake she'd made, from the day she took Jack with her to meet with Connor, to the night he showed up at her parenting class, changed her tire, and even her suspicions that he had slashed it. She had given him a copy of the police report to read and explained the legalities of a restraining order.

When she finished he had only one thing to say to her.

"Don't ever take any of our kids to that clinic. Ever."

In doing the right thing, she had succeeded only in alienating her husband even further.

When she had told him she was going into work today, he had no comment. Just a wounded look.

———

Kimberley yawned, stretching in her chair. She had finished writing up the notes from her last session and had a free half hour before her next client. A cup of coconut chai tea would be perfect right now.

Down in the clinic's kitchen, she saw Jon Robinson's wife, Ann, talking with three other well-dressed women at the Formica table. They stopped their conversation as she came in.

"Don't let me disturb you," Kimberley said, reaching for the tea kettle.

Ann laughed and introduced her to the group as the facilitator of the Parenting Group sessions. "We're discussing possible topics for the new Emotional Transition from Prison program. It might be useful to have a fresh set of ears, if you have a minute. Dr. Brower-Crawford was just telling us about a very promising idea."

The elderly woman inclined her head modestly at the compliment, adjusting her magenta patterned silk scarf against her wool jacket. She explained that she used to teach inmates at the Mid-Orange Correctional Facility.

"One of the things I noticed was their inability to convey their emotions in a measured way," Dr. Brower-Crawford explained. "They lacked what you might call a facility with language skills, and so, were unable to express themselves. Their frustration could quickly escalate into a tirade of expletives and violent gestures."

"Yes." Kimberley nodded to show her interest. "You can see that even with toddlers who don't have a facility with language."

Dr. Brower-Crawford explained her idea to compile a list of acceptable expressions for them to practice when speaking, say, to a social worker or parole officer, or their own family members.

"What do you think?" asked one of the other women.

"Maybe it could go further than just one night's topic," suggested Kimberley, pouring the now steaming water from the kettle into her mug. "Each week, they could spend ten minutes practicing a key phrase in the right tone. I truly believe that modeling behavior and having them act it out over and over is very beneficial. That's what we're doing in the weekly parenting sessions."

"What a good idea!" said Ann, turning to a younger woman on her left. "Ericka, what about having some of your students from the high school drama club videotape some short skits that could be played during the meetings?"

"I think they'd be—" began Ericka.

She was cut off by the sound of a loud backfire.

The sound echoed in the street outside. A screech of wheels. Another backfire. Or was it gun fire? The sound of a car speeding off.

For a moment, no one spoke. They barely breathed. Then they heard the sound of wailing and a woman screaming.

"Oh, God above!" Ann Robertson whispered, bowing her head.

"Not another one," Ericka murmured, pressing her hand to her chest.

Uncomprehending for a moment, Kimberley tried to decode the other women's reactions."Another what?" she blurted out, gripping the handle of her mug of hot tea so violently, the hot liquid sloshed onto her dress and dribbled down her hand.

The women stared blankly back at her.

Jon Robinson burst into the room. "You all right, Ann? Everybody all right?"

Ann nodded, gripping her husband's hand.

"Call an ambulance," he said. "Someone's been shot. Keep everyone inside!"

Ann Robinson jumped up, reaching for the phone mounted near the door, as Jon disappeared.

Dr. Brower-Crawford lowered her head onto her folded arms at the table and began to sob. Another women patted her shoulders, murmuring something intended to soothe her. "It's gonna be all right, you'll see, God has this in his hands, Emeline."

The teacher, Ericka, looked over at Kimberley, her mouth drawn into a tight line. "Her nephew was shot two months ago. This brings it all back."

In shock, Kimberley drifted out to the waiting room. The

receptionist was gone. Men and women were crammed together at the front window, mesmerized by the chaos in the street. The front door stood wide open. Kimberley was drawn to it as if pulled by a magnet. Outside, a small huddle of people were gathered by a figure lying crumpled on the sidewalk. Near them, a woman was crying, rocking back and forth, her eyes fixed on Jon Robinson, who was hunched over the prone boy, giving a measured mouth-to-mouth resuscitation. Emma Wu was at Jon's side, timing him with a stopwatch.

A siren began to wail in the distance.

Dazed, Kimberley moved back inside, and shut the door against a swarm of flies. Two women turned away from the window, looking at her as if she might have something to report.

Kimberley shook her head, not knowing what to say.

The younger woman, who wore a paisley blouse and silk hair scarf, put her arm around the older woman, who was dressed in the pink scrubs of a pediatrician's office.

"This has got to stop!" muttered the older one, shaking her fist in the air to punctuate her lilting Caribbean patois. "Bold as brass, in broad daylight, now. They killing children in the street, these wicked boys!" She glared at Kimberley, caught up in the grip of her anger.

"I'm so sorry," Kimberley said quietly. "I'm so sorry."

The old woman grunted. "It's a sad thing when a ten-year-old boy can't walk down the street in his own neighborhood. A sad thing."

"He's...?" Kimberley gasped, turning back to the door. "The boy...out there. He's only ten?"

"His name is Vernon," answered the younger woman, tears streaming down her broad cheeks. "He was in my Sunday school class. Such a nice boy."

"It's his older brother who stirred up the trouble by joining that gang," added the nurse, scowling. "Wicked, wicked."

"Wicked," echoed Kimberley, overcome by these women's faces, streaked with tears, one born of grief, the other of paralyzing anger. Their helpless expressions kindled some faint sparks of her professional demeanor.

She reached out for their hands, and to her surprise, they clasped hers in return.

"Let us gather here as witnesses. Let us gather here to comfort each other," Kimberley heard herself say. Her voice grew more powerful and sure as she invited everyone in the room to come into the circle of compassion. As people drifted over, one by one, the circle widened, and hands clasped.

Kimberley had no idea what to say, but the words came from somewhere deep, deep inside her as she encouraged everyone to bear witness to the community's past and future. Ann Robinson took over, as the residents responded with an emotional outpouring about the victim, about their anger at the gangs, about their fears for their family, and their hopes for the future.

Out of the corner of her eye, she saw Jon Robinson walk through the door. He looked grim. His wife held out her hand. Jon hesitated, then seemed to collect himself enough to take her hand and join the circle. Everyone quieted, all eyes turned to Jon, waiting for him to say something.

But the look on his face told them everything they didn't want to hear. And the tears began to roll down their cheeks again, as they gripped each other's hands for support.

For the first time, Kimberley understood something about the strength and the burdens of this community. The 'wicked boys' had taken another innocent victim, leaving another hole in the already shattered hearts of these good. If they could bear up under the strain, Kimberley thought, so could she. She could help them. And she would like to be a useful part of their world.

But she had promised Ammon that she would find another job. And she still deeply regretted that promise.

"This way, Abuelita!" Alexia Mackenzie tugged on her grand-mother's hand as they entered the clinic. "We have to sign in at the big desk." She waved excitedly at the receptionist. "Hi, Miss Emma!"

"Well hello there, Miss Alexia!" The receptionist greeted her with a warm smile. "And how are you this evening?"

"Good," Alexia said. "Look at my new sweater! This is my Abuelita! She knitted it for me! And she's teaching me how to knit!" She twirled around to show off her pink cardigan.

"Very pretty! And who do I see hiding back there? Hello, Jayleen!"

The younger sister waved shyly back at the receptionist, then buried her face in the folds of her grandmother's navy-blue skirt, which she wore with a crisp white blouse.

"I'm Mrs. Rodriguez," Beatriz said, smiling politely. "My daughter asked me to bring the girls today."

"Mama's at school!" Alexia said. "She has a test."

"Good for her," Emma said. "I hope she does well. I'll just sign the girls in. Mrs. Mason should be down in about ten minutes."

"I heard about the, you know, what happened this morning."

"It was a terrible thing." Emma nodded gravely. "But everyone here is coping. Did you know the family?"

"No. I don't think so." Beatrice expressed her sympathies, and Emma thanked her.

Alexia steered her grandmother and sister back to the waiting room. "Come sit here, Abuelita! This is the nice couch." She climbed onto the brown plaid couch and patted the cushion. As the others settled in, she leaned over and whispered in her grand-mother's ear. "The other one sags!"

Beatriz smiled. She was pleased that Alexia seemed so confi-dent here. It was a sign that the therapy was working. She fished out a library book from the deep recesses of her quilted tote bag. "Should I read you the rest of 'I Love Saturdays y domingos'?" The girls nodded, snuggling closer as she read the bilingual book about a family with American and Mexican grandparents. "Abuelita, how come we don't have grandparents from Daddy's side?" Alexia asked at the end of the book.

Beatriz hesitated. "They died. It's sad."

Alexia looked up, catching sight of Kimberley coming down the stairs. "That's Miss Kimberley, Abuelita! That's her!" She bolted up, tugging on her grandmother's hand. "Come on. We're next!"

Beatriz struggled to rise, but Jayleen clung to her arm.

"Miss Kimberley!" Alexia wriggled with excitement as the therapist approached. "This is my Abuelita!"

"She's my Abuelita, too!" Jayleen pouted, crawling onto Beatriz' lap to prevent her from rising.

"Sshhh, girls. Inside voices," Beatriz admonished. "There are other patients."

"How lovely to meet you," Kimberley said, extending her hand toward the woman. "The girls have told me so much about you."

"Good things, I hope," Beatriz replied. Unable to rise, she offered an apologetic smile to the therapist. "I'm sorry. Jayleen is very clingy today."

"That's fine," Kimberley said. "If you prefer, I can just work with Alexia. She's making tremendous progress," she added. "Isabella couldn't make it today? I had time blocked out for her."

"I'm so sorry, she should have called to cancel," Beatriz apologized. "She has a final examination today."

"That's fine," Kimberley said. "Would you like to wait here with Jayleen, or come upstairs?"

"I would prefer to come upstairs for a moment," Beatriz said. "I have something I would care to discuss with you."

"Of course," Kimberley said. Then she laughed. "Come on, Jayleen! Would you like to show your grandmother the game you like to play? You can do that in my office."

The girls normally flew upstairs ahead of Isabella, but Beatriz kept them firmly in hand, letting go of their hands only when

Kimberley opened the door to the children's therapy room. While the girls looked for the *Feed the Woozle* game, with the snack-guzzling orange Muppet-like creature that always made Jayleen giggle, Beatriz remained just inside the door frame.

"Can we speak privately for just a moment?"

Kimberley nodded. "Of course."

Beatriz glanced at her granddaughters. "These sessions. What would they cost if someone didn't have insurance or Medicaid?"

"I'd have to ask the receptionist. She would have the rates and be able to help you with any paperwork."

"Certainly. The receptionist. I will ask her," Beatrice said. But she didn't move. Her steady gaze held Kimberley's.

"Is something wrong?" Kimberley asked gently.

"How much would it cost for a ten-minute consultation?" Beatriz's fingers tightened around the handle of her bag. "I could pay out of pocket."

"Oh, that's not necessary," Kimberley said. "How about we talk for a few minutes after Alexia's session? I have the time open for Isabella. In the meantime, you and Jayleen can take the game into my office and play it at my desk."

"Thank you." Beatriz hesitated shyly. Then she inclined her head and said in a low voice, "You're very kind. My granddaughters, they like you very much. You're good for them."

———

Kimberly ended the session early, sending the girls downstairs to wait by the receptionist's desk. She had been very impressed by Alexia's openness today. Her grandmother's presence seemed to have a calming and centering effect on both children. Kimberley instinctively liked Mrs. Rodriguez. There was a deep family resemblance between her and Isabella, both outwardly graceful and slender. But Mrs. Rodriguez seemed to be well-grounded, sensible, and practical. She radiated strength and a quiet dignity. Kimberley wanted to hear what this woman had to say.

"Emma, could you just keep an eye on them while I chat with their grandmother for ten minutes?"

"No problem."

"And could you find out the cost for the girls' sessions, in case Isabella has to pay out of pocket?"

"Wait one sec and I'll check the rate card." Emma flipped open a folder, then jotted down a figure on a slip of paper for Kimberley to take upstairs.

Glancing at the cost, Kimberley realized how little it was compared to most therapy centers. Yet, as she climbed the stairs, she thought it would still be far too much for Mrs. Rodriguez to afford.

"I don't know," Beatriz murmured a few minutes later, staring glumly at the price. Perched at the edge of her chair, she looked as if ready to bolt. "I just don't know. I have a hearing coming up soon, about my becoming the girl's guardian. But I want them to continue the therapy. Did Medicaid say why the girls can't come anymore? They are just starting to make progress." She sighed heavily, her expression pained. "They can't end up like their father. They must not end up like their father."

"I agree they need more time," Kimberley said. "I just sent a follow-up report to the team to ask for more sessions. But . . ."

"I know how things work in the health care system," Beatriz interrupted. Her tone was bitter. "If my girls were white, they'd have everything they need."

"Not always," Kimberley tried to console her. "I know it seems that way, but…"

Beatriz cut her off with a wave of the hand. "If Isabella had fallen in love with any other white boy but Connor…any other. But having a white father like Connor is worse than having no father at all. My daughter doesn't see it that way, of course."

The venom in her tone of voice startled Kimberley. "Mrs. Rodriguez, why do you dislike Connor so much?"

He's an addict." Beatriz gave a snort of derision. "His whole family are addicts. It's in his genes—in his father's genes, his mother's genes, his sister and brothers' genes. And now, in *my grandchildren*'s genes."

Beatriz was quiet for a moment, lost in thought.

"I have a theory," the older woman finally said. "It's always there, maybe, the addiction gene. It may run in the family." She grimaced. "With his mother, maybe he was born an addict. Or if not, maybe the gene was waiting for the weak moment."

She shifted in her seat, hugging her bag closer to her. "Once his grandfather died, *that* was the weak moment. That was where the cousin comes rushing in, with all sorts of bad ideas and worse habits. And so, he becomes what he was born to be."

"You don't really believe that, do you?" Kimberly was stunned. "That people are preprogrammed and can't change their destiny?"

"You, being a therapist, you have to believe people can change. Or why would they bother to come to you?" Beatriz shrugged. "But I'll tell you what I have seen as a nurse. I have seen people, smart people, professional people, do things you'd never believe in a million years. Patients come in with lung cancer, diabetes, liver problems. They know that they are doing this to themselves, and yet? They don't change. I have to ask myself why? Why are they addicted to alcohol? To heroin? To painkillers? To cigarettes? To junk food? We got patients coming in for throat cancer, lung cancer, and they still can't quit the cigarettes!"

Beatriz shook her head, touching two fingers to her temple. "They are crazy?" Her voice rose in frustration. "They are stupid? No. No, I think not."

She leaned in toward Kimberley for emphasis. "I meet hundreds of people just like them who don't smoke. Who don't do drugs. Who don't eat themselves sick." She raised her hand, pointing to the ceiling as if the proof was written on it. "It's in the genes. It's got to be. What else is the difference?"

Kimberley sat back, not sure how to answer.

"I'm not a geneticist. If that's true, then how can I help your daughter and granddaughters?"

The grandmother leaned in eagerly, suddenly animated. "Oh, but if you can shut down those genes, the signals to turn on those genes, then you can stop the whole cycle. That's what I think it's all about. I read that researchers now think you can change the brain. Rewire the brain. Change those genes, somehow, especially in a young person. Especially in a child." She reached out, rapping the table with her knuckles.

"Knock on wood, it's not too late for Isabella. She didn't start out like that. She only did it a couple of times. She's good. She goes faithfully. The little ones' brains? You could rewire them even easier. The gene, *his gene*, might be inside them, but you could train them to turn it off."

Kimberley stared at this woman. Her face was absolutely grave, her intelligent eyes imploring Kimberley to agree.

Could it be true, she wondered, that most addicts had a gene that would take over reason? Over consciousness? Over every other instinct toward decency and survival? And could it be overcome? Could the brain be rewired to turn that gene off? She too had read the latest literature, seen webinars. Was everything just a matter of biology? Weren't human beings more complicated than that?

"You could be right," Kimberley admitted. "The research is all so new."

Beatriz nodded back eagerly, as though she were about to impart an important piece of the puzzle.

"I think you know how important this therapy is for my girls," Beatriz said softly. "I think you are the only one who can help them escape their fate."

Kimberley took in a deep breath. She was thinking of her promise to Ammon. Of the morning's frightening events. Was it wrong not to tell this woman that she might not work here much longer?

"I'm not a miracle worker," she said instead. "I'm not even the most experienced therapist here."

"God is the one who will work the miracle," Beatriz insisted, looking her right in the eye. "But I have prayed about this. And I believe, he will work it through you."

CHAPTER TWENTY-SEVEN

It was a warm June day when Kimberley met again with the school team. She was greeted warmly by Lisa DeLaney, the school psychologist, who once again ran the meeting briskly with the same team, including Alexia's kindergarten teacher, the school principal, the school district social worker, and Dolores Fuentes.

Everyone agreed that Alexia had made great progress. In fact, they talked about it as though this was a case that needed to go no further.

"I can't agree," Kimberley said, pulling out a sheaf of papers. "I was going to recommend that Alexia receive another ten weeks of therapy, every other week. I'm hoping to see her through the summer vacation, so she won't lose ground. I've got a formal assessment here, and although she is much better, there are things going on with her home situation now that I think could send her back into a panic stage. I understand that the father has been removed or removed himself from the home and is now living in his car. I'm also concerned that Isabella may slip back into her depression and will lean on the girls too much for comfort. Whether they will be able to handle that, is at best, uncertain."

She handed the assessment to the school psychologist, giving another set to the school social worker.

"Yes, I understand that the home situation is rapidly evolving," Lisa Delaney said, turning to the Alisson Moureau, the school social worker. "Could you fill us in on the changes?"

"Perhaps Ms. Fuentes is better able to do that. What I understand is that the father is indeed out of the house. The grandmother, Beatriz Rodriguez, is petitioning for guardianship of the two girls."

Kimberley nodded. Isabella's mother had mentioned that to her during their meeting. "Which is another reason I would strongly suggest extending the therapy until those changes are set."

"The hearing is set for next week," Dolores Fuentes interjected. She shuffled through a few papers, pulling one out. "Excuse me. In two weeks."

"And can you tell me when your agency will make a determination on when Mr. Mackenzie can return home?" Kimberley asked.

"I have no firm date." Dolores glanced her way. "It depends on a number of factors, which I won't go into here."

"I'd like to hear what they are," Kimberley insisted. She looked around the room. The principal, Dr. Cruz, looked at her with a puzzled expression. Lisa Delaney said nothing. Neither did the teacher or the social worker. "So I can understand how to prepare the girls for the situation that's coming. They are asking why their daddy is gone."

"I have no date to give you," Dolores Fuentes reiterated. "It's dependent on a number of factors, on judges, on hearings, and other factors I can't go into right now."

The rest seemed satisfied with her statement, but Kimberley was angry. "Well, can you tell me if the family will be allowed to stay in the house with Connor gone?"

"I think so, for the moment."

"For the moment?"

Lisa Delaney interrupted. "I think we'll have to let the course of that play out in the courts. With a custody hearing, this is going to take a while. So I agree, I'll recommend an extension of therapy sessions for the girls. It's up to Social Services and Medicaid whether they can extend the sessions for the mother."

"And the father?" Kimberley looked at the social workers.

"I don't believe he is eligible," said Allison Moureau, writing something in her notebook. "But I can get back to you on that, Mrs. Mason."

The rest of the meeting concluded quickly after that. Kimberley chatted for a few minutes with Alexia's teacher, to find out how she was doing in class.

"Oh, she's much more willing to participate with the other children," Trish Sherman said. "We are not having meltdowns anymore. And I believe she has two friends, now. A little boy and a girl. They seem to get along nicely. Has she mentioned any bullying?"

"No," Kimberley said with a smile. "She did mention a Meyers and a Camille. She called them her besties."

"I know." The teacher laughed. "So cute."

Kimberley wanted to stay and chat for another minute, but she saw that Dolores Fuentes was on her way out the door. She excused herself and hurried after her, determined to get a straight answer out of the social worker who had treated her so dismissively.

On the walk out to the parking lot, Kimberley was conscious of a rising anger as she caught up to the social worker. She didn't want to come off as unprofessional. But she was angry at the entire situation this woman had placed her in.

"Mrs. Fuentes," she began.

"It's Ms., but you can call me Dolores." The social worker's smile was pleasant, but she continued walking briskly.

"I need to clear something up, Dolores." Kimberley adopted a professional tone. "Something we didn't get to touch on in the meeting. It's about the report I wrote. The one that led to Connor being asked to leave the house. I need to know what happens next. My clients are very anxious and confused."

"Confused? About what specifically?"

"About when or under what circumstances Connor will be allowed to come home."

"That's out of my hands."

"Out of your hands?" Kimberley echoed, stopping in mid-gait to stare at the social worker. "What do you mean? Whose *hands* is this case in, if not yours?"

"Right now, it's in the DA's and the medical examiner's hands, I believe," Dolores said calmly, fingering the straps on her leather briefcase. "I gave Connor a list of what has to happen next. One," she held up a finger. "He has to prove he is on the methadone program and not using again. Two." She ticked off another finger. "He has to be cleared by the medical examiner's office for any part in his son's death. And three!" She held up a third. "He has to prove he is not a danger to his remaining two daughters."

"And how long is all that going to take?"

"I really don't know. As long as he is not around the children except for supervised visitation, the situation is considered stable."

"Stable?" Kimberley was stunned. "Are you telling me that now that Connor's out of the house, the case is no longer urgent? You gave me the impression that him leaving would speed things up."

"No. I never said that," Dolores corrected, walking away. "But it will make it better for Isabella and the girls."

"Better? How?" Kimberley ran after her. Every muscle in her body was pulsing with fury and indignation. She wanted to throttle the child protection worker, but all she could do was try to make her see what she had done. "She has no money. She has no car. That house isn't hers, legally, so she could be evicted. She can't afford the taxes and the heat. They could end up losing the house in the end. And he is homeless. He's living out of his car. Which might mean, he could lose his job for all I know. How is any of that *better*?"

"It is better," Dolores said patiently, her expression neutral as she pulled out her keys. She stopped before a silver Honda Accord. "Isabella can apply for welfare. She'll be eligible for Medicaid insurance. She'll get free tuition, which will help her mother, and probably be able to take classes full time. And get a job sooner."

"But Connor isn't around to watch the girls anymore," Kimberley protested. "And the grandmother works at the hospital."

"She'll qualify for day care through the college." She shook her head and gave a little laugh as she pressed the key fob to open the car door. "Believe me, he wasn't doing a great job of watching them anyway."

"How do you know?"

She paused to open the passenger door and deposit her briefcase inside. "If we were in my office, I could show you a long list of calls from the neighbors about Connor leaving them on their own once Isabella left." Dolores gave her a meaningful look as she shut the rear door. "And I could show you the reports from the methadone clinic saying how many times Connor missed his doses."

Kimberley sobered. But she was still furious that she hadn't made a dent in the social worker's assessment of the situation.

"I know you're upset," Dolores continued calmly. "There's a bench over there. If you need to talk, let's go and sit down. Please."

Kimberley followed the social worker across the parking lot to the lawn, then perched on the edge of the bench. Her anxiety and frustration wouldn't allow her to relax.

"There's something you need to understand," Dolores said gently. "Isabella's been isolated from all the people who value education and family, all the people who would be willing to look after the children and give them more positive guidance and help. All the people Connor has shut her away from all these years. It's not because he's a monster, he's not. At least, I don't think he is. It's because he doesn't trust anybody. And so he isolates his family from the very people who can help. And he was ready to take off, anyway. Uproot his family to a new state, miles from her relatives, without a job or a house to go to. Probably, where they wouldn't be eligible for any benefits that she gets now."

"Why wouldn't they be eligible for the same federal benefits in another state?"

"Every state makes its own rules about how to administer the benefits and who is eligible," Dolores shot back.

Kimberley took a breath, realizing her mistake. "Yes, of course. I know that. It's just…just an insane system."

"Of course it is." Dolores shifted on the bench, looking out over the fields to the baseball diamond in the distance. Her eyes glittered with anger. Her jaw worked as if she were chewing over her thoughts. "Truth is, it's a broken system. It's an absolutely *punishing* system." Her hands moved apart, as if she were dropping a weight onto her lap. "And God help me, I have seen more families ripped apart. . . destroyed, really." She pressed her lips together and inhaled as though fighting back a torrent of emotions. "Then again, I've seen a lot of women who actually were helped by the system, too."

"But not the men," Kimberley persisted. "Not men like Connor?"

"No… Not most men," Dolores said softly. Tears filled her dark eyes. She raised her pinky fingers to the corners of her eyes, delicately blotting away the tears before they could smear her kohl eyeliner. Wiping her fingers on a tissue, she looked up.

"It's not fair," Kimberley said quietly.

"Ain't that the truth!" Dolores gave a short, cynical laugh. "This system is designed to *punish* certain kind of men. Pretty much cuts them down to their knees." Dolores spoke softly, as if admitting something to herself. "Cuts them completely out of the cloth of the family and throws them away. It's true. It's always been true in one way or another."

"But it doesn't make sense not to help the men. The fathers."

"Capitalist systems have no mercy for men who don't achieve," Dolores said. "That's the truth. And that's not to say there isn't a percentage of men who don't bring it all on themselves. But I'm talking about *cycles* of poverty that just get totally entrenched, especially as the economy and technology keeps shedding good jobs and making everyone fight for the ones that are left."

"That's all fine. That's all philosophical, but I'm not talking about the system," Kimberley interrupted. "I am talking about four specific human beings. How does removing Connor from the only safe place, the only sanctuary he's ever had, make sense?" She stood up, turning to face Dolores. "And in doing so, you've thrown him right into the arms of his doomed, drugged-up family. So now, *he* gets to be the aggrieved victim. Now, *he* gets to justify every single one of his paranoid, negative images of the world. That women are bitches; that the system will screw you even if you do try; that he can't trust any outsider, especially us. And that there is no use in trying to be drug free, or trying to provide for your family, because as soon as you make one little mistake, you'll get thrown out of your own home and have your kids taken away."

"I agree." Dolores's expression became sad. "But we have to do the right thing by the law. It was Connor's choice to put his kids in harm's way, not ours. It's Connor's choice whether he can fix his situation. Frankly?" She sighed and raised her hands. "I don't know if he can."

"That's not good enough!" Kimberley exploded.

The social worker folded her arms across her chest. She gazed at Kimberley, her mouth tightening, barely concealing her frustration.

"You know, you're acting like you're the aggrieved party here," she said. "You're not. I've always wondered how therapists could feel like they know someone when they never went to the client's house. Never saw the reality of how they lived. One of my cases, the mother? She seared her baby's stomach with an iron, for bothering her when she was doing the laundry. Another case? The father ties his children to a post in the basement and leaves them there until they behave. That's what he thinks good parenting is. That's the reality of what social workers deal with every single day."

Kimberley gasped.

"I don't think private therapists even look up the client's history, especially when you're dealing with people in poor neighborhoods. Relying on your client to volunteer the facts is a fairly useless strategy."

Kimberley was flummoxed. "Are you saying this is my fault?"

"No. But it damn well isn't mine!" Dolores shrugged. "I've been doing this for thirty-five years. And in all that time, I just haven't seen many of my clients helped by going to therapy. Sometimes a psychiatrist can help the really mentally ill ones by prescribing drugs. In fact, that's why I think so many people in Newburgh are on drugs. Self-medicating."

"And you don't believe that behavioral therapy supplements the medicine? Medicine alone can't change an entire lifetime's worth of problems."

The social worker shrugged. "You're new at this." Shaking her head, she added. "My mother used to have a saying: Innocence can be a dangerous thing. Stay in this business long enough and that innocence will trick you up every time."

CHAPTER TWENTY-EIGHT

Isabella sat on the bench in the hallway of the police station, one leg crossed, her arms wrapped around her knee. She was cold, even though it was summer now. She propped her chin on her hand and stared at her watch. Two o'clock. She'd been waiting here since noon. They probably did that to make you nervous, she told herself. She had been studying from her nutrition textbook, but her eyes ached in this dim light, and she was starving.

A policeman walked by.

"Excuse me?" she asked. "Is there, is there anywhere to get a cup of coffee and a roll? I haven't had lunch. I'm feeling a little light-headed."

The policeman, older, slightly balding, tilted his head, as if appraising her.

Isabella sat up straight, placing both feet demurely on the ground and smoothing her tee shirt.

"I'll see if somebody can find you something," he said. "Coffee with milk and sugar?"

Isabella nodded and thanked him. Then, she opened her textbook to the right chapter, and tried to study for the unit test coming up at the end of the week.

"Bella?"

She looked up at the sound of Connor's voice. "Oh Connor!" she cried. Jumping up, she rushed to him and flung her arms around him. She felt his rib bones beneath his tee shirt. He'd lost weight.

"Are you eating, baby?" she murmured.

"Don't worry about me," he said, tightening his arms around her waist. He kissed her neck.

She kissed his cheek, startled by the rough beard he had grown. Still, it felt good to stand next to him, to lean her body against his, to nuzzle her cheek into the hollow of his neck.

"I'm scared, Connor," she whispered. "I don't want to say the wrong thing."

"Me, too," he whispered back, stroking her hair with his long fingers. "Me, too."

She looked into his eyes and saw that he was sober. "I miss you."

"Me, too."

They stood like that for a moment longer, then sank down onto the bench, his arm around hers.

"I was studying," she said as she moved the book aside. "Unit test on Thursday."

"Good. Yeah, you'll do good." He laced his fingers into hers. "You always ace them. You're the smart one in the family."

"How you doing?" She noticed bruises on Connor's cheek; cigarette burns on his arm. Alarmed, she stroked his wrist, noticing the strange rubber bracelet he wore. He twisted it to show her what it said: LANDO in capital letters burned into the black rubber. She kissed it, then his hand, smiling up at him through tear-filled eyes. "Where you staying?"

"On the boat."

"In the warehouse? Not Gil's?"

"Sometimes." He rubbed the velvety skin on the inside of her wrist, then kissed it. "Wherever. It sucks though."

"I want you to come home," she murmured.

"Soon."

A policeman, younger than the first, came by with a Styrofoam cup of coffee and a buttered roll. "Here's some sugar and creamers," he said, handing her a plastic baggie. "Stirrer's in there, too."

"Hey," Connor asked. "Anymore?"

"You'll have to wait, buddy. I got to take this little lady here with me." He turned to Isabella. "You can leave the book. Okay?"

Nodding, Isabella stood up. Her hands started shaking. She felt numb. She didn't want to leave Connor. Didn't want to go with the officer. She fumbled as she tried to hold the bagel, the baggie and the cup.

"Be calm," Connor said, raising his eyebrows and giving her a slight nod. "Just stay calm. You don't have to say a word, you know. Not a word. That's your right."

Isabella knew he didn't want her to say anything to the police. But how the hell could she do that? It wasn't in her nature to lie. She stood up and began walking, with heavy steps and heart.

———

By the time Isabella reached the interrogation room, her body was trembling so badly that she was afraid she would drop the coffee.

The atmosphere felt suffocating, the air stale. The officer gestured to the first seat in front of a brown table. Placing her coffee cup down, she pulled out the metal chair, conscious of the scraping sound it made on the floor. Her hands started to shake. She let the bagel and baggie drop to the table.

"Detective Varas will be in soon," he said. He smiled. "You got a few minutes to eat your bagel."

Isabella nodded. She tried to take a bite of the bagel. Her throat had gone dry. It tasted like sawdust, and the lumps of butter stuck to her tongue. She chewed and chewed but didn't seem to be able to swallow. A sip of coffee helped, but it was too hot. Defeated, she set the food down, folded her hands on her lap to try and keep them steady, and stared at the wall.

Hail Mary, full of Grace.

Two detectives, one male, the other female, entered the room. They sat down. The man, who was dressed in a black suit and silver tie, leaned over to switch on the video machine.

The male officer was saying something now. But Isabella couldn't hear him. Her ears had stopped up, muting other voices and enlarging the sound of her own breath and heartbeat. Her prayers played like a soundtrack to the proceedings. Just like the day they buried Lando.

Pray for us sinners. . .

The detective leaned forward. She could see his lips moving. He had a handsome face, an older man with kind eyes. *Now and at the hour of our death. Amen.*

The detective snapped his fingers in front of her eyes. She blinked.

"Are you okay, Miss?"

"Uh-huh," she managed to reply.

"State your name, please, for the record."

"Oh. *Si.* Isabella Rodriguez."

"Where do you live?"

Hesitantly, she gave her address.

"And who lives there with you?"

Unclasping her hands, she touched her locket and burst into tears.

"My babies. My girls." She moaned, her chest filling with the pressure of nerves, loss and pain. She began to cough. The perpetual tickle in the back of her throat grew into a monstrous gagging reflex that wracked her body. She held her hand over her heart as if she could stop herself from falling apart. But she couldn't. She sat there and cried, while the two officers looked at each other, and then at her.

"Do you need some water?" Detective Varas asked.

He sounded genuinely nice, Isabella thought. She nodded, still unable to speak. When the other officer returned with a bottle of water, uncapped, Isabella reached for it gratefully, and took a sip.

She coughed again, sipped some more, and slowly quieted her cough.

"I'm sorry. So sorry," Isabella finally said.

"It's okay," the detective said quietly, offering her a box of tissues. He wasn't exactly smiling at her, but Isabella felt that he was a caring person. Something about him made her feel calmer.

"It's hard not to cry about my baby. About all of it. Everything." She dabbed at her eyes, then blew the mucus from her nose. Gingerly, she cleared her throat, taking another sip of water.

"Better?" the female officer said.

Isabella nodded.

"Okay, now," Detective Varas said. "The subject will continue the interview now. Let's go back to the day your son died, Miss Rodriguez. Tell me about your day. How did it start?"

Isabella shook her head. "Like any other day," she said. "Like every other day of our lives."

She went through the day as best as she could remember. The baby was sick. The girls had oatmeal with orange sections and a glass of milk, the same breakfast they had every day. She packed their lunch bags for school. Combed their hair and walked them to school.

"Who was home with the baby?" the female officer asked.

"Connor."

"State his full name."

"Connor Mackenzie."

"He was home?"

"Yeah. He didn't have any work then. It was January. He works at the docks in Newburgh. Sometimes he works on cars, but mostly boats. When he gets work. It's seasonal, you know."

The questioning went on. Bit by bit, Isabella was telling them as much as she could remember. In the back of her head, she was still reciting prayers. They asked her many questions about the baby, about Connor, about her classes. What time she left. What time she got back. Did she give the baby any medications that day. Did she use any medications that day.

"Well, baby aspirin, sure. For Lando. And nothing for me."

"No oxycodone?"

"No. No, I don't use any medications. Only the methadone."

Detective Varas pushed a piece of paper in front of her, telling her it was the autopsy report.

Isabella eyed it nervously, afraid to say a word.

"Go ahead. Read it. Read it out loud, please."

With a trembling hand, Isabella touched the paper and pulled it toward her. Voice trembling, she started to scan it first. The words began to sink in. The baby's stomach was filled with crushed oxycodone.

She looked up, mute. "I... I don't understand. How could that be?"

"Did you have it the house?"

"No. No," she insisted.

"And the only thing you gave the baby that night before you left was baby aspirin?"

Isabella nodded, barely able to swallow. "I swear. I... I did. I crushed up a tablet and put it in his bottle. But it was aspirin. I *know* it was aspirin. I'm sure it was aspirin. I would never give the baby anything else. I..." Tears began to stream down her cheeks.

The questions went on. When did she come home? What time did she find the baby? Why didn't she go straight to check on the baby?

"Connor. He waved me off. He'd just gotten Lando to sleep. I... I didn't go in." She was sobbing now, the full weight of what she had read in the report finally settling on her heart like a stone weight. "That's why he didn't wake up. For his two a.m. feeding, I mean. I...my breasts were...pretty swollen. Full of milk... I woke up."

She hesitated. Should she say Connor wasn't there? He hadn't been in their bed. She didn't know where he had gone.

"What, Miss Rodriguez? What happened. Where was your husband?"

"I don't remember. I don't...it's all confused. All I know is, I went to the girl's room. When I went to pick up Lando, he was... he wasn't...he was...dead."

They asked her a hundred more questions. She answered all of them, but she never said where Connor was. Only that she had fainted. That when she came to, he was there, and the EMTs were in their house. But all the while she was telling them what happened, a small part of her brain was on fire, knowing that the only way those drugs could have gotten into the baby is if Connor put them there. And finally, she could no longer hold the thought back.

So when they asked her again, she said the only thing she could. "He had some pills for his back when he came out of . . . He had a bad back. So maybe, maybe he dropped one. Or maybe..."

Now that she thought about it, she began to convince herself that maybe it wasn't true. "Maybe my Alexia, my oldest, she's such a Mommy to Lando when I'm not home, maybe she got mixed up and took the wrong pills from my dresser."

Round and round the questions went again until finally Isabella could only say, "If it happened that way, it was an accident. I know my daughter would never do anything like that on purpose."

"And your husband?"

"No." Isabella shook her head. "He loved his baby boy. He loved him. He would never hurt his children."

"Even when he was using?" Detective Varas said.

"He doesn't use," Isabella insisted. "He's on methadone. He's been on methadone for a year now. Voluntarily. We both go. *Both of us*. I would know. He doesn't *need* drugs anymore. He's clean."

The answer seemed to satisfy the detective. He switched off the videotape.

Isabella collapsed on the table. She wouldn't allow herself to blame Connor. She couldn't allow herself to. She recalled the bruises on his arm, the wristband, the cigarette burns and scabs on his arm.

Because if he had given the baby crushed up oxy that night... If he was using while taking methadone... Then their entire life was a lie.

————

Connor was led into a small interrogation room. The last time he'd been in one of these, he'd been driving a stolen car for Gil. Back then, he was young, inexperienced, and scared. He figured if he told the truth, it would go easier. Now he knew better. His only duty was to save himself and Bella, if he could. He was not going back to jail.

Detective Varas strode in, unbuttoned his black jacket, then leaned over to switch on the video machine, announcing the time and date and names of the participants. Then he sat down, his back ramrod straight, his face composed, a cool customer. Opening a leather notebook, he began to flip through the pages.

"I want to take you back, to the night your baby died." He looked at Connor, cool and collected. No trace of emotion, just a friendly interest. "You said you put him to bed at about eight." The detective looked up at Connor and smiled. "Is that right?"

"If that's what I told you, then that's what happened."

"Your wife was at her class at the Orange County Community College campus in Newburgh?"

Connor nodded. He bit the inside of his cheek, holding the skin between his teeth as a reminder not to say too much.

"I need to you say yes or no into the recorder," the detective said firmly.

Connor shrugged. "Yes."

"And your little girls were home at the time?" Detective Varas' voice was still calm.

"Yeah," Connor said. "Both of them." That was information he wanted to make sure got on record.

"And your oldest daughter is Alexia? Right? That's her name?"

Connor nodded, biting down just a bit harder to keep himself grounded.

"Yes or no." Varas' voice was a bit sharper now.

"Yes. Alexia, five. Jayleen, four."

"You said someone was at the door, and you told your daughter to go upstairs and take the baby."

Connor nodded again. "Yes."

Stick to the story you gave them the first time, he thought.

"And the person at the door was someone you didn't want to talk to?"

Connor said nothing. But he shook his head.

"Let the record show, the witness is shaking his head no," Varas said. "So, who was it?"

"My old man," Connor said, allowing a trace of anger to leak out. "He's an ex-con. A real bastard. And you guys…" He stared accusingly at Varas, leaning slightly toward him. "The law let him out. I didn't want him hanging around my kids. So I told everybody to go upstairs and take the baby."

"That must have shook you up, Connor," Detective Varas agreed. "I can understand that. I'm with you. We work hard to lock the bad guys up, and then they just let them out."

Connor knew the cop's game. Show a little sympathy and catch him off his guard. But he wasn't playing. He was just trying to figure out if he needed to lawyer up, or if he could play out this little drama the right way, to throw suspicion off himself.

When he didn't speak, Varas leaned forward. "Okay. So, tell me about your father? How long was he in?"

"Long time."

"Where?"

"Don't know." Connor looked at him. "Don't care."

"So I guess you didn't let him in," Varas said, leaning forward.

Connor leaned back, keeping his expression as blank as a

stone wall. "Whatever I said that night to the police, that's what happened."

Detective Varas sighed. The door opened to let another policeman in, who sat down next to him. Connor saw they were going to do the "good cop, bad cop" routine. He said nothing as Varas announced the newcomer.

"Let's go over it again," the new cop said. He gave a quick snort, staring hard at Connor.

Connor remained silent, bracing his feet against the floor, chewing harder on the inside flap of his lower lip. He wasn't going to give an inch.

"Your daughter gave him a bottle?" the new cop asked.

Connor stared at the blank wall, imagining himself rising up out of his chair, and floating through the wall, on up to the sky, leaving everything and everybody behind him.

"You're accusing your own daughter of putting one of your pills, your oxycodone, into the bottle?"

Connor kept staring at the wall.

"Why?" the cop pounced. "Why the hell would a little girl do that?"

Connor lowered his eyes. He tried to keep a blank stare, but he couldn't quite hide his contempt for this new guy. "She's got it in her head that she's his Mommy and his nurse. You know? He was sick and she was just doing what Bella does, crushing up baby aspirin in his bottle."

"But this wasn't baby aspirin," the cop pressed.

"Maybe she thought it was," Connor said. "Not her fault. I was busy trying to keep the Bastard outta my house. That's all."

Varas interrupted. "So you're saying, the baby was fine when you put him in the crib at eight p.m."

Connor nodded.

"And that you didn't check on him again that night?"

Connor nodded.

"Because you were high?"

Connor shook his head no.

"Do you want to know what I think?" Detective Varas closed the notebook and laid it on the table. Standing up, he took a few steps to Connor's right side, leaning in toward him.

Connor stared at the wall, avoiding both of the cops' eyes. He willed his face to be a blank mask, his eyes to go dead, his body to be still. But he bit down even harder on the lining of his cheek. The pain was a reminder of what role he had to play.

"I think you're lying," Detective Varas said, leaning over him.

Connor drew in a deep breath.

"Why would you give your baby crushed up pills in his bottle?" the other cop accused.

Connor snorted. "I wouldn't."

"Yet, funny thing," the other cop said. "Your baby boy, little Lando, right? He was full of oxy."

Connor nodded. "So I heard."

"So where did it come from?"

"It wasn't me." He looked the detective in the eye, willing himself to be calm. "I told you, that's something Bella and Alexia do."

"So, you feel like one of them fed the baby narcotics."

"Not on purpose," Connor said, allowing his voice to rise. "Fuck it!"

He willed his eyes to tear up. That wasn't hard. He did regret that night. He did miss his son for real. He drew in a deep, ragged breath through his nose, then shook his head slowly.

"You think I like saying that? You think it doesn't hurt me to say that? But yeah, it happened." Connor eyed each of the cops in turn, willing them to see his pain. "She's little. She don't know what she's doing. And every day…" Connor clenched his fist and hit the table one short blow. "Every fuckin' day, I can't help thinking if the fuckin' Bastard hadn't been knockin' on my fuckin' door, I would have been the one to give Lando the baby aspirin!" He rubbed his forehead and then his eyes. "He'd be fuckin' alive right now!"

Varas shook his head. "So, it wasn't your fault."

"No sir." Connor hung his head and took in a deep breath. "The only thing that was my fault was answering the door."

———

The second officer stood up suddenly and walked out of the room, leaving Varas alone with Connor. But Connor wasn't fooled. He knew the game. They were still recording everything he said. Every move he made.

"My officer, who just left. He was at your house that night. Shook him up. He's got kids. I got kids."

Connor cocked his head to one side, wanting to scratch his itchy scalp. "Yeah, so?"

"Forensics found Oxy. Traces of it, all over the house. But no pills that we could find." Varas moved behind Connor. "Yeah. No pill bottle either. No carton. No foil cards. No packaging of any kind."

"That's because I don't take it."

The detective remained behind Connor. "Hard to believe, when your cousin Gil sells it."

Connor stayed silent. He wasn't about to defend Gil. But he wasn't about to give him up as some sacrifice, either. His cousin had always helped him out. He owed him that much.

"So, no response?" the detective said.

Connor remained silent.

"Am I gonna have to bring Gil in, too?" the detective asked. "Was he there that night?"

"No. He's not a..." Connor frowned. "He's not into kids."

"Right," Varas said. "Ever buy Oxy from him?"

Connor shook his head.

"Yes or no," the detective continued patiently. "For the tape."

"No." And it was the truth, he thought. He didn't buy it. He earned it.

"So, you're sticking with your story. It was your daughter. Where'd she get it from?"

Connor didn't flinch, but he did bite the tender area near his bottom lip harder, as if in penance. He looked down, conscious of the detective hovering behind him. "I don't know."

Varas moved to his left side. "Your wife said she didn't have a prescription."

Connor shrugged. He could see the detective now out of the corner of his left eye.

"The nipple of the bottle had traces of the drug. Funny thing. The bottom of the bottle, on the outside, had traces of crushed oxcy on it, too. How would that happen, you think?"

"I don't know." Connor looked stonily into space.

The detective sat back down and looked up into Connor's face. "Do you really want me to bring in your little girl, who's having a hard enough time of it. She's only, what? Five? I gotta granddaughter who's five." Eyebrows raised, Varas' cool gray eyes stared directly into Connor's. "You really saying it was her? You're gonna blame it on your baby girl?"

"I didn't give my son something I didn't have on me." Connor didn't flinch. He didn't break down. He didn't move an inch. He didn't even scratch the scab on his arm.

"Wow." Varas stood up slowly. "You're something else, Connor. Something else."

Then he walked out of the room to consult with his boss, leaving Connor to sit alone, with only his guilt and shame for company.

CHAPTER TWENTY-NINE

Another ten sessions for Alexia had been approved, and Kimberley had decided to parcel them out every other week, to last through most of the summer. She also included Jayleen in each session, now that she was slated to enter kindergarten next September.

She was grateful for the extension, because the girls were just at the point where they were able to talk about the night their brother died with some comfort. The girls haltingly talked about how scary it was and chose cards that were more positive and less ominous. Kimberley wanted to make sure that no matter what they experienced that night, they understood that none of it was their fault.

Using the doll house characters, the girls showed what happened. It was when Alexia pretended to crush up some baby aspirin and put it in the baby bottle, that Kimberley suddenly realized the importance of what the child was trying to tell her.

"Did mommy or daddy tell you to do that? Crush up aspirin to give to Lando?" she asked.

Alexia froze. Immediately, she put the bottle down. "I'm not allowed to say."

Jayleen also froze, her head pivoting to the door, where

Kimberley could hear some commotion outside. Voices were raised. Someone pounded up the stairs. Then the door to the play-room burst open.

Connor looked around, suspended for a moment against the painted blue door. "Okay, enough of this shit!" he yelled at Kimberley. "The girls are coming with me. We are moving out of this place, girls. Come on, Mama's waiting."

The girls shrank back, clutching each other. Kimberley stood up and swiftly moved between the sisters and their father. "Connor, this is not the right way to..."

But Connor cut her off. "Don't fuck with me, Missy Kimberley. No. Don't you fuck with me." He was weaving slightly, his eyes out of focus as he swayed back and forth.

"You need to leave," she said. "You're out of control."

Jon appeared behind Connor, slightly out of breath, his long frame filling up the doorway.

"Connor, you need to leave now," he said in a quiet but firm voice. "This is not acceptable. Come on buddy. I don't want to have to call the police."

"I'm not your buddy." Connor didn't even turn around, but continued to glare at Kimberley, as if he were talking just to her. "You already called the police on me. So go ahead. Do it again."

His blank, zombie-like expression chilled her. She understood the volcanic anger underneath it. She hoped he didn't have a weapon on him.

Kimberly and Jon exchanged glances. He mimed putting a phone to his ear and mouthed the words nine-one-one. Behind him, another face appeared: Beatriz Rodriguez had heard the commotion and come to protect her granddaughters.

"You're scaring your daughters, Connor," Kimberley said, managing to keep her voice calm and professional. It was as if some other side of her, the brave side, had taken over, and her real self was watching it all unfold. "They are innocents, the way you were when you were small. You're better than this. You're not a violent man."

"Only when I'm pushed, Kimberley." He took another step, Jon right behind him. "You swore out a complaint on me. About that note I left. I didn't harm anyone. I was telling you how I felt. The only one who's harming anyone is you people."

A retort, about whether he slit her tires that night, almost came out of her mouth. But she didn't want the girls to know that about their father.

"Don't be like your father, Connor." As soon as Kimberley said it, she realized it was the wrong thing to say.

"You better hope not." Abruptly Connor turned, pushed Jon out of the way, and thundered down the stairs. A few seconds later, they heard the front door slam.

The girls collapsed in a heap on the floor. Beatrice Rodriguez rushed to them, sinking to the floor and gathering them in her arms, cooing and murmuring endearments in soothing Spanish.

Kimberley stood by, helpless, and glanced at Jon.

"We called the police," he told her. "We'll both need to talk to them, sign a statement."

Kimberley nodded. Maybe it was time to write that resume. Maybe she was way in over her head, unable to help people with this level of trauma.

Everything falls to pieces, she thought. But can it be put together again?

———

Ammon was feeding the kids supper, when he noticed a white Ford F-150 truck with a rusted side panel parked across the street from his driveway. It looked pretty beat up. He knew it wasn't his neighbor's vehicle. Paul Anderson kept his cars in pristine condition.

Suspicious, he grabbed his cell phone and dialed the Andersons, while the kids ate the lasagna that Kimberley had left for them.

"More cheese, please!" Tony cried, lunging for the bowl that Paige was holding.

She whipped it away, and half the contents spilled across the table.

"Daddy! Look what Tony made me do."

"Sshhh! I'm on the phone," Ammon said. "Paul? It's Ammon Mason. How are you? We're fine. Say, I'm sitting here looking out my window and there's an old white Ford F-150 parked in front of your lawn. That's the second time I've seen it. Do you know whose it is? Okay, go take a look."

He waited, switching over to camera mode to snap a picture through the window. Jack was snacking on Cheerios. Tony had darted to the spot where the cheese had fallen. He scooped it up in his hands, while Paige made faces at him. Tony scooted back to his plate and dumped the cheese onto his lasagna.

"Yuck!" Paige said, giving an exaggerated shudder. "You're gross, Tony."

Ammon continued to look out the window. To his surprise, he saw Paul Anderson's front door open. The older man walked down the lawn toward the truck.

"Oh, no!" Ammon jumped up. "Stay here. Paige, Tony, you watch over Jack. Don't leave. I'll be right back."

Phone in hand, he bolted through his own front door.

Paul was at the driver's side window now, standing on the grass, partially obscured. Ammon couldn't see what he was doing, but he had a bad feeling. He kicked into a run, heart pumping, moving fast. Speeding around the back, he stopped to snap a photo of the license plate.

"You can't just park here!" Anderson shouted. He banged on the window.

Ammon hurried to Anderson. From the driver's seat, a startled pair of blue eyes stared back out of an angry face. Instinctively, Ammon brought his camera up again, shooting through the glass.

The motor revved up.

Ammon banged on the window. "Roll down your window. I want to talk to you."

The truck lurched forward, screeched precariously, and careened off.

"You know him?" Anderson asked.

"Not sure," Ammon said, checking to make sure the photos were legible. "I didn't mean for you to go out and confront the guy. I only wondered, because Kim and I have seen that same white F-150 before, parked the same way."

"Mary's seen it before, too. Somebody trying to rob the house, you think."

"Don't know," Ammon said. "But I got the license. I'm going to find out just who the hell it is. If you or Mary see it again, don't hesitate to call the police."

———

Kimberley pulled into the driveway later that evening. The night air was warm. She could hear music and voices from the decks and patios in the neighborhood. With only a week left till graduation, soon Ammon would spend less time grading papers for his summer classes and have more time to enjoy with the kids.

She expected to see him at the dining room table, grading the final exams. Instead, he was sitting at the kitchen window, looking through a pair of binoculars.

"What are you doing, Ammon?"

"Keeping watch."

"Over what?"

"That white truck was parked across the street again. This time Paul Anderson and I both went out there and chased him off."

"When?" Kimberley put down her handbag and slipped into an adjacent chair.

"When we were eating dinner." He turned to look at her. "I

called the license plate in to the police." He lifted the binoculars again, training them on the window.

"Is that what you texted me today?" Kimberley already knew what he would say.

"Sure was. It was registered to a Connor Makenzie of Newburgh." His voice was grim. "That's your client, isn't it?"

"Yes."

"That's what I thought. Police said it violates his court order. They could pull him in for that. If they find him."

Kimberley was trembling. She reluctantly told Ammon what Connor had done today, and how Jon had reported him to the police.

"He isn't listed in the phone book," Ammon said, still gazing out the window. "But I did some sleuthing and found an address for him. He's got a criminal record. Did you know you can find almost anything online?"

"He's not living at the house anymore, Ammon. Just his family. Please don't go over there."

Lowering his binoculars, Ammon observed her thoughtfully. "If I ever see him again, he's gonna wish he never heard of therapy."

CHAPTER THIRTY

"Goin' to see a mo-vie! Goin' to see a mo-vie!" Paige and Tony had been chanting the refrain the whole way to the Newburgh shopping mall, until Ammon, stopped for a light, finally turned around to shush them. It was the July Fourth weekend, and they were on their way to meet Kimberley's parents at the movie theater. The traffic to the popular mall was heavy.

"Tell us about the movie, Mommy!" Paige demanded.

"Mum's already described it twice," Ammon said, as he waited for the traffic light to change at the mall entrance. He adjusted the car visor to shade his eyes against the low-hanging sun that blinded him despite his sunglasses.

"Tell it again," Tony insisted.

"Okay, okay," Kimberley said, reaching into the diaper bag. "First, pass this to Jack." She handed a pacifier to Paige. "His fell on the floor." She smiled as Jack sucked contentedly on the pacifier.

"I wanna see 'Cars'!" Tony cried, swishing his Lightning McQueen toy car through the air. "Zoom, zoom!"

"That's only on DVD, doufus," said Paige, primly smoothing the ruffled hem of her pink summer dress.

The car lurched forward, as Ammon turned into the mall.

Tony zoomed his toy car right up the side of his sister's leg and over her dress.

"Hey!" Paige cuffed him on the shoulder. "Stop messin' with me!"

"Behave, the both of you!" Kimberley said. "Otherwise, we'll have to go home. Grammy and Granddad will be very lonely at the movies without you. And we'll miss the fireworks tonight."

"Look for a spot," Ammon asked, as he squinted against the sun. "This place is packed today."

"Ooh, there's a car going out," Kimberley said, before noticing that another car was waiting to pull in. "Sorry. Try the next aisle."

Ammon finally got a break by following a couple to their spot near the movie theater entrance. He flipped on his turn signal to claim the spot, waiting while the couple stowed their shopping bags away. The car behind him honked sharply. Ammon rolled his window down to waved at it to pass him, but it stayed behind him.

Kimberley looked out the rear-view mirror into the glaring sun. She could make out a white truck, rusty with a missing front fender.

"Idiot," Ammon grumbled. The horn blared again. He threw up his hands. "G'day to you too! Ah, finally," Ammon added, as the parked car slowly backed out, freeing up the space for him to pull in.

"Okay kids, we're here!" Kimberley gathered up her belongings. "Don't unbuckle until I get you."

Ammon turned off the engine. "I'll take Jack."

Kimberley helped Paige out first. "Not one step into the road, young lady," Kimberley warned. "Don't move until I get Tony out."

"I see Grammy and Granddad!" Paige cried, waving madly and hopping up and down as Kimberley finished unbuckling Tony. "I see them. They're waving, Mommy!"

"Go on ahead, Kimmy," Ammon said. "I'll get Jack's stroller and meet you at the entrance."

Kimberley gripped her children's hands firmly as they walked toward the mall entrance where her parents were waiting.

"Oh, I forgot," she said, turning back toward Ammon, who was lifting the stroller out of the hatchback. "Don't forget Jack's blanket! The air conditioning gets cold."

That's when she noticed the rusty white truck again, stopped just beyond their parking space. A man stepped out of the driver's side, his face in profile, half covered by a black hoodie.

Strange thing to be wearing on such a hot day.

He turned suddenly, leaping toward Ammon, raised his hands over his head, then smashed them down on top of Ammon's back.

"Ammon!" Kimberley screamed, watching the scene in disbelief as it played out not five yards away. Ammon crumpled to the pavement. The man yanked open the side door. The door where Jack was.

At once she knew who it was. Connor!

Caught in the grip of fear and paralysis, Kimberley clutched her children's hands, unwilling to let them go, yet straining toward her husband and her baby. Someone ran up behind her, touching her shoulder.

"I've got Paige and Tony." Kimberley recognized her mother's voice, breaking the spell. "Let go now, Kimberley," her mother gently commanded. "I'll keep them safe."

Her father was right behind her and Kimberley fell in with his stride as they ran.

Connor hauled out Jack in his car seat, then shoved it into his truck.

"Connor!" Kimberley screamed, her lungs bursting. "Don't do this!" Her heart was pounding, her breath came in ragged bursts.

Connor looked back at her for one moment, his features twisted into a mask of rage. He scrambled into his car, slammed the door shut, and gunned the motor. Kimberley lunged for the car, managing only to slam the flat of her palm against the rear fender as it sped off.

Her father was already dialing 911, kneeling at Ammon's side, feeling for a pulse. Kimberley knelt next to him and listening for his breath. Her tears fell on his cheek.

"He's got a pulse!" Ian said, rising. He began speaking to the emergency operator.

This cannot be happening! Don't fall apart. Stay strong. Stay strong.

Kimberley looked back down at Ammon, his dear face bloodless white. He was in shock. He couldn't do anything for Jack. She glanced up, scanning the lot for the white truck, spotting it headed for the exit. It was all her fault that this had happened. Now it was up to her to fix it.

"I'll find Jack," she whispered in Ammon's ear. "I promise, I'll put this right."

"They're sending an ambulance and the police," her father said in a husky voice.

"Dad, stay with Ammon, please," she told him, rising. "I'm going after Jack. I think I know where he'll take him."

Her father held her arm. "Wait for the police."

"There's no time." Kimberley stared into her father's anguished gray eyes. "I have to go now. I can't lose Jack, too."

———

Keep my baby safe. Keep Jackie safe.

The prayer played over and over in Kimberly's head, as she worked her way through the bumper-to-bumper mall traffic, while keeping Connor in her sight.

The only blessing was that the unbroken procession of cars also cut off any quick escape for Connor's white truck, mere yards from the exit ramp that led to Route 302.

She looked for a short cut. There was none. If she could just jump ahead to force him off the road. But she was too far back.

All she could do was inch her way forward, braking anxiously, pounding on her steering wheel in frustration as Connor finally turned onto the exit ramp.

Soon he'd be at the traffic light.

After that he'd reach the highway and turn onto Interstate 84. Then he'd be out of sight, taking Jack away forever.

The car ahead of her turned left, away from the exit ramp. Kimberley surged forward to fill the space and keep other cars out.

Just nine cars between her and Connor now.

Her hands stopped shaking. She stopped cursing; stopped pounding the steering wheel; focusing solely on the white Ford truck.

A second car ahead of her turned left. Kimberley gunned the motor, covering the gap instantly.

Only eight cars behind him.

Inch by inch, she was gaining on Connor and Jack. Her fear morphed into anger. How dare Connor attack *her* husband? How dare he steal *her* precious child. She *would* find Jack. She *would* bring him home. And she didn't care what she had to do to make it happen.

A third car turned off.

Just seven cars between her and her prey.

She could see Connor more clearly. Black smoke belched intermittently from the tail pipe. The passenger door was dented near the hinge. From her angle, she couldn't see the license plate numbers. But she didn't have to. She felt as if there was a radar connection between her and her Jack. She would follow him straight to hell, if she had to.

She was shaking, yelling at Connor again and again, until her rage was spent, and her heart held no mercy.

———

The light up ahead turned green and Connor gunned the motor, shoulders twitching and fingers tensing as he gripped the wheel.

"Hey asshole, move your car. Gotta make the light."

If he were playing Grand Theft Auto, he could just dodge around the cars, careen up the grass meridian, smashing and charging his way out of traffic, past the light, onto the highway, slam over the guard rails, and free sail into eternal oblivion.

But in video games, you got more than one life. Not in this game.

Fuck that. We're going to get the boat, move to Florida, start over. Start my own fishing boat rental company. That's what we're going to do.

"Hey, little Jack. How'd you like to live in Florida. Huh?" Connor glanced over at the baby on the floor of the passenger seat. The kid wasn't crying anymore; just laying quietly, staring up at Connor. He wasn't Lando by a long shot. But with his dark hair and blue eyes, he could pass for a Mackenzie kid. Why not?

"You like the name Lando? We'll call you that. That was my son's name. Lando."

Jack made no sound.

"Yeah, this is a little bit of payback, that's all," Connor continued, talking more to himself than the kid. "We'll see how your mom likes having her kid taken away."

The line of traffic started moving. Connor's eyes were on the road now, his foot pressing down as hard as he dared, willing the light to stay green.

Two cars more. He was picking up momentum.

The light turned yellow. One car left.

"Almost through," he said to Jack. The light changed.

Connor gunned the engine. In a second, he shot through the red light, jamming the wheel hard, tires squealing as he took a hard right, speeding home free down a suddenly clear stretch of highway.

Sitting high in her SUV, heading toward Newburgh, Kimberley felt like a predator, scanning the light traffic for any sign of Connor's white Ford truck.

But there was nothing. He had eluded her.

Maybe he'd turned off an exit or was just too far ahead. She was already pushing past the speed limit, something she never did. She didn't care. Her mind was occupied with other thoughts.

Where the hell would he take Jack? To his home?

Start with that.

She had the address somewhere in her phone list. She'd look it up if she had to, unless she caught up with his car before the Newburgh exit. She pressed down on the accelerator until the speedometer hit eighty.

Watch out, you'll get stopped by the police.

And what if one did pull her over? Would she tell him what happened? Ask him to put an alert out for Connor? She pressed down a bit harder on the accelerator.

———

Kimberley lost sight of the white truck long before she hit the last exit before the bridge.

She pulled off the road, and thumbed through her cell phone contacts, searching for Connor's number and address. She punched the address into the car's GPS, the map appearing instantly. Less than nine minutes from here. Should she call the house?

If he knows I am after him, he might hurt Jack.

Preserving the element of surprise made more sense.

The GPS guided Kimberley toward Connor's address, taking her back toward Broadway, and onto the south side of town. Turning onto the first side street, the neighborhood seemed normal. Working class houses with small yards and cars parked in the driveways and lining the street. The aroma of barbecuing chicken and hamburgers filled the air. People perched on front porch railings, lawn chairs, and front stoops, some with paper plates of food.

But with each turn, the houses became more dilapidated. Front yards were filled with weeds, brown grass, and scraggly shrubs.

She felt as if she were driving into one of those dystopic video game landscapes. She gripped the wheel, feeling more despair by the minute. Scanning the cars parked on the street, she saw they were increasingly older, more rusted, with huge dents in the doors, missing fenders and even windows. The people who hung out on the stoops looked as if they were stoned, eyeing her with boredom or suspicion.

Feeling conspicuous, Kimberley locked her doors with a definitive click. She kept driving until she came to Connor's house. It was the last one on a dead-end street. High scruffy hedges blocked most of the house behind it.

Looking closer, she saw a mailbox stuck in front of one of the hedges. It sat on a post, connected to a narrow, wrought iron gate. She pushed at it, but it wouldn't budge. Looking closer, she saw there was a padlock on it.

How the hell do they get in?

Kimberley looked up above the hedges and saw windows on the top story of the house. They were hung with heavy blinds that blotted out any access.

Prowling along the perimeter, she found a break in the hedge by the corner. Squeezing through, scratched by overhead branches and prickly barberry, she found herself in a front yard. It was patchy with crab grass and dirt. The wood siding was painted a garish green on the left side, and gray on the front. The front door was a blank, white square, the kind that would be hung on a warehouse or shed.

Kimberley wandered around the yard for a moment, raising her hand to touch the clothesline, moving under it toward a battered Playskool playhouse. She squatted next to the tricycle, trying to imagine Jayleen and Alexia playing here. Repulsed by the bleakness of the property, a shudder went through her body as Jack's face came into her mind.

"Jack!" She wailed the words out loud, looking up at the house, hands clenched by her side.

Her cell phone rang as if answering her question. Scrambling for it inside her bag, she thumbed the code to unlock it. It was an unknown number, and she was tempted to let it ring, but her intuition, some unnamed feeling of dread, made her answer. Trembling, she held the phone to her ear.

"Yes," she answered tensely, standing up.

"Kimberley?"

The voice was Connor's.

"Where's my son!"

"He's okay. I'm in the warehouse. On the boat." Connor's voice sounded flat, deflated of all emotion.

"Connor, you're just making everything worse."

"I need two-thousand dollars."

"Where the hell am I going to get two-thousand dollars, Connor?"

"ATM's on Broadway. Plenty of ATMs on the riverfront. Your choice."

"I'll get it!" She was moving fast now, heading back to the car.

"No police, Kimberley. I'm not going to jail. I'll kill myself and your kid if you bring the police."

CHAPTER THIRTY-ONE

Connor approached the warehouse, holding a sleeping Jack in his carrier. With every step, he expected someone to stop him, but no one paid any attention. Most of the people were here only for overflow parking, intent on walking down to the restaurants and stores and boats along the wide, welcoming riverfront.

Connor kept running his mental list. Meet Kimberley here, collect her money in exchange for Jack. Pack up Gil's stash of Chinese prescription meds from the boat and pack it in his car to deliver to his cousin's partner in Georgia. Once there, get paid and buy a plane ticket for Mexico.

He was not, ever, going to stand trial for Lando's death. Even if it meant leaving Isabella to face charges alone.

She didn't do nothing, so there's no chance she'll go to jail. Sure. She'll be fine.

He opened the door, which creaked on its hinges. With his flashlight, he picked his way over toward his grandfather's boat. He could almost navigate it in the dark but holding Jack's baby carrier made it awkward. And the last thing he wanted was to wake him up. With any luck, he was so exhausted that he'd sleep until his mother got here.

The boat loomed up large in the warehouse.

Setting Jack's seat on the floor, Connor switched on a small work light, and went to raise the ladder to the side of the boat. He grabbed the baby seat and swung it up as he climbed up to the first deck, then hopped the staircase up to the pilot's house on the top. He left Jack there before heading back down to the lower compartment to pack up his cousin's stash of fentanyl and oxycodone drugs. Gil had told him it was worth a quarter million dollars on the street. Their take might be twenty thousand. He had already hidden the shrink-wrapped packets in empty paint cans with fitted false tops and an inch of paint as camouflage. Now he just had to load them in his car, drive them to Gil's, and everything would be fine.

He heard the creak of the door, and scrambled down the ladder, relieved that the therapist had come. She was his ticket out of this nightmare.

"So this old pile of junk is still here?"

Connor froze at the sound of the Bastard's voice. He turned to face the intruder.

He knew his father's features well, even though time had reduced the once handsome square-jawed, Scottish face to a mass of wrinkles, a swollen purple nose, and lanky gray hair. He looked old, but his physique was still massive and intimidating, his muscled arms and wrestler's torso straining against his black tee shirt.

Gilead Mackenzie squinted back at his son, then slowly made his way toward the ladder. "Surprised Arnie lets you keep her here. You know, I saw him the other day. He told me to get out. Said he'd call the cops on me. Can you imagine, him threatening me?"

Connor said nothing. He kept his head low, monitoring The Bastard out of the corner of his eye, totally thrown off balance by his presence here.

"You paying him rent?"

Connor ignored him.

His father kicked at the ladder. It fell to the ground, clattering against the cement.

Connor flinched. From above came a whimper, then a soft cry. Would The Bastard notice?

But his father was focused on Connor. "I asked you a question," he said with exaggerated politeness. "Are you paying the gentleman rent?"

Connor ground his teeth. "No."

"Nice of him," his father said dryly. He eyed the boat up and down. "Pick up the ladder. Let's go inside."

Connor's arm twitched, but he didn't move. He didn't want The Bastard to see Jack. He'd want a piece of the money. Or he'd fuck it up.

"Pick up the ladder, I told you!" He clenched his fist and shook it, the way he used when Connor was small. "I want to take a look inside!"

"Don't want you on my boat," Connor mumbled, standing his ground.

"*Your* boat?"

"Yeah, *my* boat." Connor stood up straighter.

His father stared him and a grin spread over his face. "You mean Andrew's boat, don't cha?"

Connor said nothing.

"If that old jackass didn't die, it wouldn't be yours now, would it?"

"He wasn't a jackass!" Connor was breathing hard, staring straight into The Bastard's eyes. "You were the jackass!"

His father smiled, like a fisherman who had just gotten a nip on his hook. "I admit I was the jackass," he said. "A jackass for marrying his whore of a daughter." The old man's eyes sparkled as he warmed to his verbal assault. "And my son takes after me. You never even married your Mexican whore."

"She's no whore!" Connor cried.

The old man laughed.

"Fuck you," Connor mumbled.

The Bastard did a little shuffle with his feet.

He's enjoying this. I ought to bash his brains out.

"I'm surprised immigration hasn't rounded her up yet. They're getting rid of a lot of Mexicans, God love 'em."

"She was born here," Connor said, turning away. He wished he had a crowbar to smash his father's head into the cement; smash it until it was nothing more than pulp. He deserved it. Every wrong thing in his entire life really was The Bastard's fault, wasn't it?

"Yup, they'll be rounding your whole family enough," Gilead McKenzie said, rubbing his hands together, his mouth twisted into a smirk. "The two girls are bastards. Well, that's what they would have called them in my day. And the baby. Dead. Whadja do to him?"

Connor whipped around. "Get the fuck out!"

His father planted himself firmly in front of Connor, stance wide, arms akimbo.

"Make me," he taunted softly.

As Kimberley drew nearer to the waterfront, the parking lot was packed. Snaking her way down River Road, she cursed at the drivers who tried to cut in and out of traffic in their hunt for a parking space. She glanced at her phone.

Should she alert her father? Should she try to contact Connor? An opening in the line allowed her to spurt through to the next parking lot, a bit closer to the warehouse. Everywhere, she saw families and couples, happily making their way down to the waterfront restaurants and shops.

She saw a police car. Inhaling, she found herself unable to breathe for a moment. What if she told them? What would they do?

She conjured up feverish images of the police calling on a bull horn, of Connor yelling at her, of gunfire, of Jack dead . . .

Stop thinking! Stop projecting!

Kimberley drove past the police car without looking at it. She wouldn't put Jack in any more danger.

What makes you think you can bring him out safely? What makes you think Connor will actually give him back? Why kidnap him then?

She tried to remember her training: People did desperate things when there was a disconnect between their real self and their false self.

She snorted. What did that even mean? And how could she, in a few minutes, or even an hour, bring back Connor to his real self? What if the real self was the broken part, the psychopath, and the false self was only the veneer of how he thought people should act? What hope was there then?

"Go to hell," Connor told his father. He was shaking all over.

"Make me," the Bastard said again.

Connor turned away. He took a deep breath to steady his nerves.

His father laughed. "You and all your cousins together couldn't make me."

Connor exploded, quivering with rage as he turned to face him. "Nobody gives a shit about you!" He balled up his fists. "Not one! Not me! So go to hell! Just go to hell! No one cares if you die in the gutter."

His father stood back for a moment, eyeing Connor. Slowly, he shook his head. "Look at you. What a miserable piece of putz you turned out to be. Got the courage of a goddamn mouse. Christ. Goddamn daughter got more courage than you. See this?"

He stepped closer toward Connor, then stuck his hand in front of his face. "See what your brat did to her own grandda? She stabbed me, the little bitch. Made me bleed like a stuck pig."

Connor pulled his fist back. But the Bastard only sneered.

"Take a swing at me. Go ahead. I'll even put my hands behind my back and spot you a free one." He swung his arms back and stuck his chest out. "Come on, take a swing."

Filled with rage and a newfound courage, Connor rushed at his father, his fist aimed at his face. The Bastard grabbed his hand and spun him around, throwing him into a choke hold.

"You can't beat me, boy!" he said, as Connor struggled. "I can crush your larynx and snap your neck easy as pie."

Connor went limp. He thought he might pass out.

Go ahead, kill me, you bastard. I'm the last, and you always wanted to kill us all.

His father released his chokehold, grabbing him by his collar. He shook him. "Now do what I asked you to do," he said calmly. "Get the ladder. Put it up against the boat, because I wanna go inside!"

His father shoved hard, sending Connor sprawling backwards on the concrete. Scrambling to right himself, he stood up and faced down his father, though he was shaking all over and breathing hard.

"I don't...want you...in my...boat!" He kept his voice low, his head down, knowing that his father could deck him any moment he felt like it. But he was done being pushed around.

Connor's father snorted. "So you do got a spark of fight in you! That's something." He looked amused. "So why you keeping this hunk a junk?"

Connor didn't answer.

"Using it to hide Young Gil's stash? Hmmm?"

He took a step closer to his son, who stood his ground. "I hear things." He took another step. "I make it my business to know things, right?"

Connor didn't answer.

"For instance, I know you're back on heroin. Oxy, Percodan, whatever you can get. Yeah, heard about what happened to you in jail. Fractured vertebrae and coccyx. That hurts!" He patted his own butt, and smirked. "Yeah, hurts bad, huh?"

Connor stared at him, wondering what he wanted.

I could kill him. If I had the big wrench.

"Got nothing to say for yourself?"

"Nothing to you!" Connor said evenly.

"Don't matter." Suddenly the Bastard was calm. "I know you're keeping Gil's stash here. Mikey told me. That kid's a good weasel. Rats out his friends for a few beers."

"Bullshit. Mikey don't know nothing. He's just telling you what he thinks you want to hear. Gil's got better places to hide his stash."

His father chuckled again, his hands in his pockets. He grinned. "So he does have a stash, then."

Connor felt the familiar wrench in his stomach, realizing that the Bastard hadn't known for sure, until he tricked him.

Goddamn him!

His father began to whistle a tune that Connor recognized from his childhood. It meant he was scheming, thinking up some new plan to make trouble. Inching backwards, Connor retreated slowly toward his gearbox, where he might find a weapon.

"Where you going, boy?"

"Just giving you space," Connor said sullenly.

"Well, if you aren't hiding Gil's stash here, then I have a proposition for you, Connor. You and me, father and son, as it were, doing some business together." He stopped walking and eyed his son. "You owe me."

"I don't owe you nothin'." Connor kept easing backwards. He was almost in reach of the toolbox. The big wrench was laying on the floor next to it.

"I'm your father."

"Still don't owe you nothin'." Connor felt around behind him and brushed against the wrench.

The elder Mackenzie grimaced. Then he chuckled and resumed his whistling. Suddenly, he turned and rushed at his son, his head down, charging straight into Connor's gut.

Connor went over backward, flat on his back on the cement,

his breath knocked out of him like the wind going out of the sails. His head cracked against the floor. He felt dizzy with the weight of his much larger, much heavier father on top of him. He couldn't breathe.

In the distance, somewhere above his head, a baby screamed. It confused Connor for moment.

Lando?.... No...therapist's kid.

Then a searing pain blotted out the world, as his father dug his knee hard into Connor's groin.

"No son of mine disses me that way." His voice was low, controlled, menacing. "You owe me everything! Your life. Your breath. Every fuckin' cell in your body. You owe me forever! That's a debt you never repay."

Connor's entire nervous system was paralyzed. Like being five again. He wanted to curl up in a fetal position and just die. Before, he would have begged his father to stop. He would have cried.

But now, a deeper primal urge, a murderous, cold, calculating instinct for revenge took, over, even as he gasped for air; even as he felt himself being pummeled. Connor reached over his head, grabbed the wrench with both his hands, and brought it down hard against his father's temple, once, twice, three times.

He lost track of how many times he hit him. He just kept battering him until his father's body stiffened, then sagged.

Rolling the old man off him, Connor sat up, gasping, sputtering, doubled over with pain. With his heels, he scooted backwards away from his father's body.

Is he alive? Did I kill him?

He didn't know which would be worse.

"Oh My God! Oh My God! You stupid bastard!" Connor screamed at the body, which hadn't moved. "Look what you made me do! Just look at what you made me do!"

CHAPTER THIRTY-TWO

Kimberley's scream echoed through the dark warehouse, horrified as she watched Connor roll off his father's prostrate body. She could hear Jack bawling, scared and hungry.

Terrified that Connor might hurt her son, she picked up a piece of pipe leaning against the wall, then advanced on Connor.

"Where is Jack?" she asked softly, brandishing the pipe.

Connor turned to look at her, then groaned. "You!"

"Tell me where he is!" She stood her ground, holding her head high, even though her whole body was shaking.

Connor groaned again, getting to his knees. "Then what? You'll go to the police?" He stared up at her. "Great testimony; I saw Connor Mackenzie beat his father to death."

"It was self-defense," Kimberley said firmly, grasping the pipe hard to stop her hands from shaking. "That's what I'll say. Self-defense. He would have killed you."

"Interfering bitches!" Connor rose like a wounded animal, clutching his arm against his stomach, his rage throwing Kimberley off balance for a moment.

"You came to me," Kimberley defended herself. "You sought me out."

"I had no choice! You! Beatrizz! Mizz Fuentezzzz!" Connor

exaggerated the consonants so that it sounded like an angry swarm of bees. "What a trio! Fuentes throws us in a series of foster homes; like she ever gave a damn about keeping us together! Mamacita's always angling to get Isabella and the girls away from me. And you, turning my girls against me!"

"You're right. I couldn't help you." Kimberley kept her voice low, using her mimicking technique. "I was useless to you. It wasn't fair, Connor."

"Not fair? What the fuck is fair in this life?" He kicked at his father's leg. "Not him. I got the wrong father. That ain't fair. My kid's dead. That ain't fair."

"No, it isn't." She took a step closer.

"I hear you lost a baby, too, hey Kimberley?" He staggered to a wooden crate, and sank onto it, wincing. "Some fuckin' mother you are. What'd you do to it? Huh? Neglected it? Huh? Was it SIDs? Was it SUDs? Did it die in mysterious circumstances? How'd you like it when the police accused you? Huh? Huh? Did you kill it?"

He was pointing his finger at her. His accusation had zeroed in on her deepest wound. She started to shake. Not with fear this time, but with a murderous urge to smash him down. She clenched her fists around the pipe, digging her nails into the flesh of her thumbs to stop her from shaking. To stop her from feeling emotion that would interfere with her finding Jack.

"She died two hours after she was born," she answered evenly.

"Oh, sure," Connor continued, his voice mocking her. "Right. The police would never question you, right? Nah, 'cause you're middle class, with your nice clothes, and your regular paycheck, and your big house, and your shiny new car, and your college degree. So they believe you. But not us. 'Cause we're poor. Didn't go to college. Live in the city. Work under the table. Have to work at some not-so-legal jobs. Our kids don't have nice clothes."

He was weeping now, his voice ragged and hoarse. "We're on

methadone. Food stamps. My Pop's a con, Mom and sister were 'hos and junkies. Gil's a dealer. And me? I'm a, a, junkie. And I'm fuckin' Jonesing out here! God I'm Jonesing out."

Kimberley glanced everywhere, sizing up the hiding places, knowing it was best to let him rant on. *Where are you Jackie?*

She had an idea. She began to whistle the tune she loved to sing to her children, the one she had made up to go with the words from the A. A. Milne poem.

Where am I going, I don't know where?

"Mama!" The cry came from above Kimberley, far up in the top of the boat.

Jack! He was alive!

Kimberley ran forward, but Connor rose on unsteady feet.

"Not that easy," Connor said. "Where's the money?"

Kimberly stopped, her skin turning cold and clammy. She dug into her pocket, pulled out the packet of fifty-dollar bills, and held it out to him. He snatched it, like a greedy child, and began to count it.

Maybe now that his father was dead, he didn't care anymore if he killed her and Jack. She had to get him talking. Had to trick him somehow. Or distract him.

"How did it happen, Connor? How did Lando's stomach get filled with crushed oxycodone? I read the autopsy report. The residue was on the bottom of the bottle, too. What did you do? Use the bottle to crush the pills?"

Connor didn't answer.

"I know you were a good father," Kimberley lied. "I know your father came to the house that night. He made you crazy, didn't he. You wouldn't have done that unless you weren't thinking straight. Was it a mistake? You thought it was baby aspirin? I can testify on your behalf. I can help you, as long as nothing happens to Jack. I can testify about your father being self-defense. We can say it was all his fault."

"It *was* all the Bastard's fault!" Connor cried, lurching forward. "He was there that night. He was pounding on my door.

Gil let me know he was out of jail that day. He spotted him in town, heard he was asking around."

Connor touched the back of his head and groaned, collapsing to the floor. He hung his head and began to sob, great gulps of air and cries that sounded in a bass counterpoint to Jack's higher pitched wails.

"Mama! Mama!"

Every fiber in Kimberley's body strained toward the sound. She moved to the ladder on the floor, steady and deliberately, watching Connor's prostrate body heave out his misery.

"It's not your fault, Connor. It's all your father's fault. I know you didn't mean to hurt Lando, or Jack. I know," she said.

Her words were calculated. She did believe he meant to hurt her and Ammon through Jack. But she wasn't going to say it. She kept up a sympathetic patter as she inched closer, her body shaking; her courage trembling, yet remaining intact.

God, give me courage. Keep my baby safe.

She reached the fallen ladder. Keeping her eye on Connor, she squatted down to pick it up. It was about six feet tall, and awkward to handle. She prayed.

Help me get to Jack. Keep Connor in a daze until I get to my baby.

She began to drag the ladder toward the boat.

Connor jerked his head up. He eyed her sullenly, saying nothing.

Jack wailed again. "Mama! Mama!"

With a surge of adrenaline, Kimberley swung the ladder up and let it fall against the boat. "It's okay, Jack baby. I'm coming," she called out.

She put one foot up on the first rung, then another, then the next, climbing steadily toward her child, expecting that any minute Connor would come after her.

———

Connor watched Kimberley climb the ladder, feeling too exhausted and defeated to do anything about it. Inside, his head swam with a running dialogue with himself.

I could leave.

You won't get far.

I could run.

I could ask Gil.

Gil let you down before.

I could turn myself in.

Not going back to jail. Ever!

I could go to Mexico.

They'll find you there. And the gangs. The cartels. No man. No.

There's only one way out.

He looked around the warehouse. At the cans of paint, and thinner, the oil, and the gasoline cans.

Yeah. That's what I'll do.

He turned to watch Kimberly climbing.

"Tell me the whole story, Connor," Kimberley said. "Tell me what really happened. I'm sure it wasn't your fault."

"It wasn't." He sat back on his hands, still dazed, but wanting, no needing, to talk.

"Gil texted me. The Bastard was spotted in town," he began. "I was spooked. I locked the doors after Isabella left. I told the girls to go to bed, no TV. Alexia was upset, but I took them up to their room. Lando was crying. He was always crying."

He watched Kimberley to see if his words were having any effect. She had reached the first deck and was climbing up the next ladder.

Her baby's cries brought Connor back in time.

"I hate it when they cry," Connor said. "It freaks me out. I was so freaked, so fucking scared, I just couldn't cope with it. I was Jonesing out."

"What does that mean, Jonesing out?" Kimberley asked, desperate to keep him distracted.

"Getting that feeling that you're gonna need a fix. So I crushed up some oxy, figuring it would calm him down. Alex was yammering at me. The baby's sick, Daddy. He's sick. So I said, 'So fuckin' give him something.' I had the pills in my pocket. I was Jonesing. I wasn't thinking straight, or I wouldn't have *never* done it. And then the Bastard was knocking at the door. I just whacked out."

"Which door?" came Kimberley's voice.

"The front door." Connor could hear it all in his mind, as if it were happening all over again. "I couldn't move. You get like that, sometimes, when you're coming down off the high. Or you're starting to need one. Ever read The Walking Dead? It's like that. Alex was standing at the top of the stairs, staring down to the door. The Bastard was pounding. 'You good for nothing shit,' he's saying. 'I see you there, wasted on heroin, still with that Mexican whore!' That's what he said."

Kimberley was climbing the third ladder now. The one that led up to the pilot house.

Connor started to shake, exactly like he had that night.

He could see it all happening again.

Alexia creeping down the stairs.

"Daddy, somebody's at the door."

"Don't...don't open...don't..." Connor mumbled, not sure whether he is talking to Alex or to her ghost.

"Daddy," Alexia says, hesitating at the bottom of the stairs.

The Bastard's yelling. His fists are pounding on my door.

Connor shook his head and stared at his father's body on the floor of the warehouse. Still, he could still hear the sound of the Bastard's voice and the pounding of his fists echoing in his ear.

You son-of-a-whore, let me in, Goddamn you! I'm your fucking father, goddamn you. Let me in!

———

Connor was caught up in the flashback, as real in his memory as it had been on that first night.

Alexia is shaking him, unresponsive on the couch.

Daddy! Daddy!

"Go...back...to bed," Connor mumbled to the air. He looked up. His eyesight was blurry. Darkness was closing in around his eyes. He was blacking out. He was blacking out, just like he did as Alexia tried to pull him off the couch that night.

Daddy! Daddy. Come on. We have to get upstairs and hide.

"Aaah, ahh." Connor tried to get to his feet, tried to balance, collapsing back to the floor as a stab of pain dug into his side. Maybe the Bastard broke one of his ribs.

He heard a little scream. Or thought he heard a scream, the same one Alex gave that night, when she saw the Bastard peeking in at the window. She had pulled the blind. He remembered that, thinking now of how brave she was. Damn, Alex was a brave little girl. He remembered that she wanted to call the police.

No police. Had he said that to his daughter then? Or was he thinking that now?

Confused, Connor began to crawl toward the right side of the boat, where he had piled cans of oils and paints.

Get down on the floor, where it's safe, Alex.

Should I call Mamma? Daddy, are you sick?

Connor continued crawling toward the paint cans. One part of his mind was hunting for a solution to this problem. The other was back in the past, with Alexia standing over him on the stairs.

Come on, Daddy. You can do it. One step at a time, Daddy, she was telling him as he crawled up the stairs on his hands and knees. He can hear pounding on the back door. He knows it's locked. All the doors are solid, with heavy bolt locks he installed himself.

With Alexis' help, he gets to the top. He is clutching his vial of Oxycodone that his cousin gave him.

"Go back...bed..." he mumbles to Alexia.

"Daddy?"

Connor peeks out the windows of the bedroom, staggering around the room. He bumps into the crib. Lando wakes, begins crying.

"Sshhh, Sshhh!" Connor is desperate. He sees the top of his father's head out the window.

At the sound of the baby crying, the Bastard looks up. Connor quickly moves away from the window. He shuts all the blinds.

"Keep him quiet!" Connor slurs his words.

Alexia climbs into the crib with Lando and tries to comfort him, but he keeps crying.

The sounds of something splintering makes them all freeze. The Bastard is using something heavy to batter in the door.

Neighbors scream from the house across the way. "Shut up out there. I'm calling the cops!"

The battering continues.

Desperate to shut up the baby, Connor grabs a bottle of juice on the bureau. He tries to open the top but can't.

He shoves it in Alexia's hands. "Open it," he commands.

Alexia unscrews the top, and holds it up to Connor, who fumbles with the vial of pills. He shakes one out in his hand, then two. He tries to crush them using one of the baby's juice bottles on the bureau. He sweeps the crushed pills into the bottle, screws back the top, then hands it back to Alexia.

"Daddy, it's not working."

Connor grabs the bottle from her, and using his teeth, bites at the hole, widening it. He hands it back, sloshing some of the liquid onto the sheets.

Lando screams and flails. The battering continues. The neighbor keeps yelling.

Connor is weeping. "Please Alex, please," he begs. "Make him be quiet. Please."

Alexia struggles to feed Lando, who chokes at first, then starts to quiet down.

The battering stops. Connor is peeking through the blinds, listening.

Everything outside goes quiet.

The menace is gone, for the moment.

Shooing Alexia back to her own bunk bed, he takes the bottle and flushes the plastic insert down the toilet. Collapsing into bed, his brain still on high alert, Connor stares into the darkness, every fiber of his body alert for any sign of danger from outside.

It's only later, much later, when he hears Isabella scream from the kid's room, and rushes in to see that Lando is dead, that he remembers he left the pills on the baby's bureau. He lays Isabella on the floor, screams at Alex to call 911, and looks around to hide the pills.

Where better, than inside Floppy Dog? He's good with canvas and a needle, and there the sewing kit is on the bureau. In a minute, he's got the vial stuffed deep inside the puppy's stomach and he's stitching up the neck and adjusting the ribbon to hide the seam. He tosses the toy on top of Alex's bunk, just before the wail of the ambulance stops at his door.

CHAPTER THIRTY-THREE

As Connor droned on about the night Lando died, Kimberly reached the top step, stepped off the ladder onto the pilot house. Running to Jack's baby seat, she fell to the floor, covering her son with soft kisses. The she grasped the baby seat and carried her son to the ladder.

Below her, she could see that Connor was still on the ground, clutching his side, sobbing.

"I never meant to hurt Lando," he cried. "I was just scared of the Bastard, what he could do to me. To us."

Kimberly felt nothing for Connor, just a coldness and numbness about the whole affair. She had to get out of the warehouse, past him, and to freedom. So she began to placate him with words, bidding for time as she carried Jack down the steep flight of steps, balancing her son precariously so as not to fall.

"Anybody would have been scared."

"Not Gil. He wanted to have the Bastard killed. I didn't want that."

"That's because you have a conscience, Connor. You are at heart a decent person deep down," she said, finally reaching the first deck. "It's just that nobody ever taught you how to stand up for yourself."

Reaching the last ladder, she peered down. Connor gazed up at her, still clutching his ribs, crouched on the floor.

"You're going to call the police, right?" he said quietly. "You're going to have to tell them what I did."

"I don't want to," Kimberley said.

"But you'll have to," Connor interrupted. "After what I did to your husband, snatching the baby."

"If you let me leave, I'll wait until I get home to report you." Kimberley pleaded with him.

Connor stared at her for a long time. "Yeah. Alright. That's how it'll work." He made a gesture with his hand.

Kimberley took it as his giving her permission to climb down. This was a balancing act that was worse than climbing the first ladder. She held the baby seat with her left hand, steadying herself with her right hand against the ladder. She tried to breathe deeply, feeling her way down each rung of the ladder, worrying that her wrist would give out.

Once she stumbled, almost losing her grip on the baby seat. It seemed an eternity when she finally placed both feet on solid ground, then turned to look at him.

"Are you hurt, Connor?" She gestured to his side. "Should I call the ambulance?"

He seemed amused by that. "I'm not going to jail again, Kim. You can tell that to the police. And you can give Fuentes a message for me. Tell her she was wrong. You were wrong. You can't fix broken families. But you sure can screw them up even more."

———

Kimberley lifted Jack from his baby seat into her arms, protectively cradling her son against her. Slinging the lightweight seat over her shoulder, she began walking toward the warehouse door.

Jack buried his face in the hollow of her neck, gripping a lock of her hair. "It's all right, my sweet baby Jack, you're safe and

Mommy's here now," she murmured, kissing the top of his head with every step. "We're going home. We'll see Daddy. And Paige and Tony and Granddad and…" Her heart was pounding. Her head felt as if it would explode.

One step after another. Concentrate on that.

Pushing through the door, she broke into a trot, wanting only to get far away from danger. Then she stopped, disoriented to see people staring back at her… No, she realized: Not staring at her; staring up into the sky. They were waiting for the fireworks to begin.

She fished her cell phone from her pocket, quickly thumbing up Ammon's number, holding it to her ear as she pushed her way back through the crowd.

Ammon's voice came through, faint but clear. "Kimberly!"

"Ammon? Are you all right? Are you…?"

"I'm good," he said. "I'm fine. Jack?"

"Yes, yes. I've got him. Oh God, Ammon, I'm sorry. You were so right. I put you all in danger and…"

"You bring Jack home. That's all that matters, my girl."

Kimberly smiled; hugging Jack closer to her. Her eyes filled with tears. "I'll come straight to the hospital. I'll. . ."

"I love you, Kim. You and the kids. That's all that matters. Take Jack home."

A sharp crack followed by a high-pitched whizzing sound made Kimberley turn back in time to see a bright explosion of color in the sky. The crowd sighed with pleasure. As the colors faded, there was a loud bang. Startled, Jack screamed.

"What's that?" Ammon demanded.

"Fireworks." Kimberley nudged her way through the crowd, as the rhythmic staccato of fireworks built, each bang and pop eliciting a fresh wail from Jack.

"You know how Jack gets with fireworks," she said. "Poor baby. It's all right. We're almost there," she murmured to soothe Jack. "We're almost to the car, Ammon."

There was a deep whooshing sound, and then a bang, deeper

in pitch than the individual fireworks. Kimberley froze, trying to make sense of what her body had already registered. She turned around.

The warehouse exploded.

———

As Kimberley watched, the corner of the building blew out in chunks. Sheet metal was torn from the facade like crepe paper, exposing the concrete block construction and rubble. Flames shot through the roof as it collapsed in on itself.

Connor's in there.

She froze, took a few steps forward, but the crowd had pressed in tighter. Some people were still staring at the fireworks, as a giant ball of glittering red, white and blue bloomed against the sky. Others were turning their heads toward the warehouse, where black clouds billowed out of the roof and open doorway.

Kimberley closed her eyes. "Oh God," she whispered into the cell phone.

"Kimberley! Answer me!" Ammon said.

"I'm fine. We're fine. But the warehouse…it… It blew up. Connor was in there."

Connor's last words to her played in her mind: *I'm not going to jail again, Kim. You can tell that to the police.*

"Kimmy. Listen to me," Ammon told her. "Do not go back there."

In the distance, the firehouse siren began to wail. The crowd was moving, jostling to let a few men through. A police car inched past Kimberley, lights whirling. It parked a few feet from her, and two officers jumped out.

"Stay back!" one yelled, as he began to direct the crowd away from the building.

Kimberley was frozen, still staring at the door. Inside, Connor was burning, or dead already.

"I can't not let them know, Ammon. It would be wrong."

Kimberley approached the police officer. "Sir! Officer! Somebody went inside the warehouse before it blew up."

The officer glanced at her, then waved her along. "Okay, Miss. We'll check it out."

"You can give them a statement later." Ammon was saying. "Kimmy. Get in the car. Bring Jack home."

She hesitated, torn between a duty to her client and a duty to her family. What was her duty as a citizen? As a witness?

Jack whimpered and clutched a lock of her hair, his normal way of making Mommy pay attention.

Forced to gaze down at his upturned face, Kimberly studied her son's expression: tiny chin thrust forward into a pout, eyes glistening and red-rimmed from crying, his rosebud lips quivering with distress. As she leaned forward to kiss his forehead, she experienced Deja vu: brought back to the exact moment she had kissed her sweet Gabrielle's face for the last time, her heart leaden with the misery of knowing she had not been able to save her precious life. Closing her eyes, Kimberley relived the sharp anguish of helplessness, like a knife wedged into her spine, disabling and paralyzing her with guilt. She felt a second of vertigo, a sudden loss of balance.

It was Jack, tugging at her hair, who brought her back to the present. Opening her eyes, she smiled at this little boy, so brave, so trusting, and pressed his sturdy little body against her heart. She was overwhelmed by a surge of loving emotions. In that moment, her internal struggle between duty to client and family dissolved. Her body felt lighter. Her mind cleared. She knew what mattered most.

As she walked toward her car, she dug her cell phone from her pocket.

"Ammon? Are you still there?"

"I'm still here."

"No worries, mate," she assured him, appropriating his favorite saying. "We're on our way home."

CHAPTER THIRTY-FOUR

Alexia Rodriguez-Mackenzie sat in a metal folding chair, her hand clasped in Abuelita's as the hot July sun beat down on her family. The collar of her new summer dress, the one with the purple butterflies on the skirt, made her itch. She squirmed, scratching the back of her neck with her free hand.

"*Miha!* Sit still," Abuelita whispered.

Mama was next to them, holding Jayleen on her lap. Mama's face was all blotchy from crying too much. Jayleen cried, too. Her face was buried in Mama's shoulder, her legs sticking out from her bunched up pink skirt.

There was no big white box, this time, like the one for Lando's funeral. Just a blue jar, nicer than the ones her art teacher had taught her class to make out of clay last week. It had a little brass plaque stuck on, with Daddy's name.

At their last session, Miss Kimberley had called it an 'urn'. She said Daddy's ashes were inside it. Daddy had got all burned up in a warehouse fire, just like her grandpa did.

"I understand," she had told Miss Kimberley. "Now can we play with the therapy toys?"

One thing Alexia did understand. Daddy wasn't coming home no more. He was going to stay with Lando in Heaven. But she and Mama and Jayleen were all going to live with Abuelita in a new apartment. One that had a playground and a pool where they could swim all summer! They had gone to see it. It was nice.

She turned to scan the faces of her cousins and aunts and uncles to look for Miss Kimberley. There she was, standing to one side next to Mr. Robinson, who ran the clinic and the nice reception lady, Miss Emma. Alexia waved, hoping to catch their attention. Miss Kimberley smiled back, blowing Alexia a kiss.

But when Alexia asked if she could say hi to Miss Kimberley, Abuelita told her to be patient.

The child sighed, resigning herself to be quiet until Father Estanzia was finished. Then she smiled, thinking of a song that Miss Kimberley had taught her. Alexia hummed the tune, thinking the words to herself.

Where am I going, I don't quite know. Down to the trees where the king-cups grow. . .

She sang the entire song, and finally, the man in the black suit gave a white carnation to everyone, like they had at Lando's funeral.

This time, Alexia didn't refuse. She waited until it was her turn, then dropped the flower on the table next to the urn. She would have liked to lift the lid and peek inside, to see what ashes were. Instead, she leaned forward to whisper: "Goodbye, Daddy. Be real nice to Lando."

When everyone had laid their flowers next to the urn, the priest said the final blessing.

"Can I talk to Miss Kimberley now?" Alexia asked.

"Yes," said Abuelita, letting go of her hand. "Stay near!"

Alexia sped over to Miss Kimberley, who knelt down to scoop her up. Alexia put her arms around her neck in bear hug and kissed her cheek. "You have pretty lipstick on."

"And you have a pretty dress," Miss Kimberley said.

"It's new."

"I know."

"Are you coming back to the house, Miss Kimberley?"

"No, honey. I'm going to say something to your Mama and Grandma here—"

"Abuelita," Alexia corrected her.

"Yes, your Abuelita," Miss Kimberley said. "How are you doing? Are you sad?"

Alexia nodded. "A little."

"You know your Daddy is dead and he's in Heaven now. Like we talked about?" Miss Kimberley squeezed her in a gentle hug. "And that the bad man, the one who banged on the door and called you bad names is dead too. He can't bother you again."

"The bad man can't go to Heaven, right?"

"No. He can't bother anyone again. Here or in Heaven."

"Yeah," Alexia said. "He is in the bad place. That's where the bad people go."

"That's right," the therapist said.

"Only…" Alexia looked into Miss Kimberley's eyes.

"What? Is something bothering you?"

Alexia leaned forward to whisper in Miss Kimberley's ear. "God won't let Daddy give Lando any bad medicine in Heaven, right?"

Kimberley shook her head. "Everyone in heaven is healthy. They don't need any medicines."

"Hmmm." Alexia thought about this. Then she nodded. "So now both our babies are happy. Do you think they get to play together in Heaven?"

"Yes," Kimberley said. "I think they do." She swung Alexia gently to the ground. "Now let's go find your Mama, so I can say goodbye."

"Okay," Alexia said, taking her hand. One thing still worried her. She grew solemn. "Are you gonna keep being my therapy lady?"

Kimberley gazed reassuringly into the wide brown eyes of this beautiful child, who had her innocence stolen from her. She couldn't explain it rationally, but from the first moment she'd seen the two girls, it was as if her own Gabrielle had whispered in her ear: *Mummy, they need your help.*

How could she deny such a request from the child she had not been able to save?

"Yes, I will see you every Tuesday all summer long," Miss Kimberley promised. "That's a promise."

Alexia wrapped her arms around Kimberley, holding her so tightly that Kimberley could feel the child's heartbeat. "Oh, Miss Kimberley! Daddy said you didn't like us. But I knew he was wrong because you told me I was special."

The child gazed up at the therapist, her eyes wide with longing, hungry to hear the words that would ease her into a more confident path.

"Oh, sweetie," Kimberley reassured her, choosing her words carefully. "You are a special, brave, smart girl. And I am honored to call you my friend, Alexia."

They stood like that for another moment, holding Kimberley's words between them like a benediction. Then Alexia took Kimberley's hand in hers, and they walked off to find Alexia's family, and the promise of a new start.

———

Don't miss out on your next favorite book!
Join the Melange Books mailing list at
www.melange-books.com/mail.html

THANK YOU FOR READING

———

Did you enjoy this book?

We invite you to leave a review at your favorite book site, such as Goodreads, Amazon, Barnes & Noble, etc.

DID YOU KNOW THAT LEAVING A REVIEW...

- Helps other readers find books they may enjoy.
- Gives you a chance to let your voice be heard.
- Gives authors recognition for their hard work.
- Doesn't have to be long. A sentence or two about why you liked the book will do.

ABOUT S.K. MASON

Behind the pen name, S.K. Mason is a real-life therapist, with years of practice working with families. However, when she isn't working as a professional, she is writing fiction stories about her experiences, and translating these into out-of-this-world thought provoking accounts. With a gift for setting scenes in health and medical settings, her books aim to be intense, adventurous and thrilling novels. She lives in Australia with her five children.

www.skmasonauthor.com
www.facebook.com/skmasonauthor
www.instagram.com/skmasonauthor
www.twitter.com/skmasonauthor

ABOUT DEBRA SCACCIAFERRO

Debra Scacciaferro is a former newspaper reporter and arts critic, who lives in the Hudson Valley of New York, where State of Innocence is set. After leaving the newspaper business, she worked as a researcher and assistant to her husband, bestselling author Jim DeFelice, and raised her son, Robert. In between, she joined several writers groups, finished three unpublished novels, and began helping other writers polish their books and novels through her business DebraS Novel Services. She is grateful to her dear friend and colleague, Lorraine Ash, author of "Life Touches Life," for introducing her to S.K. Mason, who was looking for a writing partner.

www.debrascacciaferro.com
www.facebook.com/debrascacciaferro
www.facebook.com/debrasnovelservices